Also by Brenda Hasse

The Moment Of Trust

~

Brenda Hasse

The Moment Of Trust

ISBN: 978-1-7347786-0-1 (pbk)

ISBN: 978-1-7347786-1-8 (ebk)

To my mother, Alyce, for always having my best interests at heart

Chapter 1

A bead of sweat trickled down the center of her forehead and dangled on the tip of her nose as Rhoslyn bent to pull another weed from the row of beans. Not wanting to dirty the white sleeves of her habit, she used the bottom of her gray wool tunic to wipe away the dampness from her face, regretting her decision as the material pricked her skin. She stood dropping the weed into the basket and arched her aching back. The nuns working alongside her seemed content with the laborious task. For Rhoslyn, it was her punishment. She had been caught doodling rabbits donning shields and fighting with swords in the margin of the book she was copying, a much worse offense than the forewarning curses she normally added. The abbess, Mother Margaret, ordered her to spend several days in the Misericord, a small windowless room with a single lit candle to help her reflect on her misdoing. Her penance was to weed the vegetable and herb gardens, which was quite different from her normal tasks of reproducing books with the monks, embroidering, and sewing.

"Rhoslyn, stop daydreaming and return to your work."

Rhoslyn turned to see the abbess standing at the edge of the garden in her black habit with her hands folded beneath her tunic, unsmiling like a black cat ready to devour its prey. To protect her royal identity, the abbess insisted on addressing her by her given name.

She sighed before glancing at the blazing sun to estimate the time of day and forced her reply to sound sincere.

"Yes, Mother Margaret." Secretly, she despised the woman, resented her father's decision to send her to the Sisters of Charity, and hated the retched rules of the abbey.

Grabbing the nearest weed with both hands, she pulled, but it remained firmly in the ground. Picking up the hoe where it lay on the dirt, she hacked and chopped at the dry soil with a vengeance to loosen it. Bracing her feet, she yanked on the weed and nearly fell backward as its roots gave way. Tossing it onto the overflowing wooden bushel basket, she watched as it rolled off the small mountain of pulled weeds and onto the ground. She flexed her blistered gloved hands and looked at the compost pile on the other side of the garden. Rhoslyn retrieved the wayward weed, placed it atop the basket, and pushed it into place ensuring it would not fall before hoisting the basket onto her hip. She stepped over each row of vegetables as she lumbered to the compost and dumped the contents of her basket. Pausing to catch her breath, she watched the resident monks in the alfalfa field turning the first cutting with their pitchforks to ensure it was properly dried.

Rhoslyn scanned the pasture and discovered her dapple-gray mare was absent. She looked over her shoulder at the nuns in the garden and the convent windows and doors for any watchful eyes. Confident she would remain unnoticed, she set the empty basket on the ground, casually walked toward the stable, and went inside.

Even though the monks kept the stone stable immaculately clean, the odor of musty straw and horse dung calmed her temperament as she entered. She passed several empty stalls and found her horse under the shelter of the inner corral at the opposite end of the aisle. Laila looked toward her mistress, stepped to the gate, and lowered her head for some needed attention.

"Hello, Laila, my big girl." Rhoslyn laid the side of her face on the horse's cheek and stroked the mare's nose. "I've missed you." In truth, she missed having the freedom to climb atop her mare and ride through trails in the woods and tall grass in the fields. She missed shooting her bow on the practice field with her father's garrison. She yearned to spend time with her mother, dress in beautiful gowns, and sit at the High Table in the Great Hall at Bardenham for the evening meal. "It's been six months, Laila. Do you want to go home as much as I do?"

At the insistence of her father, she was escorted by his knight, Sir Cedric, to the abbey, and watched as he handed the abbess a chest containing coins. More than likely it was a payment for her stay, but it made her feel like a fattened pig being sold for slaughter. Her father refused to divulge the reason for forcing her to leave Bardenham. She assumed it was for her protection, but protection from what? How long must she remain at the abbey?

"There you are." Sister Patricia stepped into the stable. "Mother Margaret sent me to fetch you. Come quickly or we will be late for None." The nun turned and began walking toward the church.

"Sorry Laila, but I must attend Mass again." She kissed her horse on the nose and patted her face farewell. She looked toward the field as she stepped into the sunshine. The monks were gone. They were already in the church. If she was late for Mass, it would give the abbess another reason to be angry with her. She quickened her steps to catch up to Sister Patricia so they could enter the church together.

Chapter 2

Lord Atherton returned the red wax candle to his desk drawer while the seal on the missive cooled and became ridged. He ignored his wife, who paced the floor of the solar with her arms crossed over her chest, picked up the missive, and presented it to his trusted knight standing before his desk.

"Deliver this to Aldwinster." He pointed to the chest filled with coins on the corner of his desk. "And the chest as well."

"Yes, my lord." Sir Cedric tucked the missive inside his tunic, picked up the heavy brass chest, and left the solar.

Lord Atherton glanced over his shoulder at his wife. "Our daughter's future is safe and secure."

Lady Eugenia was not as confident but took comfort in knowing Rhoslyn would be cared for if they were both sentenced to death. Her husband's misdoings had caught up with him. Whatever he had done to offend the baron was far worse a crime than the unfaithful and estranged husband she had endured during their marriage.

She often wondered how her life would have turned out differently if she had been allowed to wed the young man she loved. Even though he was lower in rank, she assumed her life would have been happier.

She clasped her hands together to stop them from trembling and took a deep breath to calm her rapidly beating heart. With doubt settling within her mind that her plea of innocence would be taken into consideration, her stomach soured as she turned toward the solar door to meet the fate awaiting them in the Great Hall.

Lord Atherton opened the desk drawer, took out a vial filled with a liquid, and drank its contents. He dropped the empty bottle on the floor before exiting the chamber.

The Lord and Lady of Bardenham descended the staircase to the Great Hall where the baron's man-at-arms, Lester, and his guards waited.

The Keep's staff peeked around pillars and through doorways as rumors of the conspiracy had reached their ears. They watched as guards surrounded their lord and lady. Lester stepped forward. He thrust his chest outward displaying the many dirks attached to his leather belt strung from his shoulder to the opposite hip.

"Lord Atherton, Lady Eugenia, you are under arrest for crimes committed against the crown."

"Surely, you're mistaken." Lady Eugenia stared at the man-at-arms, glanced at her husband, and turned in a circle as she looked at each guard. "What is the accusation, the charge? I do not know of any transgression."

Lester remained stern, committed to following the baron's orders. He sneered. "There is no mistake, my lady. The evidence is quite solid."

Lord Atherton grabbed his stomach with both hands and cringed. His face drained of color as he looked to his wife. "I'm afraid, Eugenia, this is where we shall part, permanently."

Her head snapped toward her husband. "Part? What?" Lady Eugenia watched her husband doubled over in pain.

"Augh." The Lord of Bardenham dropped to his hands and knees before rolling onto his back.

Lady Eugenia thought it best to portray the loyal wife and display a trifle bit of compassion. She sat on her heels as she knelt and placed her husband's head upon her lap. He gasped for air; his eyes wide as he tried to inhale but only wheezed before his body stilled. She glared at his lifeless open orbs. *Coward, you leave me to face the consequence of your transgressions.*

Lester stepped to Lady Eugenia, towering over her. He pulled his long black hair away from his equally dark eyes and looked down at the pair. "My lady, we must leave for Somerville immediately."

She looked up at the man and laughed shaking her head. "Am I not allowed to bury my husband?"

He lifted his chin and thrust out his chest. "No."

Bentley, the steward, came forward from the doorway of the kitchen. "My lady, I will see that Lord Atherton has a proper burial."

Lady Eugenia looked into the baby blue eyes of the elderly steward. His dark hair had grayed above his ears over the years. She nodded accepting his kind offer, rolling her lips inward making a straight line. "Very well." She closed her husband's eyes, lifted his head from her lap, and placed it upon the stone floor. She stood and took a deep breath trying to gather the strength to face her dismal future. She looked toward Lester. "May I be allowed the time to pack a bag before we leave?"

"Only if you are accompanied by my men."

"Very well." Lady Eugenia ascended the staircase and went to her bedchamber with two guards trailing closely behind her.

Chapter 3

Shadow crouched in the vegetation of the forest. The gray Irish wolfhound stared at the large buck while remaining perfectly still near the feet of his master.

Drawing back his bow ever so slowly, Jayden held his breath as he aimed at the twelve-point deer. As if catching the scent of the young lord in the still air, the animal turned his head and looked him directly in the eye. With his heart thumping in his chest, Jayden let his arrow fly. It struck its mark. Shadow rose onto all fours as he watched the buck staggered before dropping to the ground.

Sir Darwin stepped out from behind a tree. "Well done, my lord."

Jayden signaled to the two peasant men crouched behind him. They darted forward. One of the men whistled as he kicked his toe against the stomach of the deer. "It's a large one, my lord. It'll feed many."

Leaving the men to dress out the deer, the lord and his knight wove their way around trees and underbrush to their tethered horses on the fringe of the forest. Jayden set one end of the longbow on his boot, compressed its ends, and unstrung it. He attached the weapon to the back of his saddle before untying the reins from a sapling and climbing atop his ebony warhorse, Beval. Shadow waited as Sir Darwin mounted his chestnut destrier. The trio traveled in the shadow of the trees cast by the setting sun. Once on the dirt road, they turned toward the castle of Aldwinster.

They passed fertile fields dotted with dedicated peasants tending the kingdom's crops. Those who were heading home for the evening waved to their young lord, who nodded in return.

Jayden admired the village with its quaint dwellings and castle in the distance. He remembered when it was not so well kept.

"Aldwinster has become a fine kingdom under Father's reign."

The knight looked toward his young lord, who had yet to reach a score in age. His elder by a decade, Sir Darwin's responsibility was to advise, protect, and train Jayden for combat. His biggest challenge, however, was to keep the young lord's mind focused on following in his father's footsteps as the next Lord of Aldwinster and not on the flirtatious women who seemed under a magical spell when the tall, broad-shouldered, handsome lord glanced their way. His striking sky-blue eyes framed with curly charcoal hair and chiseled chin invoked the silliest promiscuous behavior in the women. The knight insisted his understudy remain polite and respectful no matter how foolish his admirers behaved.

Sir Darwin redirected his line of vision to the village and distant castle. "Yes, Lord Filmore and Lady Myla have improved it greatly over the years."

On their way to the castle, they passed the cottages lining the dirt road of the village. Shadow lifted his nose in the air and inhaled the various aromas of the peasant's evening meals cooking over their fireplaces. They crossed the drawbridge at the gatehouse and entered the bailey with its diverse shops of talented crafters along the castle's interior walls. Many of the crafters were closing their shops for the day and settling in for the evening. Jayden reined his horse around several people who stood in his pathway to the stable.

Kolby, the stableboy, came forward and grabbed the bridles of the horses as he watched the two men dismount. Just past a decade old, the lanky lad's inquisitive hazel eyes looked to his lord. "Did you have any success, my lord?"

"Yes, a large buck." Jayden tussled the stableboy's brunette hair before the lad encouraged the warhorses forward to the stable for a bucket of oats and water.

Jayden patted Beval's dusty rump as his stallion passed by clearing his line of vision at the alewives, who were busy brewing a batch of ale. A young woman with long dark hair batted her eyes at the young lord as she ran her hand along her body to accentuate her curves. He smiled and nodded in her direction while winking in acknowledgment.

Sir Darwin's head turned toward his lord, the woman, and back to his lord like a loose shutter. Sighing in disgust, he stepped between the two blocking his lord's view and attempted to redirect his present train of thought. "Will you be practicing your sword with the garrison tomorrow, my lord?"

Jayden tried to keep the beautiful woman in his sight by peeking around the knight, but Sir Darwin moved to block his view.

"Yes, an excellent idea." Jayden stepped over the threshold of the Keep.

Sir Darwin looked back to the woman, who stuck out her bottom lip in a pout.

"I couldn't agree more." He followed his lord.

With a journal tucked under his arm, Pearson, the steward, stepped before Jayden as he entered the Great Hall. Tall, lean, and well-organized, he was a few years younger than Lord Filmore. He tiled his head to the side clearing his mousey-brown hair from his gray eyes, apprehensive to break the news to the young lord.

"My lord, I thought you should know Lady Carling and her servant have arrived and will be staying for several weeks."

Jayden's mouth fell open. "Several weeks?" A chill ran up his spine as he recalled the woman's false affection for him and her laugh, so piercing it could shatter glass. "I failed to spot her coach when we passed through the bailey."

Pearson sighed as he looked to the ceiling to emphasize his sarcasm. "I believe it is at the blacksmith for repairs."

Jayden understood the steward's implication and the lame excuse for her stay. "I see. Well then, Father had no other choice than to accommodate her and her servant."

The steward nodded.

Jayden looked about the room at the adjoining corridors. "Where is she now?"

"She is in the garden, my lord, taking in the view of the flowers. Oh, and Lord Thornton has stopped by for a visit as well."

Jayden cringed clenching his teeth. He was somehow related to the man but forgot the connection. He recalled Lord Thornton's reputation as a taker. He took advantage of everyone around him, always wanting something for nothing, showing up at Aldwinster for a free meal, and continually hinting of his dire need for money. Without the ambition or the willingness to work, he weaseled hand-outs from others. His bulbous belly conveyed his gluttony of food. His dilapidated kingdom, Pembroke, reflected his laziness. Seldom could Jayden manage to converse with the man without focusing on the crumbs of food dotting his unkempt beard. Those within the Great Hall tried to ignore his repulsive habit of sniffing his food with his pig-like nose and grunting while he dined like a boar. Seldom did he chew his food with his mouth closed.

"I shall hide in the library until the evening meal is served." Jayden turned to his knight. "Sir Darwin, will you join me?"

"Yes, my lord." The knight and Shadow followed their lord to the library while the steward returned to the kitchen to supervise.

Chapter 4

The Sisters of Charity left the church without speaking, walked along the arched cloister, and entered the convent.

Rhoslyn waited in line as each nun washed their hands before going to the kitchen. She drew in her breath as she dipped her blistered hands in the bowl of water and washed them gently. She patted them dry with a cloth, entered the kitchen, and selecting the stack of wooden plates from a shelf, her given task for the evening meal. She circled the long wooden table in the dining room placing a plate before each seat. As she set the last plate on the table, she stood before her assigned seat and waited for the remainder of the nuns and monks to finish their tasks. Sister Patricia filled the last mug with watered ale and set the pitcher upon the table before standing in her place. The abbess stood at one end of the table and Abbot Andrew at the opposite end, then everyone sat in unison. They pressed the palms of their hands together and bowed their heads as they muttered a prayer of thanks.

The protocol for the meal operated like a well-oiled machine. A loaf of bread was passed around the table, followed by a small plate of butter and a knife with each person placing a dab of butter on the side of their plate. The abbot cut a slice of cheese from the round and placed it upon his plate before passing the cutting board to another. Lastly, the bowl of strawberries traced the same circle clockwise around the table.

Rhoslyn looked at the sparse, bland food on her plate. Her stomach grumbled. She missed the variety of food available at Bardenham. Most of all, she missed the sweet cakes. Picking up the cheese, she took a healthy bite and peeked at the others at the table. Their heads were bowed toward their plates and no one spoke. Rhoslyn glanced toward the abbess as she reached for her mug of ale. Miscalculating, her knuckles brushed the side of the vessel tipping it over and spilling its contents.

Sister Patricia, who sat across from Rhoslyn, bolted from her seat as the ale dribbled onto her tunic.

"Oh, Sister Patricia, I'm so sorry." Rhoslyn looked toward the abbess, whose stern expression conveyed her displeasure in having the silence of the meal broken.

Mother Margaret sighed, calming her anger. "Rhoslyn, you will remove yourself from the table and go to your cell until Vespers begins."

Rhoslyn's eyes widened. "It was an accident. I said I was sorry."

"I don't want an explanation. You will go now."

"Yes, Mother Margaret." Rhoslyn rose from her seat. She took one last look at her plate knowing the contents would most likely be fed to the pigs. Her cheeks grew warm and she imagined they were flushed rosy. With her head bowed toward the floor, she left the room. Tears welled in her eyes as she walked through the halls of the dormitory, entered her cell, and lay upon her straw mattress staring blankly at the ceiling.

"I hate this place." A tear trickled from her eye and disappeared into her hairline by her ear. "I want to go home." Her stomach grumbled as she devised a plan to return to Bardenham. She would take food from the kitchen larder and hide it in her cell until the night of the new moon, sneak into the stable to saddle Laila, and ride through the night. She was certain she could find her way home, even though it would take several days of traveling.

Rhoslyn imagined her parents' happiness upon her arrival, of lying in her soft bed and eating delicious food once again. No more attending Mass eight times a day. No more working in the garden. No more wearing scratchy clothing. No more having the abbess watching over her.

A knock upon her cell door brought her back to reality.

"Rhoslyn, it is time for Compline."

Rhoslyn groaned inwardly. *Not Sister Patricia. She is the last person I want to see.* She remained silent.

"Rhoslyn?"

Rhoslyn rose from the bed, wiped the dampness from her face, and opened the door. "Sister Patricia, I'm so very sorry."

"It was an accident. No need to apologize. I changed my habit, good as new." The nun held out her gray tunic for Rhoslyn to see. "The abbess asked me to retrieve you for Mass."

"Time for Compline already?" The two hours passed by quickly. Rhoslyn stepped into the hallway closing the door to her cell behind her. The only positive aspect of attending Compline was the promise of returning to her bed at its completion.

~

Conversations echoed within the Great Hall of Aldwinster. With its candelabras emanating the room in a golden glow and its long tables donned with trays of meats and vegetables, those in attendance sat on benches and enjoyed a meal of plenty and mugs filled with ale.

Jayden sat to his father's left with Shadow near his feet. He was thankful Lady Carling sat at the opposite end of the table next to his mother's lady in waiting. He leaned toward his father. "I see we have a guest."

"I know you aren't fond of Lady Carling, but her coach needs repairs, or so I have been informed. Nevertheless, we must be hospitable toward our guests." He nodded toward the opposite end of the table toward Lord Thornton.

"Yes, Father." Jayden looked toward the hog-like man at the end of the table as he slopped his food into his mouth. He looked back to Lord Filmore. "Tell me again how we are related to Lord Thornton."

"He is your mother's cousin. A distant cousin, thankfully."

Jayden picked up his tankard of ale from the table and turned to Sir Darwin, who sat to his left. "The room seems lively tonight, such conversation." He drank nearly half of the tankard before returning it to the table.

"Yes, my lord, perhaps everyone has had a productive day and they're eager to share a story or two to celebrate." Out of the corner of his eye, the knight watched his lord wink at a passing serving girl, who carried two pitchers of ale. She paused before Jayden, batted her eyelashes, and dipped her chest low enough for her cleavage to nearly spill as she refilled his mug. The knight admitted, she was quite pretty.

Jayden grinned as the servant winked before leaving the High Table to refill another empty tankard. He watched her hips sway with each step she took.

Sir Darwin sighed as he looked toward the ceiling.

With his tankard filled to the brim, Jayden lifted it from the table, paused to look in the direction of the cackle that rang out from the other end of the table, and cringed internally. Lady Carling was staring at him. She misunderstood his gesture and lifted her mug as if toasting to his good health. She forced a fake smile displaying her crooked yellow teeth and extended her pinky finger before sipping her drink. Physically, he thought of her as attractive with thick blonde hair the color of straw pinned in pristine curls, her blue eyes reminded him of the color of the ocean, and her figure turned many of men's heads when she passed by them. He estimated her age to be over a dozen years his senior and discovered, in one of his close encounters, she possessed the most horrid breath. He assumed a rotting tooth was the cause of her odious mouth.

Sir Darwin realized Lady Carling had entrapped the young lord in her venomous stare. It was unfortunate the young lord had earned the reputation as a womanizer, but Sir Darwin was determined to redirect him toward a more noble legacy. He knew Jayden planned to practice his sword with the garrison in the morning, but it was the only topic that came to mind. "My lord, what's on the agenda for tomorrow?"

Jayden looked to his knight. "As we previously discussed, I will be training with the garrison tomorrow."

"Ah, yes. May I speak freely?"

"Please do."

"You have been known to pursue a few women, well, maybe more than a few. Perhaps Lady Carling is aware of your reputation and thinks of you as a stud for hire. It may be wise for you to curtail your public adoration for women, especially during the duration of her stay." Sir Darwin hoped he conveyed the importance of the matter without overstepping his bounds.

"Even though Father remains faithful to Mother, many men, even those who are wed, have their way with women outside of the marriage, especially noblemen of rank."

"Your parents' marriage is a marriage built on trust and love. Those in arranged marriages are not always as fortunate. You, however, must uphold your honor, for someday you will become the Lord of Aldwinster."

Jayden glanced at Lady Carling, who stuffed a sweet cake into her mouth. "I shall do as you wish and avoid Lady Carling at all cost."

"And for the other women?"

"Very well."

"Let us hope when the time comes for you to sit on the throne, your reputation as a leader will outweigh your current one as a rake." Sir Darwin picked up his tankard and took a long drink. By stating the truth bluntly, he hoped his words were taken to heart, but he had his doubts.

Chapter 5

As nightfall brought the day to a close, the man-at-arms and his guards found a suitable campsite along the roadside and dismounted. A guard helped Lady Eugenia dismount from her horse. Her stiff body ached. She could ride for hours when she was younger without any repercussions, but her responsibilities at Bardenham kept her from enjoying such activities over the years.

She straightened her wrinkled dress and wrapped her cloak around her before sitting upon a nearby log and looking at the stars in the cloudless sky. The men unsaddled the horses, placed them and the blankets in a circle on the ground, and built a fire in the center to ward off the coolness of the night. Sleep, a priority, allowed no time to hunt for their evening meal. A guard handed Lady Eugenia a flask of ale, jerky, and bread made from barley.

"Thank you." She watched as each man sat before their saddle around the fire. The warmth from the flickering flames invited her forward. Sitting on the ground near her saddle, she ignored the guard's conversation and her mind drifted to her entrapment while she nibbled on the sparse meal and stared at the dancing flames. What travesty had her husband committed against the baron? A dreadful heaviness settled within her heart. She extended her fingers confirming her hand was shaking. Was she chilled or fear of her future that cause her to shake? She was thankful her daughter was not implicated in the offense and remained safe and well cared for by the Sisters of Charity. She prayed the decision her husband made for Rhoslyn's future would bring her happiness even though she may not approve of his choice.

A man bellowed with laughter. She looked at him as she bit into the dry meat. It was tough and tasteless; the bread was stale. She ate what she could before throwing the remainder into the fire. She lay against her saddle and covered herself with the horse blanket. As her eyelids lowered, she listened to the men's conversation. Their topic was crude as if they disregarded the presence of a lady. After all, to them, she was nothing more than a prisoner.

~

With the last of the dirty plates and platters gathered, the tables and benches in the Great Hall of Aldwinster were pushed aside, and the minstrels began to play. Lord Filmore and Lady Myla took their traditional turn around the floor before returning to their carved wooden chairs at the High Table and those in attendance followed their lead.

Jayden leaned toward his knight. "I suppose it's too early for me to retire to my bedchamber."

"If you did, it would appear inhospitable." Sir Darwin glanced toward Lady Carling, who wore a sour look on her face as she sipped her drink and stared at the dancers. Should he ask her to dance and fulfill the lack of attention she wished to receive from the young lord?

Jayden resisted the urge to look toward the other end of the table and chose to stare at the pretty wench who filled his tankard earlier. He wished he could ask her to dance, whisk her off to a darkened corner, and taste her sweet lips.

Sir Darwin glanced at the young lord, reading his mind. "It would be inappropriate to ask her to dance."

"I know." He took another swig from his tankard.

Out of the corner of his eye, Lord Filmore saw Lady Carling rise from her seat and turn toward the opposite end of the table. He tilted his head toward his son. "Be polite. Lady Carling is coming toward you."

Jayden felt a tap on his right shoulder as he was lowering his tankard from his lips. He turned toward Lady Carling, who gushed with false sweetness. He stood respectfully. Shadow lifted his head from the floor and watched his master bow and the woman curtsy.

"My, my, but you have been involved in such conversation tonight. I have yet to speak to you. I do hope you are feeling well." She took a step closer trapping him against the High Table.

"I'm well. And you?" His recoiled as she tapped her index finger under his chin, turning his face away from the decaying odor of her rancid breath. He wished he could back away, but the High Table blocked his escape.

"I'm well too. However, my coach seems to have fallen apart during my journey. Luckily, I happened to be near Aldwinster and knew I could rely on your excellent blacksmith to repair it."

"It's unfortunate you've experienced a delay in your journey. Rest assured, you can rely on our blacksmith, who is quite skilled in his craft. I'm certain he will have the repairs finished quickly and you will be on your way soon." He made a mental note to speak to the blacksmith and offer him a bribe to hasten the repairs.

Lady Carling placed her hands upon his chest, leaned toward him, and whispered into his ear.

"I've heard nasty rumors about you." She leaned away and smiled raising her eyebrows suggestively.

"How so?"

She glanced at the pretty serving wench as she passed by the table. "You've been a busy boy." She poked her finger at his chest and began to cackle like a chicken who just laid an egg.

Eavesdropping on the conversation, Sir Darwin sighed. Just as he had assumed, Jayden's reputation as a rake was common knowledge. It was unfortunate the confirmation came from such a loose woman.

Jayden almost grinned as if proud. "Well, practice makes perfect, or so I have been told."

Enticed by the possibility of being held in his strong arms for the night, Lady Carling looked to the dancing couples. "Shall we take a turn around the floor?"

Obligated to end his lord's torment, Sir Darwin rose and turned toward Lady Carling, took her hand within his, and pressed his lips to its back. "My lady, I fear my lord has a taxing day scheduled for tomorrow and must save his strength. Perhaps I may be of assistance and escort you to the dance floor instead?" He offered his bent right arm.

Lady Carling looked to the offered arm, to Jayden, and hoped he would rescind his knight's offer, but he remained silent. She pursed her lips in a pout and stared at the young lord with askance eyes. "I guess if I have no other available partners." She redirected her attention to the knight. "Then yes, Sir Darwin, I will accept your offer." She threaded her arm through his and allowed him to lead her to the floor to join the dancing couples.

Jayden returned to his seat and picked up his tankard. He planned to celebrate his narrow escape by drinking what remained within his tankard. The flirtatious serving woman offered a refill, but he declined and departed for his bedchamber before the song ended.

Chapter 6

Rhoslyn opened her eyes as the tapping on her cell door registered within her mind. She looked to the tiny barred window on the door and saw the glow of flickering candlelight.

"Rhoslyn, time for Matins."

"Yes, Mother Margaret, I'm coming." She sat up in bed and watched the light fade from the window as the abbess went to the next cell to wake its occupant. She slipped on her habit, tightened her belt, and placed her gray tunic over her head. She donned the linen veil, fastened the cloth under her chin, and wished she had time to use the garderobe but dare not be late.

The sisters were lining up behind the abbess as Rhoslyn emerged from her cell and fell into line. Attending Mass had become her way of life since arriving at the convent. Curious, she dared not question why there was a need to attend it so many times a day.

In single file, the sisters followed the abbess to the dark narrow night stairs, descended carefully, and entered the church. It was a faster route and was only used for the earliest Mass of the day. The sisters sat in their assigned pews on one side of the church while the monks sat on the opposite side. Rhoslyn had yet to grow accustomed to beginning her day so early and she prayed she would stay awake throughout the Mass.

~

The men roused at daybreak. Lester nudged Lady Eugenia's shoulder waking her from her restless night's sleep. She sat upright pulling the horse blanket close to her body to ward off the chill in the air. A guard handed her the same meal as the previous evening before pulling the blanket away from her shoulders and saddling her horse. Once atop of their horses, the wicked pace set by the man-at-arms sent lightning bolts of pain throughout her body adding insult to agony. She tried to reposition herself upon the saddle searching for relief, but shifting her weight made little difference.

They rode in silence along the dirt road through valleys, forests, and fields. It was just past midday when the baron's castle, Somerville, came into view.

Lady Eugenia's heartbeat quickened, and her palms became damp causing her to tighten her grip on the reins as she stared at the immaculate and large kingdom in the distance. Clenching her teeth, she thought of her husband and wondered what penalty she would pay for his transgression.

As the small party rode through the village, people stopped to stare at the lady of some significant importance on horseback surrounded by guards. Seldom was a lady arrested for a crime.

Lady Eugenia looked at each peasant's questioning glare and watched as dwelling doorways filled with curious peasants eager to see who the guards were escorting. To convey her innocence, she ignored her aching body as it protested the straightening of her back. She lifted her chin and ignored the inquisitive stares.

Crossing over the drawbridge, the party was detained momentarily at the gatehouse before permitted to enter Somerville's castle. They passed through the crowded bailey reining their horses to avoid the vendors pushing their carts and people wandering the streets. Several stableboys came forward to take the reins of their horses as they dismounted before the stable. After enduring the vigorous pace of their journey, Lady Eugenia remained atop of her mare fearing she may fall in her attempt to dismount. A stableboy came forward with a set of steps and placed them to the side of her horse.

"Thank you." Lady Eugenia gingerly straightened her cramped left leg to lift herself from the saddle. She swung her right leg over the horse's rump and lowered herself until her foot touched the step. Breathing a sigh of relief to be on solid ground once again, she turned and descended the three small steps.

"This way, my lady." Lester motioned toward the Keep.

Lady Eugenia tilted her head backward to take in the full height of the majestic residence with its towers on each side resembling pointed bookends. The detailed architecture was magnificent and several windows larger than any she had ever seen. One panel of windows displayed a patterned of stained glass, possibly where the chapel was located.

A guard opened the embellished wooden door of the Keep. She followed Lester through the portal, along a hallway, and emerged into the Great Hall. She gasped upon seeing the immense size and beauty of the room decorated with many tapestries and paintings. Countless candelabras lined its walls. There was a large fireplace on one wall with a mantel made of carved stone. Above it hung a portrait. She assumed it was of the baron.

"And who is this?"

Everyone turned toward the short, little man descending the grand staircase. He was dressed in a plum tunic embroidered with gold, his sword at his side tapping on the top of each step as he descended and stared directly at Lady Eugenia.

Lester stepped forward to meet Baron Roldan as he stepped onto the stone floor. "My lord, this is Lady Eugenia. She is being charged with…."

Baron Roldan held up his hand, palm facing outward. "I know what she is being charged with, Lester. The question is whether she is guilty of the charges or not."

Lady Eugenia curtsied and rose. "My lord, I am innocent."

The baron smirked as he stopped before her and looked up into her face. "That's what they all say."

Lady Eugenia, estimating the man was a dozen or more years older than she, ignored his sarcastic comment. Her situation was no laughing matter, at least, not to her.

"Your lordship, I do not know of my husband's transgression. I am ignorant of the crime he has committed. However, I assume he was guilty of the offense and avoided prosecution by ingesting poison while in our solar before our arrest. He died in my arms before we departed from Bardenham."

Baron Roldan looked to Lester, who indicated she told the truth with a single nod of his head. The baron looked back to his prisoner. "And what of your daughter?"

"Lady Rhoslyn is currently residing with the Sisters of Charity. My husband and I have arranged her betrothal to Lord Jayden of Aldwinster and have asked they arrange for her transportation to the kingdom as soon as possible."

"Good. You will remain in the tower until I have reviewed the evidence, interviewed witnesses, or I receive your confession as an accomplice to the crime." He walked past the group dismissing them.

Lady Eugenia curtsied. "Yes, my lord."

Lester turned toward her. "This way, my lady." He led her up the staircase, through many hallways, and ascended the spiral stairs of a tower. He opened a door to a chamber. "Food will be sent several times a day."

She entered the tiny room. It contained a small bed, table and chair, a chamber pot in the corner, and a single window. It smelled of soap as if it had been cleaned recently. The straw mattress was plump as if never slept upon and a blanket folded at the foot of the bed. A single candle was the only adornment in the center of the table. She went to the window and looked down at the people in the bailey as Lester pulled the door closed. She heard the click of the key locking it securely. Her thoughts drifted to her daughter. She prayed the missive and dowry had reached Lord Filmore safely.

Chapter 7

Jayden widened his eyes to clear his blurred vision and focused on the ivy carved oak posts at the end of his bed. He glanced at the balcony doors to see the sparkling beveled leaded glass in the morning sunlight.

After using his private garderobe, he dressed and joined his parents for breakfast in the solar with his faithful canine following closely behind him.

"Good morning, Mother." He kissed her cheek. "Father." He sat in his usual place at the table and scanned the platters of sausages, boiled eggs, rolls with butter, cheese, and baked apples. After selecting several items filling his plate, he picked up the pitcher of ale and poured it into his tankard until the foam cascaded over the brim. Shadow sat next to his master looking toward him with askance eyes waiting for his share of the meal.

"I see Sir Darwin helped you escape the claws of Lady Carling last night." Lady Myla displayed a sly smile as she selected a sausage from a platter and put it on her pewter plate.

"Yes, I'm certain he will request a favor for his noble deed." He cut an egg in half, stabbed it with his fork, and popped it into his mouth.

Lord Filmore smirked. "Oh, Lady Carling isn't all that bad. She is just a lonely widow who has her sights on you."

"Unfortunately, I don't appreciate her 'sights' and prefer she would chase another."

"Anticipating the complication of having Lady Carling within Aldwinster's walls, I took the initiative to speak with the blacksmith. He is working as quickly as possible." Lord Filmore cut a sausage in half and paused with it midway to his mouth as a knock sounded upon the solar door. "Enter."

The trio watched as Pearson entered while struggling to carry the small, heavy chest.

Lord Filmore lowered his forked sausage to the table. "Yes, Pearson, what is it?"

"A knight delivered it and left without waiting for a reply." The steward stepped before his lord, bent close to the floor and dropped the chest next to his lord's chair. He reached inside his tunic extracting a wax-sealed missive. He ensured it was addressed to Lord Filmore before looking toward his lord and presenting the letter.

Lord Filmore accepted the missive. "Thank you, Pearson."

"You're welcome, my lord." The steward nodded and left the solar closing the door behind him.

Lord Filmore broke the wax seal, unfolded the missive, and read its message.

Lady Myla peeked at the handwriting. She did not recognize it. However, she watched as her husband's eyebrows drew together. "What is it?"

Realizing the time had finally come, Lord Filmore would discuss the terms with his wife once they were alone. He looked to his son, who was unaware of how his life would change by the contents of the missive.

"Jayden, your prayers have been answered."

Jayden paused in mid-chew. He looked to his mother then back to his father. "How so?"

"I need you and Sir Darwin to go to the Sisters of Charity and escort a woman back to Aldwinster. She is to reside with us."

Jayden's eyes widened in disbelief. "A nun?"

"No, she is a lady, who was placed by her family in the convent for her protection. The trip will distance you from the unwanted attentions of Lady Carling for nearly a week. Perhaps she will have left Aldwinster upon your return."

Jayden took a chunk of cheese and popped it in his mouth while he chewed and thought. "Very well."

His father went to his desk, comprised a missive, and sealed it. He returned to the table and handed it to his son, who tucked it into his tunic.

"When you finish eating, please tell Pearson to have enough food packed for your journey and inform Sir Darwin he is to accompany you."

"Yes, Father."

Jayden shoved the last bite of sausage into his mouth as he stood and kissed his mother on the cheek. He closed the solar door and cringed at the top of the staircase to the Great Hall upon spying Lady Carling, waiting at the bottom. She turned toward him.

"Oh, Lord Jayden. You missed such a grand time last night. I do believe I have blisters on my feet from all of the dancing." She approached him as he descended the stairs.

"That is unfortunate. You will have to be a bystander until your blisters heal properly." With Pearson absent from the Great Hall, he turned toward the kitchen.

"My lord, where are you going?" She followed him with her hand raised as if pleading for a moment of his time.

"I'm in search of our steward." He entered the kitchen leaving her behind. Pearson sat at a small table reviewing the evening menu.

"Pearson."

Hearing his name, the steward stood and looked toward the doorway. "Yes, my lord."

"Could you prepare satchels of provisions and flasks of wine for Sir Darwin and me. We shall be gone for a week or so."

"Gone!"

Both men turned to see Lady Carling standing in the doorway.

"What do you mean gone?" She stepped toward Jayden and batted her eyes.

Hoping to keep his irritation in check, he took a deep breath and exhaled.

"My father has given me an assignment away from Aldwinster."

"That is unfortunate. I look forward to your return. Godspeed." Her skirt flailed as she turned and exiting the room.

Jayden looked to the ceiling and sighed. He took a step toward the door, paused, and faced the steward with his index finger raised as if remembering something. "I misspoke. I will need provisions for three. We will be returning with another."

"Yes, my lord. When do you plan to leave?"

"Within the hour."

"Yes, my lord. It will be ready as you wish." Pearson took several satchels from a peg on the wall as the young lord left the room and gave orders to the women specifying how to pack them.

Chapter 8

Rhoslyn held the end of the strip of cloth with her teeth and pulled the opposite end securing the bandage around her right hand. She rotated her hands and examined the bandages protecting her blisters before putting on her gloves to work in the garden. Picking up the hoe where she had left it on the ground, she chopped the dry soil to loosen the weeds, place them in the basket, and hacked the clumps of soil until they were tiny and smooth.

Her attention was drawn to a full bucket of water appearing next to her feet. She glanced up at the chubby nun whose face was red and breathing heavily. Beads of perspiration dotted Sister Theresa's upper lip and forehead.

"The abbess wants you to water the plants after you have weeded them. This will get you started, but you will have to refill the bucket at the well." The nun handed her the ladle.

Rhoslyn looked to the ladle in her hand, the full bucket of water, and watched the nun waddled away. She raised her hand to shield her eyes from the bright sun and looked at the well, located outside of the kitchen. Glancing at an adjacent field, she saw her dapple-gray grazing.

"Oh, Laila, I hate this place." She dropped the ladle in the bucket and returned to work. With Vespers soon approaching, she needed to quicken her pace to reach the end of the row.

~

Jayden slowed Beval to a leisurely pace as he entered the village. Accompanied by Sir Darwin and Shadow, he exhaled with a sign. "It's a relief to get away from Lady Carling." He nodded toward a peasant woman in the village who paused and curtsied to her lord.

"I agree. By the way, you're welcome, my lord." The knight smirked.

Scowling, Jayden snapped his head toward Sir Darwin. "For what?" He played ignorantly but was fully aware of what his knight was implying.

"For dancing with Lady Carling and sparing you the humiliation of her fondling hands violating your body before everyone in the Great Hall. The woman cares little for morality or modesty."

"I agree. It's a compliment to have a woman give you her undivided attention. But she is overbearing."

"I've never experienced the constant attention of a woman, my lord. I do, however, empathize with your plight."

"Come now, Sir Darwin, you must have had a few. You're a handsome devil."

"Thank you, my lord." Sir Darwin's monotone reply conveyed his growing intolerance of the subject at hand.

The sun was sinking over the horizon casting shadows upon the dirt road. The swaying treetops in the distant forest drew the knight's attention to the ominous clouds to the west.

"We will have to set camp soon, my lord. There may be rain on the way."

Jayden looked to the sky. "I agree."

~

Lady Eugenia sat at the small table eating her dinner. The sputtering of a single lit candle her only company. The food was prepared to her liking, but she had little appetite and pushed the variety of food around her plate with her fork. Certain she would soon face execution; thoughts of her daughter's future haunted her mind. Had Lord Filmore received the missive? Had he accepted the conditions of the betrothal? The large dowry almost ensured the match, but would Rhoslyn be happy with her father's choice of husband?

The patter of rain upon the lead roof interrupted her thoughts. She scrutinized the ceiling, thankful there were no leaks.

Chapter 9

Gargoyle downspouts spewed rivers of rainfall forming muddy puddles at the base of the buildings. Rhoslyn followed in line as the nuns finished attending the second Mass of the morning, walked through the cloister, and entered the convent.

Mother Margaret waited by the door. "Rhoslyn, a moment of your time."

The abbess did not ask a question, it was an order. Rhoslyn hesitated with her foot in midair before bringing it next to the other. She turned to face her superior. "Yes, Mother Margaret."

"I thought you would like to choose your task for today. It is obvious by the torrents of rain, working in the garden is out of the question unless you wish to catch your death?"

"No, Mother Margaret."

"Well then, you may choose between embroidery or copying scripture with our brothers. However, if you choose the ladder of the two, there will be no doodling or curses in the margins, understood?"

"Yes, Mother Margaret."

"Very well, your choice?"

Since her arrival, the abbess dictated and delegated task after task upon her. If she was not attending Mass, she was either baking bread, copying books, making soap, washing laundry, or gardening, never given the opportunity to choose her preference.

When she was forced to leave Bardenham, she took a partially embroidered handkerchief she was making for her mother, thought it would be nice to finish it and present it as a gift upon her return.

"I would like to work on embroidering a handkerchief for my mother."

The abbess rolled her lips inward making a straight line. She preferred Rhoslyn to embellish a vestment for the visiting priest but would be lenient of her thoughtful request. "Very well. You are dismissed."

Rhoslyn went to her cell and retrieved the unfinished handkerchief from her satchel hanging on a peg on the wall before walking to the sewing chamber. She moved a chair next to the window to make the best of the limited light of the overcast sky before searching the shelves for a needle, thread, and scissors. She pulled a shallow wooden box contained spindles of thread, sat in the chair, and placed the box in her lap. After scanning the many spindles, she selected one the loveliest shade of rose, threaded the needle, and placed the box on the floor. Picking up where she left off, she pulled the needle through the linen to continue the delicate design of various flowers. *Darn blisters.* She set her needlework in her lap and held the palms of hands toward the filtered light to inspect the blisters she had uncovered hoping they would heal quickly. *They look better. A day away from the garden will do them good.* She picked up her embroidery and continued to sew.

Sister Patricia entered the room. "What are you working on?"

Rhoslyn looked to the nun, nearly the same age as herself. "A handkerchief for my mother." She held it toward the nun so she could examine it.

"It's lovely. Such pretty flowers."

"Thank you." Rhoslyn touched the delicate stitches that captured each flower's likeness.

"My mother died several years ago." Sister Patricia glanced at the chamber door to ensure she would not be overheard. She lowered her voice. "Even though we have been kept in the dark about your true identity, many of us assume you are royalty."

Rhoslyn hesitated in confirming the nun's suspicion. She feared the wrath of the abbess both for the nuns and herself. Nevertheless, hoping to leave the Sisters of Charity sooner than later, she decided to trust her friend with the secret. "I look forward to the day I return to Bardenham."

"Since I have nowhere else to go, I've taken my vows and will remain here serving the Lord and the poor."

"An honorable profession." Rhoslyn pulled the needle through the cloth as she continued to stitch. She finished the handkerchief quickly. To avoid any menial task the abbess may assign, she chose another cloth and designed a cross embellished with lilies. She imagined it would make a nice decorative pillow.

~

Puddles dotted the muddy rutted road. Jayden shielded his eyes with the hood of his cloak as he looked toward his knight. "Will this rain ever end?" He pulled the reins as his warhorse slid sideways trying to regain his footing.

Sir Darwin slowed his horse as a gust of wind blew the hood of his cloak from his head. "My lord, shall we camp and wait until the rain stops?"

"We must be near the abbey. I would prefer to get out of this dampness and sleep in a bed for the night."

It was late afternoon when Jayden, Sir Darwin, and Shadow entered the Sisters of Charity's stable. They unsaddled and gave water and oats to their horses before approaching what they assumed to be the convent. Jayden rapped his knuckles on the door. He looked skyward in disbelief at the endless rainfall. Goosebumps rose on his flesh as he shook the droplets of rain from his cloak. Impatient to get out of the rain, he knocked again.

Sir Darwin tilted his head in the direction of a harmonious sound echoing above the patter of rain.

"My lord, is that singing I hear?"

Jayden removed his hood, listened, and walked toward the sound. He stopped in front of a large arched wooden door, pressing his ear to its oak planks.

"A church, I presume." He looked at his knight. "Does your soul needs saving?" He smiled and pulled open the door. They entered the dimly lit church.

In the shadowed darkness, the Latin chanting resonating off the stone walls sounded like a choir of angels. The flickering flames of the candelabras on the altar outlined the silhouette of its loyal congregation sitting in the pews.

The candlelight danced as the door slammed shut causing the visiting priest, who stood before the altar, to look up from his bible. He watched the men entered the last pew and sit behind the nuns.

Shadow stood transfixed by the sound with his ears perked. He turned his head right and left as if trying to identify which direction the chant had originated. Noting his master was no longer near him, the dog's toenails tapped on the stone floor as he obediently joined his master in the pew.

The lord and his knight scanned the church familiarizing themselves with their surroundings. They noted the exits, the vaulted ceiling with its intricate woodwork while searching for a balcony, and the number of people in the room. The alcoves contained statues transfixed and staring back at them. Jayden looked at the crucifix hanging on the wall above the altar with several candles illuminating it respectfully.

The voices within the church became silent. The monks rose from their pew and exited through a door while the nuns filed past Jayden and Sir Darwin and disappeared through another doorway. Looking at each shadowed face as they passed, the young lord wondered which nun he would escort back to Aldwinster.

The abbess, the last in line, turned toward the men, who stood as she approached them. She stopped before them. "How may I help you?" She evaluated the men's clothing and assumed they were royalty. The men exited the pew and stood in the aisle.

The church was cast into darkness as one by one the candles were extinguished by the youngest monk, who left a single candle lit beneath the crucifix.

"I'm Lord Jayden. This is Sir Darwin." The knight nodded his head in affirmation. Shadow peeked his head around the end of the pew drawing the abbess's attention causing her to raise one eyebrow. "And that's Shadow. We've been sent by my father to escort one of the nuns to Aldwinster." He retrieved a sealed missive from within his tunic and handed it to the abbess. They watched as she turned and went to the altar. She broke the seal, read the missive by the flickering flame, and nodded in understanding.

"Very well." She noted the excessive dampness of the men's clothing. With the rain resonating on the rooftop of the church and evening soon to fall, she was obligated as a Christian to be hospitable. "You have arrived in time for our evening meal. I will have Abbott Anthony prepare a cell in the dormitory for you to sleep. Perhaps tomorrow will greet us with better weather for your departure."

Jayden nodded. "That is very kind of you. Thank you."

"Follow me." The abbess led them through a doorway into the covered cloister. The rain cascaded from the rooftop's edge as they made their way to the convent. She opened the door and entered a greeting room. Sir Darwin grasped the door and closed it behind him.

The abbess motioned toward a bench. "Wait here. I shall notify the abbot of your need for a chamber." She left the room.

Jayden sat upon the primitive bench and patted Shadow's shoulder. "They live meekly."

His knight sighed as he sat. "No matter the accommodations, it will be better than sleeping on the wet ground."

Footsteps echoed from the hallway. They stood as the abbess entered the room.

"This way to the dining room." The abbess continued through the small room without stopping, led the men through a narrow hallway, and entered a room with a long table in its center, benches on its sides and a single chair at each end. A pair of lit candlesticks donned the table, the only light in the room.

"Please be seated." Mother Margaret motioned to the bench at the side of the table before disappearing into an adjoining room.

Jayden looked toward his knight, who shrugged his shoulders. Both men sat down, and Shadow took his usual place beneath the table.

The abbess reappeared carrying two empty tankards and a pitcher. "I hope you find our ale acceptable." She set a mug before each man, filled their tankards, and set the pitcher before them on the table.

Jayden lifted the tankard from the table. "Thank you." He tasted the high-quality ale, which the abbey had the reputation of producing. "It's very good. My compliments to the brewer."

Sir Darwin nodded in agreement after tasting the ale.

The abbess nodded and left the men alone in the room. They could hear the clatter of pots and pans echoing from the kitchen as they drank their ale and talked quietly. Their conversation was interrupted by several monks and nuns entering the room carrying various dishes of food.

Jayden watched as they kept their eyes averted for each other and went about their tasks.

Rhoslyn took the stack of plates from the shelf. She stopped short in the doorway after realizing there were two more for the evening meal. She returned to the shelf, added two plates to her stack, and entered the dining room. Quite certain the abbess would be displeased with the variation from normalcy, she circled the table placing a plate before each seat. She kept her line of vision on the table to avoid the inquisitive stare of the men.

Jayden watched the woman placing the plates on the table. She was young, close to his age, and possessed the most mesmerizing eyes the color of emeralds or were they aqua. He tried to imagine the color of her hair under her habit as he watched her stand before the bench across from him.

With the meal on the table and everyone standing in place, they waited.

Jayden and his knight questioned if they should stand as the abbot and abbess took their place at each end of the table. Everyone sat in unison and bowed their heads while a prayer of thanks was offered. The meager meal was shared by all without a word spoken. Unable to bear the silence any longer, Jayden spoke.

"Abbot Anthony, Abbess Margaret, I would like to thank you for this fine meal and accommodations for the night." He lifted his tankard of ale and nodded his head toward them.

Those at the table looked up from their plates, eyes widened at the disruption of silence and the improper address of the abbot and abbess. They looked at each end of the table for their reaction.

Aware of their guests being unaccustomed to their proper meal etiquette, Mother Margaret set her fork upon the table, wiped the sides of her mouth with her napkin to give herself time to chew and swallow her food. "It would be uncharitable of us not to do so. Unfortunately, we are unable to provide you with a meal that you are more accustomed to eating. Your cell is meek but will be warm and dry."

Feeling put in his place, Jayden nodded in acknowledgment and remained silent. Still hungry after cleaning his plate, he scanned the serving plates hoping to have a second portion but feared he would appear greedy. The abbess perceived his situation and motioned for him to obtain a second helping. He nodded in appreciation and did so.

The monks and nuns sat at the table with their hands in their laps and their heads bowed until their guests completed their meals. When the abbot placed his linen napkin on the table, everyone rose from the table and began to clear away the dishes while he and the abbess remained seated.

Rhoslyn collected the plates. As she picked up the last plate and headed toward the kitchen, Mother Margaret spoke causing her to stop in the doorway.

"Rhoslyn, place the scraps from the plates on a dish for the dog. Have Sister Patricia wash the dishes so that you can return and join us."

Rhoslyn glanced at the men before looking back to the abbess. It was her job to wash the plates. "Yes, Mother Margaret." She left the room and set the stack of dishes upon a table next to the washtub. "The abbess would like you to wash the plates after I scrape them. I've been ordered to return to the dining room."

Sister Patricia's hazel eyes widened. "Maybe she wants to talk to you about those men. I thought the abbess was going to reprimand the younger one when he spoke during the meal. They must be royalty, don't you think?" The nun picked up the scraped plates and plopped them into the dishwater.

"They look like royalty, but none that I know." Rhoslyn placed the palm of her hand on her friend's arm. "Thank you for doing the dishes for me." She picked up the plate for the dog.

"No, bother at all. Now go and see what she wants. You can tell me all about it later." Sister Patricia dipped her hands into the water and swished a rag over the first plate.

Rhoslyn paused in the doorway and glanced at the abbot's empty chair. She set the plate of scraps on the floor and stood next to the abbess.

"This is Lord Jayden and his knight, Sir Darwin." Both men nodded their heads toward her when introduced. "Lord Jayden delivered a missive which indicates you are to go with him and his knight tomorrow. You must pack your belongings and be ready at sunrise. Be sure to dress in the gown in which you arrived."

"I'll be leaving tomorrow?" Rhoslyn could hardly believe her ears.

"Yes, that is what I said. Go to your cell and pack."

Rhoslyn tried to conceal her smile as she nodded her head. She quickened her stride as she went to her cell. Once inside, she smiled in earnest.

"Oh, I'm going home. I can't wait to see Mother." She took the leather bag from a peg on the wall and put her few belongings inside, except for the cotton chemise she used as a nightgown and the clothing she would wear the next day. She packed the dainty embroidered handkerchief and the pillow she had yet to finish. She planned to complete the pillow once she arrived home and send it to the Sisters of Charity as a thank you gift for her stay.

There was a knock upon her cell door.

"Rhoslyn, it's me. Can I come in?"

Rhoslyn opened the door. The nun looked at each end of the hallway to ensure she was not seen before entering her cell.

Sister Patricia kept her voice at a whisper. "What happened?"

"I'm going home tomorrow. The men, um, Lord Jayden and Sir Darwin, are my escorts. Oh, I'm so excited." She tapped her fingertips together before her chest almost wishing she could clap her hands aloud for all to hear.

"I'm so very happy for you, but I will miss you." The nun displayed a frown as she tilted her head to the side. "It's time for Compline. We must go."

Rhoslyn nodded as she left the room with Sister Patricia. She grinned knowing it was the last time she would attend the Mass. With any luck, she would leave the abbey before having to sit through Matins.

Chapter 10

Too excited to sleep, Rhoslyn tossed and turned on her straw mattress throughout the night until she conceded, rose, and dressed in the gown in which she arrived. She sat on her bed and attached her dirk above her ankle. Unable to wear the knife while in residence, it was a familiar comfort to strap it to her leg once again. She smoothed her laundered skirt and hoped it would be presentable upon her arrival at Bardenham. She brushed her thick auburn hair and pinned it into place.

Footsteps echoed in the hallway, growing louder as someone approached her chamber. She rose and smoothed the blanket on the bed, wanting to leave it neat and tidy. She set her packed bag on the floor below her cloak hanging from a peg on the wall. As a knock sounded upon her door, she exhaled to calm herself, pulled the door open, and saw Sister Patricia's smiling kind face.

"Today is your big day, my lady. Are you excited?"

Even though she tried to contain her happiness, Rhoslyn smiled from ear to ear. "Yes, very much so."

The pair walked to the kitchen. As was her habit, Rhoslyn went to the shelf to get the plates for the morning meal, but Sister Theresa stopped her before she could collect them.

"Rhoslyn, you are to sit at the table. It is our gift to you, as our guest." The round-faced nun grinned.

Rhoslyn looked at the nuns. She had befriended many of them during her stay. Each nodded with a smile upon their face.

"That is so kind of you. Thank you." She paused in the doorway of the dining room and stared at the men sitting at the table. She wondered if it would be wise to be alone in the room with them.

Sensing someone behind him, Jayden stared as he rose from his seat scanning Rhoslyn's shapely figure from her head down to the floor. He noted the elegant copper-colored gown trimmed with gold lace and its bodice emphasized her tiny waist.

Rhoslyn scowled, balled her hands until her knuckles turned white, abashed by the man's forwardness. Her attention was drawn to the knight, who stood. Heat rose in her cheeks as she stared at the young lord again waiting for his eyes to meet hers.

He scanned her body upward admiring her auburn hair. Realizing his mouth was agape, he closed it and breathed deeply. "Your habit gave little indication as to the color of your hair. It's lovely."

"You weren't looking only at my hair." Rhoslyn took a deep breath reining in her anger. She sat in her place on the other side of the table. Accustomed to the silence of the convent, she decided it would be best to remain with her mouth shut, her head bowed slightly to the table.

Sister Patricia entered and set the table, a welcome distraction. The remaining residents of the abbey brought the breakfast meal into the room. As they stood by their seat, Rhoslyn stood. She glared at the lord and his knight, who also rose out of respect. When the abbot and abbess were in place, everyone sat in unison.

Rhoslyn kept her eyes downcast at her plate throughout the meal. She dared not glance at the young lord and discover his rude stare upon her. She needed to keep her composure in front of the abbess.

Jayden was indeed watching her. *Such a shame her habit hid her beauty.* He remained quiet throughout the meal.

The abbot placed his linen napkin on the table and left the room before the table was cleared. Rhoslyn thought it strange but assumed he needed to attend to another matter.

The abbess dabbed the corners of her mouth with her linen napkin, placed it on her plate, and looked at the person who was no longer her responsibility.

"Rhoslyn, we have enjoyed your stay and pray for your safe journey." The abbess looked to the two men. "Lord Jayden and Sir Darwin, I entrust her into your hands. Godspeed."

Jayden nodded. "Rest assured, Abbess Margaret, she will arrive at our destination safely."

The abbess rose from her seat. As was her habit, Rhoslyn began to rise, but the abbess signaled for her to sit before addressing Jayden. "I will have food prepared for your journey."

"Thank you."

The abbess nodded, took one last look at Rhoslyn, and left the room.

Rhoslyn dared to make eye contact with the lord and knight across the table. After all, she would be traveling with them for several days before arriving home. In her opinion, the knight, although older, seemed reasonable. He knew when to keep his mouth shut. The young lord, however, reeked of arrogance, or perhaps lack of maturity. Either way, she must tolerate him for the duration of the journey.

The men stood as she rose from the table.

"I will be just a moment while I retrieve my bag. I will meet you in the greeting room."

Jayden watched the sway of the petite woman's hips as she walked ahead of him to the greeting room. Her footsteps faded as she entered a corridor and the men remained in the small room.

Jayden turned to his knight. "I'll wait for her, go ahead and saddle the horses."

"Very well, my lord."

Shadow watched the knight exit the convent, looked back to his master, and back to the closed door where the knight disappeared.

"My lord."

He turned toward the nun standing behind him.

"Food for the journey." Sister Theresa presented a leather satchel.

"Thank you." He accepted the bag of food. The nun nodded and returned to the kitchen. Assuming Rhoslyn needed time to gather her things, he sat on the bench and petted Shadow on his head encouraging the canine to wait patiently.

~

With her cloak over her arm and bag in hand, Rhoslyn glanced at the tiny bed, rustic nightstand, and the crucifix on the wall casting the sparse room to memory before closing the door. She promised herself to never return to the abbey.

As she entered the greeting room, Jayden stood. "Shall I take your bag?" He reached for it.

"No." She turned her body away from him to keep the bag out of his reach. "I can do it myself."

He withdrew his hand as if being bitten by a snake, staring at her with his eyes widening and his mouth agape. Women usually seemed so helpless, well, at least the women he encountered. He tilted his head and nodded once. "As you wish."

She walked past him with her nose in the air, through the door, and headed toward the stable leaving him in her wake.

Jayden stood frozen as he watched her rustling skirt bellow behind her. He placed his fisted hands upon his hips and stared at her retreating figure in the open doorway. "Truly, you're going to just walk past me?"

She glanced over her shoulder as she continued to walk. "Correction, I did walk past you."

Scoffing, he closed the door behind him as he hastened his pace to catch up with the determined young lady.

Rhoslyn was eager to climb atop her mare. It had been six months since arriving at the Sisters of Charity and equally as many months since she had ridden her horse. She entered the stable and glanced at the three horses ready for travel, two destriers and a broken-down chestnut mare, and her other traveling companion. She looked to Laila, who remained in her stall. She glared at the knight. "You saddled the wrong horse." Rhoslyn threw her bag and cloak upon the dirt floor, its dust bellowing upon impact.

Sir Darwin lifted a single eyebrow as he scratched his jaw and watched the petite woman grab a bridle from the peg on the wall, slip the bit into the dapple-gray's mouth, and buckle it proficiently.

Rhoslyn led her mare out of the stall and tied the reins to a post. Laila pawed the ground, eager to begin the journey as she watched her mistress place a set of mounting steps next to her and retrieve two saddle blankets draped over a sawhorse.

Shadow trotted into the stable followed by his master. Jayden looked to his knight, who remained silent and held up the palms of his hands with a puzzled look upon his face. The young lord was taken back by the size of the dapple-gray as Rhoslyn climbed the steps. "She is large for a mare." He stared at the horse as he blindly handed the satchel to his knight.

Rhoslyn spread the first blanket on the dapple-gray's back. "Yes, seventeen hands high."

Sir Darwin attached the satchel to his saddle as he watched the woman struggle to straighten the first blanket. He signed and stepped forward. "My lady, may I be of assistance?"

"No." She spread the second blanket atop the first and brushed it with the palms of her hands to ensure its smoothness. She descended the steps and retrieved the heavy saddle from a stand.

Fearing the woman would topple backward from the steps as she raised it high enough to place upon the horse's back, Sir Darwin stepped forward and reached for the saddle. "My lady, I insist."

She snapped her head toward the knight. Her eyes squinted and glaring. "I said no." She raised the saddle and set it upon Laila's back.

Both men watched helplessly as the woman strapped and tightened the girth belt and attached her bag to the saddle. Rhoslyn shook her cloak free from dirt and dust and draped it over her shoulders securing it with its clasp. Tossing aside the steps, she lifted her left foot hip-high inserting it into the stirrup and hoisted herself upward into the saddle. Once astride, she looked down at the men, who had yet to mount their horses. "Are we ready?" She touched her heels to Laila's belly, encouraging her horse forward, out of the barn, and into the morning sunshine.

Shadow looked to the men. His tail wagging in anticipation.

The knight detected the sarcastic undertone in the woman's question. He looked to his lord, who stared at the stunning woman as she left the stable. "My lord?"

Jayden turned to his knight, mouth agape.

Sir Darwin untied his horse's reins from the post. "Are we ready to leave, my lord?"

Jayden closed his mouth with a snap. "Apparently so."

The men climbed atop their war horses. Their sole purpose was to ensure the woman arrived safely at Aldwinster. They doubted the assignment would be an easy task.

Chapter 11

Lord Filmore turned the page of his account book. A knock on the library door pulled his attention from his work to see Pearson standing in the doorway and a man behind him. "Yes, Pearson."

"A messenger, my lord."

"Send him in."

The tall lanky man walked into the room and stood before the lord's desk. He withdrew the missive from his satchel and handed it to Lord Filmore. As instructed by Baron Roldan, he waited for a reply.

Lord Filmore broke the wax seal and read the missive. It explained the alleged crimes by the Lord and Lady of Bardenham, the death of Lord Atherton, and the incarceration of Lady Eugenia at Somerville.

"Interesting." Lord Filmore lowered the missive and set it upon his desk. He jotted a quick reply that the missive was received and understood, sealed it, and handed it to the messenger.

The man nodded and left the room.

~

Their horses stomped through puddles and kicked up clods of mud from the dirt road as they distanced themselves from the abbey. With a feeling of weightlessness in her heart, Rhoslyn ignored her traveling companions as she hummed a melody and directed Laila homeward to Bradenham. She assumed she was following the correct road since neither of the men had indicated otherwise.

Jayden hoped their leisurely pace would give the blacksmith ample time to complete the repairs to Lady Carling's carriage allowing her to depart before his arrival at Aldwinster. He looked at his knight and nodded his head toward Rhoslyn. "She seems easy to travel with and shouldn't slow us down much."

Sir Darwin stared at the petite woman atop of the large horse. "I agree, an accomplished rider." He reserved his true opinion.

Several hours later they stopped to water and rest their horses. Sir Darwin distributed food from the satchel. Rhoslyn sat on a bolder, isolating herself from the men, and ate privately.

Jayden bit off a portion of dried beef, gave it to Shadow, and turned to his knight. "So, what do you think of her?"

Sir Darwin glanced at the woman's profile. Stunning, beautiful, but he suspected there was more to her than sheer beauty. "Beneath her beauty, I think she can be a handful, a bit headstrong."

Jayden trusted his knight's insight. He watched Rhoslyn as she finished her meal and went into the woods.

~

Rhoslyn stepped into the shadowed darkness, relieved to be away from the men's scrutinizing stares. She dodged trees and underbrush in search of a private spot to relieve herself but froze in place as a grunt came from behind her. She turned toward a bush with its branches shaking. She pivoted as an adjacent bush's branches began to shake. Keeping her eye on the foliage, she bent down to retrieve her dirk, even though the small knife would be of little defense if the boar should attack.

~

Jayden stopped chewing as he watched Shadow look to the woods, perk his ears, and growl. Without hesitation, he pulled his sword from its sheath and ran to the place where Rhoslyn had disappeared into the foliage.

Sir Darwin grabbed the dog's collar before he could dart after his master and restrained the canine protectively. He was fully aware of the damage a boar could inflict on anyone let alone a dog. With his sword in hand, he stepped into the woods to assist his lord.

Jayden pushed aside sapling branches before stopping to listen. The boar grunted to his left. Snapping his head in the direction of the noise, he stepped toward it. Sir Darwin separated from his lord's side and took a wider path to the right.

Another bush moved. Rhoslyn squared herself to face the threat with her dirk ready and retreated a step backward. Her bottom bumped into a tree trunk. She reached for the trunk to determine its width but discovered what she touched was cloth.

Jayden wrapped his left arm around her waist pulling her against his body. He whispered in her ear. "Get behind me."

Without warning, the boar charged. He pushed her aside to the ground and stepped over her body protectively, leveled his sword at the boar's head, and held it steady piercing its skull. It dropped dead within inches from where Rhoslyn lay on her side.

Sir Darwin emerged from behind a bush with his sword drawn. Looking down at the beast, he released Shadow and sheathed his sword. "Well done, my lord."

Jayden nodded to his knight as he withdrew his sword, wiped the blood from his blade on the boar's fur, and replaced it in its sheath. He turned to look at Rhoslyn, who stared at the dead animal with her dirk still in her hand ready to defend herself. "Are you well?"

She did not reply as she continued to stare as the curved tusks near her chest.

Jayden placed his leg in her line of vision blocked the dead animal from her sight. "Lady Rhoslyn?" He offered a hand to help her rise.

She looked toward Jayden's offered assistance. "Quite well. Thank you." Her reply was barely audible. She sat upright. Her hand shook as she tried to insert her dirk in its sheath. Unable to refuse Jayden's unwelcome assistance, she watched as he clasped her hand, guided the blade into its protective leather case, and lifted her from the ground to stand.

Sir Darwin placed his boot upon the boar to push it back and forth estimating its weight. "My lord, shall I gut the animal and take it with us for our evening meal?"

Jayden turned and looked at the dead animal. It was small enough to strap onto the back of a horse.

"Yes, no use in letting it go to waste." He turned back to Rhoslyn, who had disappeared. "Good lord, where has she gone to now?"

Sir Darwin withdrew his dirk and paused as he looked up from the boar. "She shouldn't be alone. There may be other boars close by."

Jayden listened for the rustling of underbrush and snapping of fallen branches Rhoslyn left in her wake.

Rhoslyn needed time to pull herself together. She held her hands out before her to verify how badly she was shaking. Taking deep breaths, she tried to calm her rapidly pounding heart. She wiped her damp palms on her skirt. Tears pooled in her eyes, blurring her vision. Tripping over a fallen log hidden beneath the grass, she stumbled forward causing her tears to cascade down her cheeks. A firm hand gripped her upper arm and pulled her upward before she fell to the ground. She stared into the blue orbs of Jayden before looking away to conceal the trail of tears on her cheeks.

However, Jayden had seen her tears. Sensing she had regained balance, he released her arm and stood quietly.

Rhoslyn exhaled trying to calm herself. She looked down to his feet, unwilling to meet his inquisitive stare. "Thank you."

Hoping to ease her distress, he decided to make light of the situation. "No, thank you. You're a fine hunter."

Confused, her eyebrows narrowed as she wiped away another tear and looked to his face for clarification.

"An interesting technique to use yourself as bate." He looked down at the petite woman as he motioned in the direction of the horses encouraging her to continue walking.

Rhoslyn scowled, certain he was making fun of her. She spun around and walked in the direction he indicated.

Usually attuned to the female gender, Jayden scratched his head before following.

Rhoslyn emerged from the woods. The sight of Laila calmed her. She petted her neck while realizing she had yet to relieve herself. She turned to face Jayden, who stepped into the clearing joining her. "If you don't mind, I must be alone for a moment. Please turn around while I go behind that bush." She pointed to the other side of the clearing at a bush with thick foliage.

He nodded his head and turned his back to her.

Rhoslyn went to her destination at a quickened pace, stepped behind it, and peeked around its branches toward Jayden, whose back remained toward her. She lifted her skirt, squatted to empty her bladder, and rejoined him as the knight emerged simultaneously from the woods dragging the gutted boar by its hind leg. Shadow pranced as if the kill was his.

Eager to be on her way, Rhoslyn climbed atop Laila and waited while the knight strapped the boar over the rump of his horse. The men climbed atop their horses and they continued down the road.

Chapter 12

Rhoslyn looked skyward as she blew a stray strand of her hair away from her eyes. She had grown weary of the drone and tiresome conversation that drifted back from the men riding in front of her which involved three topics; hunting, fighting, and women. She noted the sun threatening to disappear below the horizon and assumed they would set up camp soon unless the young lord and his knight preferred to travel well into the night. Eying the boar on the rump of the knight's horse, her taste buds watered. She thought of an evening meal at Bardenham, the last time she enjoyed the savory meat.

A bellow of laughter pulled her from her pleasant thoughts. She stared at the back of Jayden's head. *Probably an exaggeration on the number of times he bedded a woman.*

Fully aware of her parent's loveless marriage and the countless times her mother was neglected and humiliated by her father, she observed other married couples who visited Bardenham and concluded they were unhappy too. Several times she stumbled upon a servant woman involved with an unfaithful lord in an alcove while their wife waited for them in their bedchamber. Rhoslyn concluded men, at least those she encountered in her lifetime, held little value in loyalty. She would have welcomed a permanent residence at the abbey if the abbess would not have made her life so miserable. She could not imagine living under her rule for a lifetime.

The men directed their horses off the road. Rhoslyn reined her horse to a stop and peered into the distance wishing she could go ahead without them, but traveling in the darkness of night was unsafe, especially for a lady, so she reined Laila to follow.

After locating a suitable spot to camp, the lord and his knight dismounted and unsaddled their horses. Rhoslyn dismounted, untied the girth belt, and pulled the saddle toward her. The horse blankets fell to the ground as she caught the saddle and set it on a fallen log. She retrieved the blankets, folding them neatly, and placing them on the saddle's seat. She interrupted the men's incessant chattering. "If you will excuse me, I shall return shortly." She turned toward the woods, not waiting for their reply.

The men looked at each other, questioning if they should accompany her, yet not wanting to encroach on her privacy. Jayden signaled for Shadow to follow her.

When Rhoslyn returned, she saw the boar rotating on a stick over the flames of a crackling campfire. The men sat on the ground drinking wine from flasks.

Jayden held up a third flask as he looked toward her. "My lady."

Scowling, she accepted the flask. "Thank you." With the flask in hand, she retreated to her saddle on the other side of the campfire, spread a horse blanket on the ground, and sat. She ignored the men's rude conversation, focused on the flickering flames as she sipped the wine, and watched the escaping tiny embers as they floated upward to the twinkling stars dotting the indigo night sky.

Jayden glanced at the woman periodically throughout his conversation with his knight.

When she lowered her line of vision, her eyes met his. She returned his stare, unwavering. He nodded his head toward her. She looked away and stared blankly into the woods.

He smirked. *There is stubbornness in her eyes or is it pride?*

Sir Darwin witnessed the silent exchange between the two. "The exterior of the meat should be cooked well enough to eat, my lord."

Jayden looked back to his knight. He nodded his head and withdrew his dirk to cut a slice.

Her mind seemed fuzzy; her reactions delayed. Drinking a good portion of the flask on an empty stomach may not have been Rhoslyn's wisest decisions. Her hand moved in slow motion as she raised it to scratch her nose. She sat stupefied, staring at the arrogant lord.

He returned her stare as he tasted the tidbit of meat ensuring it was fully cooked. "What are you looking at?"

"You, my lord." Her reply was slurred, sounding as one.

He raised his eyebrows at her reply. "Why?"

"I find your limited topic of conversations to be repetitive and boring. Furthermore, one should not boast or brag about the number of women you have seduced. Do you fornicate like an animal, rut like the pig you killed today, or do you simply charge for your stud service?"

Sir Darwin took a sip from his tankard to conceal his grin. *The lady possesses whit.*

Rhoslyn took another swig of wine and continued. "One would believe you lack education, morality, and culture."

Jayden's heartbeat quickened as he clenched his teeth. "So, this is your assumption of my character. Has it taken an indulgence in wine to loosen your tongue?"

"Perhaps the drink has lowered my senses to your level." She suggested with a smirk, giggled, and took another sip.

He scowled. "You're drunk."

"And you are a typical egotistical ass, so full of yourself, expecting women to adore you. Well, I don't adore you." Goosebumps prickled her skin. Rhoslyn looked behind her to retrieve the second blanket, but it was too far for her to reach. Capping her flask, she tossed it on the ground and stood on shaky legs. She turned toward her saddle sidestepping as she walked, retrieved the second blanket, and returned to her spot. She crossed her legs, plopped upon the ground, pulled the blankets around her. She looked toward Jayden with heavy eyelids partially obstructing her vision. He was staring at her, nostrils flaring, unsmiling.

Rhoslyn lay upon her side allowing her eyes to close and drifted off to sleep.

Chapter 13

Rhoslyn lay on her stomach with her face wedged against her saddle. Her horse blanket covered her head blocking the morning sunlight.

Shadow pushed his cold damp nose beneath the blanket, sniffed to locate Rhoslyn's face, and touched it to her cheek pulling her from her slumber. Angered by the intrusion, she lifted the blanket and squinted her eyes to shield them from the light of day as she sat up abruptly. She steadied her head between her hands to stop the landscape from spinning. Her mouth was as dry as a dessert. She looked to the wine flask on the ground but could not force herself to drink the cause of her parchedness.

With his ego bruised from her drunken comments the previous night, Jayden laughed at her plight. "My lady, I see you have awakened!" He extended his hand toward her mockingly.

Cringing from his loud chatter, she tilted her head and shaded her eyes with her hand to see his mocking grin. "No, thank you. I can do it myself." She rolled onto her hands and knees and rose slowly upright. Taking a shaky step toward the woods, she nearly walked into a tree and grasped it for support as a wave of lightheadedness blurred her vision.

Jayden chuckled to himself as he watched her stumble about and signaled for his dog to follow her. He admired her independence, or was it her stubbornness? He thought he portrayed the perfect gentlemen, offered a kindness, yet she misinterpreted his assistance. She was insulting and mysterious like a puzzle in which pieces must be assembled in order. Attuned to her present condition, the temptation to cause her additional pain with a jolting ride toward Aldwinster made him smirk. He turned to his knight, who tossed his saddle onto his horse. "Shall we push the horses and travel a greater distance today? The sooner we arrive home, the sooner we rid ourselves of Lady Rhoslyn."

Sir Darwin raised an eyebrow suspicious of the young lord's ulterior motive, assuming he was insulted by the woman's refusal. "My lord, I feel obligated to remind you that Lady Carling may be awaiting your return to Aldwinster."

Jayden cringed at the mere mention of the woman's name. He looked toward the sound of retching echoing from the woods and heeded his knight's advice. "Very well." He grabbed his saddle from the ground and flung it onto Beval's back. From the corner of his eye, he saw Rhoslyn emerge from the woods but chose to ignore her. Shadow stepped from the foliage and joined his master.

The carcass of the boar hung over the ashen embers, shriveled and dry like sunbaked roadkill. Rhoslyn glanced at the wild pig, the color drained from her face, and her stomach revolted. She turned away, emptying its contents. Rhoslyn picked up her flask of wine from the ground, winced, and took in a mouthful to rinse away the bitterness. She wiped the spittle dangling from her bottom lip before glancing toward the two men with their backs toward her. She looked from her saddle to Laila, sighed, and untied her reign. "Good morning, Laila. It's time to continue our journey home, big girl." She stroked her nose and led her to the log where her saddle lay. Laila rotated in a circle to face the war horses. Rhoslyn took the blankets from the ground, threw them on the mare's back, and smoothed the wrinkles as best she could before pulling the reins to align her horse next to the log once again.

Laila's ears flipped back and forth like a loose shutter. She took a few nervous steps forward with the reins dragging on the ground.

Rhoslyn sighed, stepped down from the log, and retrieved the reins. She pushed Laila's chest encouraged her horse to back up and stroked her neck to calm her. Retrieving her saddle, she stepped blindly onto the log and hoisted it above her head.

Beval stomped his foot, whinnied, and nodded his head up and down eager to be on his way. Laila darted forward as Rhoslyn dropped the saddle on the ground and looked to Jayden with her fists placed firmly on each hip.

Sir Darwin retrieved the skittish mare's reins and circled her around toward her mistress while Rhoslyn retrieved the saddle, stepped on the log, and placed it on the mare's back as she came alongside her. She tightened the saddle in place before climbing atop and accepting the reins from the knight. "Thank you, Sir Darwin. It's nice to have at least one gentleman accompany me during our journey." She glared at Jayden, who sat on Beval with his back toward her.

"You're welcome, my lady."

Returning to the dirt road, Rhoslyn's head throbbed with each step of her horse. She tried to ignore the whispered conversation of the men who rode ahead of her.

Sir Darwin glared at Jayden. "But she is our guest, my lord."

"I don't care. She was rude."

"She was drunk and may not remember what she said."

"Perhaps the wine loosened her tongue enough to say how she truly feels."

"She must eat something. She didn't have supper nor breakfast."

"Unfortunate for her."

Sir Darwin looked over his shoulder to see the woman's eyes closed and her face ghostly white. He turned back to his lord. "Since you have chosen to be an unsympathetic guardian, then you can pick her up from the ground once she falls from her horse. Let's pray she doesn't get hurt in doing so."

Jayden looked over his shoulder at Rhoslyn. The woman's head bobbed like a ragdoll with each stride of her horse. Was she asleep? Fearing Sir Darwin's prediction, he turned Beval toward her horse, caught Laila's reins, and pulled her to a stop.

Rhoslyn opened her bloodshot eyes lethargically, peered at Jayden, and scowled.

Jayden noted her face absent of color. "I apologize for my oversight. We will stop along the roadside so you may have something to eat."

Why does he have to shout? She nodded her head ever so slightly in agreement.

Just past a turn in the road, they directed their horses to a stream and dismounted. Rhoslyn led Laila to the water and sat on a nearby boulder. She brushed her against its mossy green surface while listening to the trickle of cascading water over a fallen log. She brushed her shoes through the lush green grass as thick as an animal's pelt. The area seemed peaceful, calm. She inhaled the fresh air and closed her eyes as she felt a tug from Laila's reins.

Sir Darwin retrieved the satchel of food and handed it to his lord, who opened it and discovered bread and cheese each wrapped in beeswax cloth. There was jerky, perhaps venison, and a flask of wine as well. He was certain Rhoslyn would turn down his offer of the drink but would offer it, nevertheless. He withdrew his dirk from its sheath on his belt and cut a wedge of cheese, sliced a thick piece of bread, and placed the cheese upon the bread. He tapped her shoulder and held it before her.

She looked at the items he offered and to his face to ensure he was sincere. "Thank you." She hoped the food would help calm her queasy stomach and alleviate her throbbing head.

Allowing the woman time to rest, Jayden and his knight indulged in a portion of the food as well. Shadow explored the area but return when his nose detected the aroma of cheese.

Roslyn looked up into the canopy of gently flowing branches as they brushed along Laila's back while she grazed. She turned around to view the trunk. A white willow. She broke off a low hanging branch, stripped it of its leaves, and put the frayed end in her mouth. She chewed loosening its bark and she watched Laila eat the vibrant green grass along the bank of the river.

Jayden secured the top of the satchel closed and handed it to his knight before going to the edge of the river. He stood with his feet shoulder-width apart and his arms crossed over his chest and observed the swift current for a moment, uncertain if the woman would speak to him. He could see in his peripheral vision the branch in her mouth bobbing up and down as she chewed. He looked above his head to the tree. "Ah, white willow. A good cure for a headache." He recalled an evening with his favorite wench who had given him the same remedy. He stared at the stubborn woman with the most beautiful auburn hair and breathtaking emerald eyes.

Growing uncomfortable in his presence, Rhoslyn's only recourse was to rise and climb atop Laila dismissing him completely.

Jayden exhaled. He was doing his best to be cordial yet was helpless in breaching her silence as he watched her rein Laila and head toward the road.

Chapter 14

The blacksmith dabbed his sweaty brow with a rag. "My lady, the repairs to your carriage are complete."

Lady Carling circled her carriage inspecting the flawless repairs. "Please have it moved to the stable. I promised Lord Jayden I would be here upon his return."

"Yes, my lady."

Lady Carling turned toward the Keep. She scanned the building's grandeur and imagined herself as the Lady of Aldwinster, wife of Lord Jayden. She strutted past the alewives and glared at a woman staring at her. *Perhaps one of his strumpets.* She snickered. *Since he is expected to return tonight or tomorrow, I'll request a bath to ensure I look my best for him. A dab or two of rose oil behind my ears should entice him too.* She entered the Keep in search of Pearson. Finding the Great Hall empty, she went to the kitchen and stood in its doorway with her fisted hands on her hips. The steward was talking to a woman, most likely the head cook.

"Pearson!" She crossed her arms over her well-endowed chest and stamped her foot on the floor. "Pearson!"

The steward looked toward the doorway, groaning internally. The woman was a guest. He was doing his best to treat her with respect, but his patience was unraveling like the end of a hemp rope. Excusing himself from the head cook, he took a deep breath and walked toward the kitchen doorway. "My lady, how may I be of help?"

"I want a bath brought to my chamber immediately. Please ensure the water is hot and include plenty of scented soaps."

"Yes, my lady." He watched her skirt flail as she turned and walked away with her nose held high. Pearson scanned his staff, who were busily preparing the evening meal, in search of idle hands to meet the woman's demands.

~

Lady Myla entered the library.

Lord Filmore looked up from the missive he held in his hand. "We received this the day I sent Jayden to escort a woman from the Sisters of Charity."

"You mean the nun."

"No, a young lady and one that you know."

Lady Myla walked around his desk, outstretched her hand, and accepted the missive. She began to scan its contents, her eyes widening, and looked to her husband. "Lady Rhoslyn?"

He nodded his head in affirmation.

"We've discussed their match for many years." She continued to read. "Oh, dear. It looks as if they have little choice in the matter now." Lord Atherton's signature was at the bottom of the contract, which stated the terms and dowry amount. "I assume you plan to add your signature."

"Yes."

"Then it is settled." She watched her husband dip the quill in the ink and add his name to the bottom of the contract. "When do you plan to tell them of the betrothal?"

"When they have become accustomed to each other."

"And what about the status of her parents? When do you plan to tell her?"

"When the baron has made his decision on Lady Eugena's case."

"Perhaps it would be wise to do it sooner. It may be her only chance to say farewell to her mother before she is sentenced."

~

Rhoslyn's headache was subsiding. She continued to chew the white willow twig, breaking off what was used and reducing the branch to a mere stub. The unfamiliar landscape was a welcomed distraction with an occasional startled rabbit scampering across the road, a scared squirrel climbing a tree, and even a raccoon waddling alongside Laila before ducking into the tall grass. She was impressed by Shadow's discipline as the canine followed his master's command and remained next to Beval. Recalling the number of days her journey from home had taken to arrive at the abbey, she assumed an additional day of riding would be necessary before arriving at Bardenham. However, since the lord and knight seemed to be traveling an alternative route, they could arrive sooner.

A rattling sound and the clip-clop of a horse's hooves forewarned of an approaching wagon on the narrow dirt road. They reined their horses to the side of the road and gave the wagon the right of way.

The driver stopped before them and looked to the young lord. "Good day, Lord Jayden."

Jayden nodded toward the round-faced man. "Cyrus, what has you out and about?"

"I'm heading to the market and hope to trade for spices and other supplies." He indicated with a nod of his head toward the back of the cart where piglets, chickens, and rabbits were caged.

"I'm confident you will trade well."

"Thank you, my lord." Cyrus slapped the reins on the horse's rump. He nodded to Rhoslyn as he passed her.

She smiled at the man and turned in her saddle to watch the wagon travel down the road. Raising an eyebrow, she looked at Jayden and his knight, who encouraged their horses forward. "Where are you taking me?"

The men reined their horses. Jayden looked over his shoulder. She had yet to follow. He turned Beval, urged him forward, and reined him beside Laila.

"With us, as we were instructed." His tone was flippant as if she should know the answer to her question.

"What is our destination?"

"Aldwinster."

"Aldwinster! You told me I was going home, home to Bardenham."

"I did no such thing."

"But I want to go home to Bardenham."

He took a deep breath and remained calm as he noticed her eyes welling with tears. "I was instructed to bring you to Aldwinster. Perhaps Aldwinster is the first leg of your journey. Maybe you will travel to Bardenham later."

Her mind searched for a logical explanation. She pried. "Who told you to escort me from the Sisters of Charity?"

"My father, Lord Filmore, Lord of Aldwinster."

With her panic subdued, she babbled. "Something is wrong. I should be returning to Bardenham." Her shoulders slumped and line of vision dropped to the road.

Jayden ventured a suggestion. "Perhaps another escort will meet you at Aldinster and you will begin the leg of your next journey once rested."

She looked to his face believing the possibility. "Perhaps."

"Either way, we shall discover the truth upon our arrival. Shall we be on our way?"

Rhoslyn stared into his eyes, searching for the truth. With the glimmer of hope that he offered, she nodded her head in agreement.

Chapter 15

Traveling at a leisurely pace, they camped for the night and continued their journey throughout the next day. Rhoslyn assumed the increased activity on the road indicated they were approaching Aldwinster.

As the sun dipped below the horizon, the small party crested a hill and the kingdom came into view.

Jayden reined Beval to a stop. "Ah, home."

She brought her horse aside Beval, staring into the distance. "It's not my home." Her voice was a mere whisper and monotoned.

Sir Darwin, his horse sandwiching the woman between him and his lord, glanced at the sullen woman before looking to his lord, hoping he would reassure her all would be well.

Jayden glanced at Rhoslyn. "True, but at least you don't have to sleep on the ground tonight. And we will be in the company of good people and eat good food, for our cook is one of the finest."

She scanned the kingdom. From what she could see in the dim light of dusk, it looked well-kept with its village, fields of abundant crops, and majestic castle. She sighed as Jayden urged his horse forward.

Rhoslyn looked from one side of the dirt street to the other as they entered the pristine village. She inhaled various aromas of prepared food lingering in the air. The illumination of candles on tables and hearths aglow allowed her to peer inside each dwelling. She spied a woman preparing the evening meal in one home. A little girl sat at a table playing with a doll in another. Many families were settling down for the evening, sharing a meal, or sitting near the warmth of their fireplaces.

They directed their horses over the drawbridge, through the bailey, and reined them at the stable. Kolby came forward, noticed the woman on horseback, and retrieved the mounting steps to aid her descent. He placed them on the ground for her to rein her horse alongside before grabbing Beval's bridle as Jayden dismounted. "I'm glad to see you've arrived home safely, my lord."

"Yes, all went well, Kolby." He glanced at Rhoslyn, displaying a sideways smile. She reined her horse next to the steps.

The stableboy looked at Laila. His mouth dropped open as Rhoslyn dismounted. "My, she's a big one. Quite large for a mare."

Rhoslyn raised her eyebrows and looked at Jayden for a proper introduction.

He looked skyward and motioned toward her. "Kolby, this is Lady Rhoslyn."

The stableboy bowed his head. "Is she yours, my lady?" Kolby grabbed the mare's bridle with his other hand.

"Yes."

"Lovely animal, she is." He led both horses inside the stable.

Sir Darwin dismounted. He patted his horse's rump. It entered the stable unassisted, eager for its share of oats.

Jayden led the way with commanding strides to the Keep. He looked at the alewives and saw one of his favorite wenches. She smiled upon seeing him and waved. He winked and nodded his head toward her.

Rhoslyn followed his line of sight. The woman was beautiful, obviously flirting. *So that's the type of woman he prefers, easy and loose.*

They stepped over the threshold of the Keep, passed through the hallway, and stood in the doorway of the Great Hall to see the evening meal in progress.

Lady Carling paused mid-chew as she saw Jayden enter the room. She wanted to cry out, to call his name. Her heartbeat quickened. She swallowed her mouthful of food, nearly choking, and gulped wine from her tankard to wash it down. She touched her hair to ensure it was perfectly pinned in place as she watched him approach the High Table, sat taller in her chair pushing her ample bosom forward, and plastered a fake smile on her face.

Rhoslyn's eyes widened and her mouth dropped open as she took in the grandeur of the room; the many tables with people eating and conversing, candelabras with their candlelight dancing on the walls as servants passed them carrying pitchers of drink or trenchers of food, the vaulted ceiling, and tapestries decorating the stone walls. A fire blazed in the large fireplace with its mantel carved of stone and a large painting displayed above. Her stomach grumbled as she inhaled the aroma of roasted venison, carrots, potatoes, cabbage, and spiced wine. She looked to the High Table on the raised dais. In its center were two high backed, wooden carved chairs where she assumed the middle-aged man to be Jayden's father and the woman his mother.

She looked down at the state of her gown. It was dusty with several smudges of dirt and quite wrinkled. She tried to tidy her hair and brush the wrinkles from her skirt as she followed Jayden and stood before the High Table. She curtsied while Jayden and Sir Darwin bowed respectfully.

Lady Carling stared at Jayden like a snake hypnotizing its prey. She was confident he would look in her direction even though she sat at the farthest seat at the High Table, but he did not. Her smile faded as she watched the stunning woman standing beside him. She had to admit, the woman was very pretty.

Lord Filmore smiled at the party of three before him. "I see you have returned safely. I assume this lovely lady is Lady Rhoslyn."

Jayden motioned toward the woman at his side. "Yes, father, we have returned with Lady Rhoslyn as requested."

"Welcome to Aldwinster." He motioned toward his right. "May I present my wife, Lady Myla."

Rhoslyn looked to the Lady of Aldwinster, who displayed a smile, her lovely ebony hair sprinkled with gray. Out of respect, Rhoslyn curtsied and bowed her head.

Lady Myla took into consideration the state of the woman's dress fully aware of the endurance needed for traveling from the Sisters of Charity. "How nice of you to join us."

Rhoslyn stood and looked to the woman. *I didn't have much choice.* She forced a grin upon her face. "Thank you for your accommodations and generosity." She watched as Jayden and Sir Darwin took their rightful place at the High Table, leaving her alone before the dais.

Lady Myla spoke to the woman seated to her right, who rose and sat on the bench next to Lady Carling. She signaled to a servant for a new place setting and looked back to Rhoslyn. "My dear, come join me." Lady Myla motioned to the empty seat as a servant set a clean pewter plate, fork, and knife. Another servant came forward, filled a silver goblet with spiced wine, and presented it to Rhoslyn, who nodded as she sat, accepted the glass, and drank. There was plenty of meat and vegetables to choose from on the platter before her. She used the two-pronged fork to select a nicely roasted piece of venison, cut a piece, and ate savoring its flavor. To round out her meal, she helped herself to potato, carrots, and a slice of warm bread in which she added a thick layer of butter.

Lady Myla picked up her goblet from the table. "I hope your trip was uneventful."

"For the most part, it was pleasant." She cut another piece of meat and paused with it midway to her mouth. "Even though I find Aldwinster to be quite lovely, I'm looking forward to going home to Bardenham to see my parents."

Lady Myla remained silent as she lifted her goblet to a passing servant indicating a needed refill. It was not the place nor the time to inform Rhoslyn about the turn of events within Bardenham. "Well, I hope you enjoy your stay while you're with us." Lady Myla took a sip of her wine. "I'll have Pearson, our steward, ready a chamber, draw a bath, ensure you have clean clothes to wear and assign one of my ladies to see to your needs."

"Thank you. I do apologize for the state of my dress. The muddy roads made it impossible to keep it tidy."

Lady Myla nodded, leaned forward placing her left elbow on the table and her chin on her fisted hand wanting to hear more of the adventure.

The sparkling ruby set in gold on the Lady of Aldwinster's finger caught Rhoslyn's eye. It was dainty in design with a thin band, an oval ruby protected by a twisted bead of gold to hold the stone in place.

"Lady Myla, your ring is stunning."

The Lady of Aldwinster extended her hand, fanned her fingers, and looked to her ring. "I received it as a gift from my husband many years ago."

Rhoslyn's smile faded. "My father never gave such gifts to my mother."

Lady Carling leaned forward and stared at Jayden. Her smiled had faded. She scowled and clenched her teeth, for he had yet to look her way.

A serving wench sauntered to the High Table and batted her eyes at the young lord.

Rhoslyn watched the encounter and nearly burst out laughing. *A strumpet.*

The servant picked up Jayden's tankard. "How was your trip, my lord?" She held it above her chest, filled it until it overflowed, and dripped onto her bulging bosom. "Oooopppppsssss." The servant smiled setting the full tankard upon the table and brushed her hand over her dampened skin.

Intrigued, Rhoslyn leaned forward to see Jayden's reaction. The peasant woman had his undivided attention. *Pathetic.* She chuckled to herself as the wench winked at him.

Jayden admired the servant's swinging hips as she walked toward the opposite end of the table. He noticed Rhoslyn leaning forward with a smirk on her face. He looked past her to see Lady Carling glaring at him with narrowed eyes. *Good Lord.* He raised his mug in a silent toast to them both. Rhoslyn looked away. Lady Carling smiled and returned the compliment.

Sir Darwin shook his head back and forth and sighed. His patience was growing thin as he watched the exchange between the wench, Lady Carling, and his ward. He leaned toward Jayden. "I was hoping she would have returned home before we arrived." Uncertain if he had the young lord's attention, he continued. "I think she aims to share your bed tonight."

Jayden nearly choked on his wine. "I'm aware of her conniving and scheming. Please have a care and do all that is possible to keep her away from me."

"I will do my best, my lord." The knight glanced at the woman again. *God help me.*

The remainder of the meal was uneventful. However, the over-attentive serving wench returned to Jayden often to ensure his tankard was always full.

Rhoslyn's attention was drawn to the woman near the end of the table and leaned forward to watch Jayden's interaction with the curvy wench. *Ah, another woman with her sights on him.*

With the meal finished, tables cleared, and pushed aside, the music began. Lord Filmore led Lady Myla to the center of the floor. All in attendance watched as their lord and lady circled about the room.

Rhoslyn admired the couple's elegance, their gracefulness. Reflecting on the many meals within Bradenham's Great Hall, her line of vision drifted to the tabletop as she remembered her parents seldomly doing the same. She looked up as the music stopped and applause filled the room. The Lord of Aldwinster presented his wife and she curtsied as if taking a bow for their performance. The next song began as the lord and lady returned to their seats.

Lord Filmore leaned toward his son. "My lord, you should ask our guest to dance."

"Lady Carling? You're not serious I hope."

"Heaven forbid, no. Ask Lady Rhoslyn."

"She has had a long journey and we don't see eye to eye. I doubt she will accept my offer."

"You don't know unless you try. Go on now."

Jayden sighed, took one last drink of his wine, and rose from the table.

Lady Carling sat a little taller, anticipating the question he would ask her. Of course, she would accept. She dreamed of his hand upon her waist as he twirled her about the floor for all to see. She watched him as he stopped behind the woman's chair next to his mother. Her mouth dropped open.

"Lady Rhoslyn, would you care to dance?" Jayden offered his hand to help her rise.

She glanced at his extended hand and to his insincere sky-blue eyes. "No, thank you."

Seizing the opportunity, Lady Carling rose from her seat. "Oh, I will be happy to accept your hand for a dance."

Jayden sighed as he withdrew his hand and turned toward the obnoxious woman. "Very well." He presented his hand.

Instead of placing her hand politely on top, she grabbed it and entwined her arm around his. Jayden's face reddened as they left the dais and took to the floor.

Rhoslyn giggled.

Lady Myla's eyebrows raised as she looked at Rhoslyn. "What are you laughing at, my dear?"

"No disrespect, Lady Myla, but your son. From the look on his face and the distance he is placing between himself and the woman he is dancing with, it's quite clear he wishes to be rid of her."

"Yes, I agree. Lady Carling has been seeking his attention ever since her husband died."

"From what I see, she doesn't seem to be his type of woman." She looked at the serving wench who had given Jayden extra attention throughout the meal.

"I agree, but she's relentless." Lady Myla reached for her goblet.

Rhoslyn covered her mouth with her hand to conceal her giggles and laughter as she was entertained by the young lord's unpleasant situation throughout the dance.

Jayden noticed her merriment at his expense. As the dance ended, he bowed to his partner and Lady Carling curtsied before leading her from the dance floor and returning her to her seat. Jayden stepped behind Rhoslyn, clasped his hand around her upper left arm, and clenched his teeth. "I would appreciate a moment of your time in private."

Rhoslyn looked at his narrowed eyes and unsmiling lips pressed tightly together as if trying to hold back what he was truly thinking. She looked to his mother, who gave a slight nod of her head in approval. The pressure from his grasp encouraged her to rise from her seat. She hastened her steps as she was pulled across the room, down the hallway, and into a room. He shut the door behind her as she looked about. There were books on shelves, too many to count, a large wooden carved desk and matching chair, a fireplace that was a smaller version of the one in the Great Hall, and several paintings upon the walls. An elegant rug covered the stone floor. "This is the most beautiful library I have ever seen."

"Do I amuse you?" His words were spiteful, angry.

She turned to face him. "Amuse me?"

"Yes, you seemed to be amused by my dancing."

"I was amused by your situation with that woman. Perceivably, you have no desire to be in her company." She covered her mouth with her hand to camouflage her smile and allow it to fade. "In truth, you dance quite well."

"I see." He began pacing the floor.

"Her goal is to weasel her way into your life, to acquire a title and position, and I'm not inferring to the many positions she is capable of in your bed." Rhoslyn crossed her arms over her chest and grinned.

He shuddered before turning toward her. "Her intention is obvious. What am I to do?"

"Don't ask me. She is your problem, but the best advice I can give you is to stay away from her. Once she gets her claws in you, she will not let go."

He paced the floor while tapping his chin with the first two fingers on his right hand. "How am I going to deter her?"

Rhoslyn sighed. "It's been a long day. I'm told there is a warm bath in my chamber. So, if you will excuse me." She pulled open the door to leave, but the latch was yanked from her hand as the door slammed shut. She turned to see Jayden leaning over her.

"You, you can help me." Jayden displayed a devilish grin, eyes wide, and a finger pointing at her nose.

"Me?" Rhoslyn shook her head back and forth. "Oh, I'm not getting involved. I plan to leave for Bardenham as soon as possible." She walked away from the door and turned toward him with her hands fisted upon each hip. "Why don't you turn to some of the other women you flirt with and lead on?"

He looked to the ceiling; his face masked with innocence. "Like who?" He took a step toward her.

"The wench in the alehouse, the wench who served you wine tonight. I'm certain they have warmed your bed multiple times."

Jayden looked toward the fireplace refraining to reveal his secret.

"Ha, I speak the truth." She went on. "You can't even look me in the eye."

He looked toward her then. "Your assumption of my character is incorrect."

"I can only surmise your character by overhearing your topic of conversation between you and Sir Darwin while we traveled. How many women you have bedded, how often, and how many times you performed in one night. I guess when it's your only accomplishment, then you have nothing else to talk about."

He stared at her, his mouth agape. The silence stretched between them.

She continued. "You value the experience between a man and a woman so little. To you, sex means nothing. But to some women who wait for a worthy man and give themselves to him, it means a lot." She motioned toward the door. "You're exasperating. All you do is walk through the Great Hall or the bailey and women wink, blow kisses, and woo at your feet. You must be quite good in bed to attract such loose and immoral women."

He smirked. "I could give you a demonstration."

She cringed and wrinkled her nose. "No, thank you." *He's utterly daft.* "Do you care so little about your reputation as a man-whore?"

Jayden's stomach ached as if being twisted by her words that struck true. "Is that what you think of me?" He began to pace. "A man-whore?"

Rhoslyn could see her words made an impact on his conscience. Not that she cared. But, after all, he would one day be the Lord of Aldwinster. He should start acting like it.

Jayden turned to face her. "Does everyone think I'm a man-whore?"

"I don't know what others think, so I can't answer that question."

"But you think I'm a man-whore?" He stared at her awaiting her reply.

She turned to look at a painting. Even though she thought of him as such, saying the truthful words to his face was beyond her means.

He read her body language. "Ah, you do." He ran his hand over the top of his head pulling his fingers through his hair. "And you don't want to be seen with me. It will label you as well."

She remained silent in agreement with his reasoning.

"Well, I thank you for shedding light on the subject." He went to the door, flung it open, and charged through the portal leaving her alone in the room. She turned toward the echoing merriment emanating through the doorway, quite relieved to be rid of his company.

Chapter 16

She backed out of the room closing the library door behind her.

"Lady Rhoslyn."

Startled, she turned around and nearly bumping into the steward. She brushed imaginary wrinkles from her skirt before looking at him. "Yes."

"I'm Pearson, my lady, the steward. I assume you are ready to retire to your chamber now." There was a twinkle in his gray eyes. "After all, you've had a long day." He smiled slightly.

"Yes, I have. Thank you." She followed the steward and ignored those who sat at the High Table, especially Jayden, as they crossed the Great Hall, ascended the staircase, and passed through a hallway. Pearson stopped before a bedchamber door, lifted the latch, and pushed the portal open allowing her to enter before standing in the doorway. "I believe you will find this room comfortable. I have readied a bath and Lydia will see to your needs." He motioned to a woman, close to her age, who rose from a chair and curtsied.

Rhoslyn nodded her head acknowledging Lydia as she stood erect. She rotated in admiration of the large room. Tapestries and paintings decorated its stone walls. A fire crackled in the fireplace warming the chamber. A cozy bench beneath the large window allowed plenty of light to sew or read. Candelabras, a dozen flickering tapers in each, illuminated the room in a golden glow. The grand bed with its carved ivy design wrapped like serpents around the four tall posts. Deep cranberry drapes hung next to each post and could be drawn closed for warmth and darkness while sleeping. The bed was high off the floor with its set of steps ready to assist the sleepy occupant of the chamber. She imagined snuggling beneath the many layers of blankets that covered the mattress and her head sinking within its fluffy pillows. A lit taper's flame danced in the draft as she passed by the nightstand.

Pearson stepped into the room and clasped the latch of the door. "There is a garderobe at the end of the hall and a chamber pot beneath the bed for your convenience."

"Thank you, Pearson, it's lovely." Rhoslyn smiled.

"Oh, the wardrobe is filled with clothing. Please feel free to use whatever you wish, my lady." He left the room closing the door.

Rhoslyn looked to the tub of warm water and her servant. "Well Lydia, let's rid my body of this dirt."

"Yes, my lady."

With the assistance of Lydia, each layer of clothing was removed and thrown into a pile to be laundered. Rhoslyn eased her body into the water, leaned her head back on the rim of the tub, and closed her eyes as her body relaxed in the envelope of warmth.

Pearson had thoughtfully left a small basket of scented soaps, a comb and brush, and soft linens on a chair near the tub.

Lydia selected a bar of soap. "Is there any particular scent you wish for you soap, my lady?"

"It matters not." Rhoslyn sighed as she sunk further beneath the water.

Lydia inhaled the fragrance of the bar in her hand and wrinkled her nose. *Lily of the Valley.* She chose another, smelled it, and smiled. *Rose.* She hoped her mistress liked the scent as well. She dipped a linen cloth in the bathwater and rubbed the soap upon it until it created a foamy lather. "My lady, I will begin with your face." She warned.

"Fine." Rhoslyn closed her eyes.

Lydia moved the cloth in small circles upon her mistress's forehead.

Rhoslyn inhaled. "Rose."

"Yes, my lady, one of my favorites."

"Mine too."

Lydia selected second linen, dipped it in the bathwater, and rinsed the soap away before using the large linen to pat away the dampness.

Rhoslyn opened her eyes. "Lydia, what can you tell me about Lord Jayden?"

Taken back by the bold question, Lydia turned away placing the towel on the chair and taking a deep breath hesitant to spread rumors. "I only know what I have heard and seen, my lady."

"From what I have observed, I've drawn my own opinion of him. I want to see if you can confirm my assessment." Rhoslyn leaned forward for Lydia to wash her back.

"Well, he is quite handsome, or so many women say. I've heard he often beds women but know of no bastards he may have produced."

"Perhaps he is incapable of having children." The cloth on her back stilled as if the servant had not drawn the same conclusion. "What of Lady Carling?"

Lydia resumed washing as she snickered. "Oh, the widow chases after him like a dog in heat. She isn't well-liked in the kingdom, but we try to be hospitable toward her just the same."

"Yes, her intentions are obvious. It is comical, thankfully my subjection to such goings on should be short lived, for I hope to leave for home soon."

"Where is your home?"

"Bardenham."

Lydia gasped dropping the washing cloth in the water. She was aware of the rumors of its lord and lady circulating throughout the castle.

"Is something wrong?" Rhoslyn looked over her shoulder.

"No, my lady, I just splashed some water on my dress." Lydia retrieved the cloth and handed it to Rhoslyn. "Lean back and I'll wash your hair." She set a bucket under the long tresses of auburn hair as it dangled over the back of the tub like a waterfall. Retrieving the small ceramic pitcher from the basket, Lydia wet, lathered and rinsed the thick locks. After blotting it dry with a linen, she combed out the tangles. "Such lovely hair, my lady."

Rhoslyn raised her leg from the water and washed her foot. "Thank you."

Assuming the woman had finished with her bath, Lydia stood and retrieved a drying towel. "Would you like to dry off or remain to soak a bit longer?"

The water was beginning to cool. Rhoslyn glanced toward the cozy bed as Lydia turned down the blankets. It looked inviting. She rose from the bathwater.

Lydia opened the towel, wrapped it around the woman's body, and laid another towel upon the floor before extending her hand to assist her mistress from the tub. She went to the wardrobe and selected a chemise and robe.

Rhoslyn removed the wrapped towel and patted it against her body sopping up droplets of bathwater. She dropped the towel to the stone floor as Lydia held the undergarment over her head. She slipped each arm into a sleeve and it unfurled as it dropped toward the floor clinging to her body where it was still damp. The chemise was of the highest quality and felt like rose petals against her skin. Donning the robe, she tied it with a cross and tuck of the matching brocade belt. She stood before the fire.

"My lady, shall I have the tub removed tonight or in the morning?" Lydia picked up the soiled clothing from the floor and gathered the linens.

Rhoslyn sighed as weariness claimed her body. It would take quite some time to empty the tub and have it removed from the bedchamber. She looked to the bed inviting her to slip between its covers.

"In the morning will be fine. Thank you, Lydia." Rhoslyn removed the robe, laid it on the end of the bed, and ascended the three steps. She nestled between the covers and pulled them over her chest as her head sunk into the softness of the pillow.

"Is there anything else you need, my lady?" Lydia extinguished the flames of the candelabras leaving a single candle on the nightstand aflame. She stoked the fire and placed another log upon it.

"No, thank you." Rhoslyn closed her eyes.

"I shall bring your breakfast in the morning." Lydia left the bedchamber and shut the door.

Rhoslyn drifted off to sleep dreaming of the day she would leave Aldwinster and return home to Bardenham.

Chapter 17

Lydia knocked on the bedchamber door and waited for permission to enter.

Rhoslyn opened her eyes a mere crack. She looked to the window which indicated it was morning and yawned. "Enter." She rolled toward the doorway, pulled the covers over her shoulder, and watch as Lydia entered carrying a tray. *Ah, the simple pleasures; a cozy bed, not rising during the night to attend mass, and breakfast served in my bedchamber.*

"Good morning, my lady." Lydia set the tray on the table.

Reluctantly, Rhoslyn sat upright shifting her legs to the side of the bed. Lydia held her robe as she inserted her arms into each sleeve and sat at the table. Hard-boiled eggs, slices of pork, bread and cheese, a small dish containing butter, another with preserves, and a tankard of watered ale made her mouth water.

"It looks delicious."

"Yes, our cook is one of the finest." Lydia went to the wardrobe and opened the door. "Do you have any plans for today, my lady?" She selected a beautiful sapphire gown and displayed it for her lady's approval.

Rhoslyn stopped in mid-chew as she stared at the elegant dress and nodded in approval. For the past six months, the abbess had dictated how she would spend her day. *What am I going to do today?* She recalled the embroidery she had tucked away in her bag.

"I brought an embroidery project with me. Do you know where my satchel is?"

Lydia turned and reached for a leather bag in the bottom of the wardrobe. "Is this it?"

"Yes, bring it here, please."

Lydia crossed the room and handed her the bag. While her mistress rummaged through it, she carefully laid out the dress on the bed.

"Ah, here it is. I plan to send it to the Sisters of Charity as a thank you gift." She spread out the cloth on the table.

Lydia touched delicate embroidery. "It's lovely and you've made such intricate stitches, some I've never seen before. Perhaps you can teach me a few of them."

"My mother taught me most of them. I will be happy to share them with you." Rhoslyn set her embroidery aside before spreading a thick slice of bread with butter and preserves and taking a large bite.

~

"Good morning, Mother." Jayden entered the solar with Shadow trailing behind.

"Good morning, Jayden." Lady Myla presented her cheek and accepted a kiss from her son.

"Good morning, Father." He nodded toward Lord Filmore as he sat at the table and began to fill his plate from the platters of food provided for breakfast.

"Jayden, I trust you were able to avoid the attentions of Lady Carling after your mother and I retired for the evening." Lord Filmore reached for a loaf of bread and tore a portion of it for himself.

"As best I could. She's persistent." He shoveled a fork full of egg into his mouth and gave his dog a bit of meat.

"I may have a solution to your problem, at least for now. Since you know Lady Rhoslyn better than any of us, I would like you to give her a tour of the kingdom today."

Jayden choked on his food. He gasped for air, grabbed his watered ale, and drank hoping to clear his throat. Breathing deeply, his eyes enlarged as they blurred with tears. "You want me to what?" He stared at his father in disbelief.

"I want you to show her around the kingdom. Pearson can pack a midday meal so you can be away from the castle the entire day." Lord Filmore grinned as if quite proud of his idea.

"Father, you jest. The woman barely tolerates my company. Her opinion of me is quite low."

"Perhaps you have misinterpreted her intention."

"She called me a man-whore!"

Lady Myla looked at her son, to her husband, and back to her son. "Well, she possesses a varied vocabulary."

Lord Filmore refrained from smiling. "Nevertheless, I need you to be her escort. With her by your side, perhaps Lady Carling will leave you alone."

"I was hoping to practice with the garrison today." Jayden returned his tankard to the table.

"Then take her with you. She can watch."

~

"My lady, the dress fits you perfectly." Lydia circled Rhoslyn and took a step backward to view her in full.

Rhoslyn brushed the palm of her hands over the skirt. "It's lovely." She held the full skirt out at each side to view it and touched the bodice with its silver thread and pearl embellishments. "Such detailed work."

"Let me pin your hair." Lydia presented a chair before retrieving a small basket from the wardrobe containing ribbons and clips.

"It seems silly to go to such a fuss about my appearance when I will be spending the day in my bedchamber sewing." Rhoslyn sat as requested.

A knock sounded on the door. The women glanced toward it before looking at each other. Rhoslyn nodded to Lydia, who went to the door and opened it.

"Lord Jayden." She curtsied, glanced at Shadow and back to his master. "How may I help you?"

"Is Lady Rhoslyn ready for the day?"

"Nearly."

"Please inform her that I will be waiting in the Great Hall for her to join me for a tour of the kingdom, as ordered by my father."

The servant detected a tone of displeasure in his voice. "Yes, my lord." Lydia closed the door.

Rhoslyn pulled a silver ribbon from the basket. "Who was at the door?"

"Lord Jayden. As ordered by Lord Filmore, he will accompany you on a tour of the kingdom today." Lydia pulled the ribbon from her mistress's tense hand.

Rhoslyn scowled. "I would rather stay in my chamber and sew."

"My lady, from what I could gather, he seemed displeased as well." Lydia wove a ribbon through her mistress's hair. She pinned a curl here and there keeping it in place with a clip donned with a single pearl. She gently patted Rhoslyn's hair ensuring it would stay pinned. "I think that will do for today." She held a mirror before her mistress so she could view her work.

Rhoslyn turned her head to the left and right. "Very nice, Lydia."

"Thank you, my lady."

Rhoslyn stood and sighed. "Well, I better not keep Lord Jayden waiting."

Lydia detected sarcasm in her mistress's comment and opened the bedchamber door.

Rhoslyn paused at the top of the staircase to observe Jayden pacing the empty Great Hall. He seemed impatient. His dog sat watching his master walk back and forth, became aware of her presence, stood, and wagged his tail.

Jayden looked toward the sound of footsteps, froze in place, and stared as she descended. The color of the gown complemented her green eyes. *Or are they aqua?* The detailed bodice emphasized her tiny waist. Her auburn hair delicately pinned into place. His mouth turned upward at one side.

She stopped before him, unsmiling. "Are we being forced to spend the day together?"

"Yes, my father was quite insistent. Since I planned to practice with the garrison, he indicated you could watch while I do so."

"Very well."

"I have taken the liberty of having our horses readied." He motioned with his hand to the exit of the Keep.

As they stepped into the warming sunlight, Jayden glanced at the alewives. His usual admirer waved, winked, and blew him a kiss.

Rhoslyn watched the repulsive exchange between the two and looked skyward in disgust. She approached Laila, tethered to a post outside of the stable. "Hello, big girl." She stroked her mare's soft nose, untied the reins, and walked away leading Laila.

Jayden untied his horse and climbed atop Beval. He scowled as Rhoslyn distanced herself. "Where are you going?"

She looked over her shoulder as she continued to walk. "If you don't mind, I would like to go through the shops."

Jayden rolled his lips inward, biting slightly, and exhaled as he reined his horse. *I could be practicing with the garrison, but no, I'm escorting her from shop to shop.* He dismounted and led Beval as he trailed in her wake with Shadow following.

The candle shop was of little interest to her, but the carved wooden boxes displayed on a bench in front of the next shop cause her to stop and stare. She tied Laila's reins to a post and approached the woodcarver, who was sitting next to a table of tools applying one to the lid of a small wooden box. She watched as he followed the lines of the scribed pattern and chipped away the unwanted wood. She leaned forward to have a closer look. The craftsman stopped working as her shadow cast over the box. He set the box and tools on the table and rose to brush away the shavings from his leather apron in order to make himself more presentable.

"My lady, may I be of service?" Wrinkles appeared at the corner of the woodcarver's eyes as he smiled.

"You have such lovely boxes. I have never seen something so delicate, yet so strong." She scanned the boxes on display. "My, it would be difficult to choose only one." She touched the top of a box, tracing her finger over the edge of the pattern.

The woodcarver picked up the box for her to examine more closely.

Jayden's eyebrows raised. It was the first time he witnessed her smile.

The pattern on the lid was intricate. It was finished with a lovely walnut stain. A small brass lock would keep its contents secure. She opened the box and discovered a key inside and inhaled the scent of cedar before closing the lid, rotating the box, and estimating its size. *Perfect for my dagger's safekeeping.* She returned the box to the table.

The woodcarver's smile faded. "My lady, you do not like it?"

"Oh, I do like it, very much. However, I do not possess the funds to purchase it at this time."

Jayden stepped forward and reached for his belt bag. "I can purchase it for you."

Rhoslyn snapped her head in his direction. Her smile disappeared. "Thank you, but no. I shall send word to my father for the funds." She looked back to the woodcarver and smiled. "Please set it aside. I shall return and purchase it, I promise. Good day." Rhoslyn retrieved Laila's reins and continued to the next shop.

Jayden stared at her as she walked away. He turned to the crafter. "Thank you for your time."

"Certainly, my lord." The man smiled and nodded his head. He resumed his seat and returned to work.

Jayden led Beval to the next shop and watched Rhoslyn disappear through the doorway. He tied the reins to a post and looked up at the sign in the shape of a knife. *What is she doing here?* He stepped through the doorway.

Rhoslyn stood before a long, narrow table. She pointed to a medium-sized dagger displayed on the wall. "May I see that one?"

The bladesmith removed the knife from the wall and presented it to her handle first.

"Thank you." She gripped the handle and twisted her arm first one way then the other as she looked down the length of her arm inspecting the straightness of the blade. She placed her fingertip where the blade met the hilt checking for balance. The dagger remained parallel to the wooden floor. "Very nice."

The bladesmith nodded his head. "Thank you, my lady."

Jayden peeked over her shoulder. He pointed to a knife he wished to see. "So, you're an expert on daggers?" He accepted the blade handed to him. "This one is superior to your choice." He gripped the handle and swished it through the air several times.

In her opinion, the blade in his hand looked off-balance. She spied a slice of tree trunk mounted on an adjacent wall with the blade marks scarring its surface. Raising an eyebrow, she smirked. "Prove it. Throw your chosen weapon at the target on the wall." She nodded toward it.

Glancing at the target, he grasped the tip of the blade and threw the knife. It drifted to the left and embedded on the edge of the target. He looked toward her with a smug look upon his face.

Rhoslyn shrugged her shoulders. "Not bad." She estimated the distance and angle where she stood from the center and looked Jayden in the eye. She raised her arm holding the blade by its tip and whipped it at the target, throwing blindly. They looked at the target upon hearing it hit its mark. The blade was dead center.

"I like my choice better." She turned and left the shop.

Jayden stood with his mouth agape. He looked toward the bladesmith, who stared at the embedded knife.

"The lady throws well, my lord." The bladesmith scratched his head impressed by her accuracy.

"Yes, she does." He left the shop to see Rhoslyn atop her mare.

"The tour, my lord, shall we begin?"

He untied Beval and placed his foot in the stirrup. "You didn't tell me you are proficient with a blade."

Rhoslyn watched as he eased himself into the saddle. "You didn't ask." She reined Laila toward the gatehouse.

"What other skills do you possess?"

"Father insisted I learn the dagger to defend myself. I'm accurate with a bow as well."

They spent the remainder of the morning touring the village, rode through the woods, and inspected the crops in the fields. Rhoslyn lost count of the number of women who winked, flirted, or raised their skirt at Jayden as they passed by them. After returning their horses at the stable, they entered the Keep for their midday meal. Pearson met them in the hallway with a satchel of food and flasks of wine.

"My lord, I had this packed for your tour, but you left without it." The steward leaned forward and lowered his voice to a whisper. "Lady Carling has been searching high and low for you all morning. I dare say, she means to track you down. Would you like to take this with you and return to your tour?"

"There you are! I've been looking all over for you, Lord Jayden."

Shadow growled. They turned around and stared at the beaming face of Lady Carling standing in the doorway of the Keep. She clapped her hands together and cackled like a fat hen.

Jayden turned back to the steward. His voice monotoned. "The Great Hall will be fine, Pearson."

"Very good, my lord." Pearson entered the Great Hall with the small group following. Jayden motioned for Rhoslyn to sit on a bench at the closest table. He sat on the opposite side. Lady Carling seized the opportunity and sat next to him leaving little space between them.

Knowing the satchel contained food for two, Pearson returned to the kitchen for an additional serving.

Lady Carling placed her hand on Jayden's forearm. "You don't want to sit at the High Table?" She batted her eyes.

Jayden unpacked the food from the satchel. "Here is fine." His eyes enlarged in a silent plea for help from Rhoslyn, who ventured a topic of conversation hoping to engage the woman in the distraction.

She directed her comment to the annoying woman across the table. "Lord Jayden has been so very kind this morning. We have toured a good portion of the kingdom thus far."

Lady Carling ignored her comment and continued to stare at Jayden.

Pearson ushered a pair of women into the room. They carried an extra plate of food and mugs filled with ale. The steward set a full pitcher upon the table. "Is there anything else, my lord?"

"Where is Sir Darwin?" He thought to pawn off the clinging female to his knight.

"At the practice field, my lord."

"Of course, he is. That will be all. Thank you, Pearson." Jayden picked up his tankard, drained it dry, and refilled it. He broke off a bit of meat pie and tossed it under the table for Shadow.

Lady Carling selected a sweet cake from the plate.

An awkward silence between the three lingered heavily in the air like a thick smog. Rhoslyn glanced from Jayden to Lady Carling and back again. Certain the young lord would be unable to rid himself of the woman, she ventured an idea. "Lady Carling, perhaps you would like to join us on the practice field after we eat." Her attention was drawn to Jayden, who nearly choked on his food.

Lady Carling's eyes widened as she looked to Jayden. "Oh, that's a splendid idea."

Anticipating their thirst, a serving wench brought a second pitcher of ale to the table.

Rhoslyn looked to the servant as she turned toward the kitchen halting her progress.

"Could you send a message to the stable. Have them ready a horse for Lady Carling, please."

"Yes, my lady." She returned to the kitchen.

Lady Carling's head snapped toward Rhoslyn. "A horse! Surely you don't expect me to ride a horse."

Fishing for the truth, Jayden peered at Lady Carling. "Is your carriage repaired?"

"Well, no." She lied.

Rhoslyn nodded. "Good. Then you shall join us on horseback." Quite satisfied with herself, she lifted her tankard as if toasting her success and looked toward Jayden displaying a devilish smirk.

Chapter 18

Rhoslyn climbed atop Laila and waited.

Kolby placed a set of mounting steps beside a black mare. He held Lady Carling's hand as she hesitantly climbed them. "Insert your left food in the stirrup, my lady."

"In the, what?" She looked to the stableboy for clarification.

Kolby had chosen a small horse that paled in comparison to Laila.

Jayden sighed. He stepped forward and grabbed the stirrup. "Put your left foot in here. Grab onto the pommel to steady yourself and push yourself upward. Then swing your right leg over and put your foot in the other stirrup." Jayden went to the other side of the horse and caught her foot before she kicked him in the head. He inserted it into the stirrup.

"Oh, I did it. Now, what do I do?" She looked to Jayden for advice.

He went to Beval and climbed atop. "Nothing. Kolby." Jayden held out his hand, an unspoken order.

The stableboy led the mare to his lord and handed him the reins. He returned to the stable as the trio and Shadow rode through the bailey and over the drawbridge.

Jayden brought his warhorse alongside Rhoslyn. He stared straight ahead, unsmiling.

She grinned as she looked toward him. "Well done." She chuckled. "There is an advantage and disadvantage in this situation."

"The advantage?"

"She will be behind you the entire way to the field."

"True. And the disadvantage?"

"Getting her back on her horse. You can only hope there is a bench or stump to assist you."

"Me?" He thought for a moment and grinned. "Perhaps I can delegate the task to Sir Darwin."

Once through the village, the clashing of wooden swords and galloping horses could be heard echoing from the practice field. Sir Darwin lowered his practice sword as the small party reined their horses on the edge of the field.

"My lord, are the ladies joining us for practice?" The knight greeted Shadow with a pat on the head.

Curious to see if Rhoslyn's skill with a bow equaled her skill with a knife, Jayden decided to give her the opportunity. He dismounted.

"Yes, they are here to practice their marksmanship in archery."
He led Lady Carling's horse to a bench. Sir Darwin held the mare's bridle
while Jayden caught the robust woman as she tumbled from her saddle.
He set her on the ground as his knees threatened to buckle beneath him.

Roslyn refrained from laughing at the comical sight. She selected
a longbow and a quiver full of arrows from a rack. Strapping the quiver
over her shoulder and onto her back, she adjusted the tension and
placement of the quiver so she could easily reach them over her right
shoulder.

Jayden observed Rhoslyn's proficiency and stared in disbelief as
she strung her bow, a difficult task for even some men. He called over
his shoulder. "Sir Darwin, please equip Lady Carling. I would like to
watch Lady Rhoslyn shoot."

"Yes, my lord." The knight directed Lady Carling toward the
equipment.

Rhoslyn scanned the field of targets, seven in all. She stepped
behind a soldier at the center target and waited for him to finish shooting
the arrows in his quiver.

Jayden stepped beside her. "That's quite a distance. Do you
think you can make it from here?"

A tone of condescension tainted his question. As the man before
her finished shooting and stepped aside, she estimated the distance of
the target ahead of her and the angle and distance of the remaining six.

"I've shot a greater distance before. Shall I sweep the field, my
lord?" She looked up into his face masked in disbelief.

"All hold while the lady shoots!" Jayden ordered. The men
lowered their bows and took a step backward, mistrusting her aim.

Rhoslyn reached over her head pulling the first arrow from the quiver as she placed her left foot at the furthest target to her left. Nocking her arrow, she positioned her right foot a shoulder-distance behind her set foot, drew the bowstring, and brought the tip of the arrow in alignment with the target. She let the arrow fly. It struck true. She selected another arrow, set her feet, let an arrow fly toward the next target in line. Dead center. She continued to shoot at the remaining targets and returned her shot in the opposite direction. When she finished, each target had two arrows within their center mark. She lowered her bow and looked to Jayden.

He exhaled unaware he had been holding his breath. "Impressive. Your father taught you well."

"Thank you. I will convey your compliment to my father in my missive. If you don't mind, I would like to return to the Keep." A page stepped forward as she removed the quiver and handed him her bow and arrows.

Jayden glanced at his knight, who was assisting Lady Carling with her bow. "Very well." He turned back to Rhoslyn, but she was gone. He turned around to see her approaching her horse with commanding strides and rushed to her side.

Hearing his approaching footsteps behind her, Rhoslyn stopped walking as Jayden joined her. She was tired of his company. Her fisted hands went to her hips as she glared at him. "I am perfectly capable of finding my way back to the Keep. Perhaps your time would be better spent instructing Lady Carling in the finer art of archery." She lifted her chin in the direction of the lady and the knight.

"My lady, my orders are to be with you throughout the day."

Rhoslyn exhaled as she scowled, inserted her foot into the stirrup, and mounted Laila with ease.

Jayden climbed atop Beval and looked toward his knight. "Sir Darwin, I shall return soon."

"Yes, my lord."

Lady Carling dropped her bow. "Lord Jayden!" She waved her hand back and forth as she watched the pair ride away and the faithful canine following.

Roslyn ignored her riding companion. As they passed the woodcarver's shop, she made a mental note to request money from her father to purchase the beautiful box before going home.

Kolby emerged from the stable, gathered Beval and Laila's reins, and looked to Jayden for instructions as he dismounted.

"You can unsaddle Laila. Leave Beval saddled. I will be returning shortly."

"Yes, my lord."

Jayden quickened his steps to catch up to Rhoslyn before they entered the Keep.

Pearson sat at a table in the Great Hall. He looked up from an inventory journal as Rhoslyn stormed past him and looked at Jayden. He stood. "My lady, my lord?"

"Pearson, where may I find Father?" Jayden glared at Rhoslyn, who ascended the staircase.

"He is in the library."

"Thank you." He crossed the Great Hall, walked down the hallway, and entered the library to find his father at his desk with paperwork in one hand and a quill in the other.

"Father, has Lady Rhoslyn any funds?"

Lord Filmore glanced at his son. "None that I'm aware of. Why do you ask?"

"She had the woodcarver set aside a box and intends to write to her father requesting money for its purchase. Why is she here and when is she going home?"

Lord Filmore dropped the paper to his desktop and returned the quill to the inkwell. He exhaled and steepled his fingers under his chin. "Please close the door. For what I'm about to tell you is for your ears only."

Jayden closed the door and stood before his father whose behavior seemed out of character.

Lord Filmore retrieved the letter from a drawer in his desk. He handed it to his son, who scanned it while his father explained its details.

"Lady Rhoslyn's home is Bardenham. Her father, Lord Atherton, was accused of a crime against the baron. Before he was taken into custody, he took poison and killed himself. Her mother, Lady Eugenia, is being held in a tower at Somerville until she is either proven guilty or innocent. If innocent, she can join her daughter, but if guilty, she will be beheaded. Either way, Lady Rhoslyn is homeless."

Jayden looked up from the missive as he folded it and handed it back. "I assume she is unaware of her parents' current status."

"You assume correctly."

"What of the letter she intends to send to her father?"

"I assume she will either give it to me or Pearson to seal and send. I will instruct Pearson to give her missive to me. I will retain or burn it. For now, we must bide some time until the baron can reach his decision. It will be best to keep the truth hidden from her until we receive word from him."

Chapter 19

Rhoslyn opened the door to her bedchamber to see Lydia sorting through gowns in the wardrobe.

The servant turned toward her mistress. "My lady, how was your tour?"

"Enjoyable. I toured the shops and practiced with the garrison. Oh, and I found the most beautifully carved wooden box. I need to send a missive to Father and ask for the money to purchase it. Do we have paper, pen, and ink in the room?"

"I believe the writing materials are in the drawer of the nightstand." Lydia crossed the room, opened the drawer, and retrieved the items. She went to the table near the window and laid them out. "There you are, my lady."

"Thank you." Rhoslyn sat in the chair, picked up the quill, and dipped the tip into the ink. She paused. *I must word this carefully.* She disliked bothering her father about such trivial things since he is such a busy man, frugal too. Many times, she had asked for a moment of his time, but he ordered her out of the library as if she had interrupted something of great importance. She secretly wished he had been at the field today to watch her archery and imagined his pride in her accomplishment.

"My lady, I find this dress quite attractive." Lydia held up a teal gown trimmed in white lace and beading. "Shall we dress you in it for the evening meal?"

Rhoslyn looked at the servant and dropped her line of vision to the gown. Its skirt was full, and the bodice decorated with beading and pearls. The sleeves appeared elbow length with wide, dainty lace as trim. She scowled at the neckline. Since living with the Sisters of Charity, the modesty a woman should possess was instilled in her mind.

"The neckline looks too low for my taste." She returned to her letter.

Lydia held the dress before her and ran her finger along the edge of the bodice. "Perhaps you can put it on and then decide." She hung the dress from the top of the wardrobe door to keep it displayed.

Rhoslyn ignored the servant's comment as she included details of Aldwinster, the box she wished to purchase, and the funds necessary to do so in her missive. She paused as she stared out the window carefully choosing the words to convince her father of her desire to return home. She sighed as she finished her request, set down the quill, and reread her message before folding it.

"Lydia, I need to ask Lord Filmore to send my letter. When I return, I would like to work on my embroidery. Would you like me to teach you a few stitches?"

"Oh, yes my lady."

Rhoslyn left the bedchamber, descended the staircase, and crossed the Great Hall with the assumption Lord Filmore was in his library. She turned into the hallway, stopped before the closed door, and straightened her skirt before knocking.

"Enter."

Lord Filmore pointed to an entry in the account book on his desk. His wife leaned over his shoulder examining it. They ignored the door as it opened.

"Very well, my dear," Lady Myla said to her husband before they both looked toward their visitor who stood before them.

Lord Filmore closed the account book. "Lady Rhoslyn, how may we help you?"

"Good day, my lord, my lady." She curtsied. "I would like to ask a favor of you."

"If it is within our ability, then we shall honor it."

"I have written a missive to my father, Lord Atherton. Could you seal and have it sent to him." She held the letter before them.

Lady Myla grinned while ignoring the truth of her father's death gnawing at her heart.

As he had been forewarned by his son, Lord Filmore held out his hand to accept the missive.

Rhoslyn stepped forward, placed the missive in his hand, and curtsied. "Thank you, my lord, my lady." She exited the room closing the door behind her.

Lord Filmore looked to his wife. "I have been put in an awkward situation, my dear. I normally respect the privacy of others, but I feel it is imperative to pry for our benefit as well as hers." He opened the missive.

Lady Myla leaned toward the letter and listened as her husband read it. "Oh, dear." She stood upright.

"Jayden had warned me of its contents. He knows Lord Atherton is dead and Lady Rhoslyn cannot return to Bradenham." Lord Filmore refolded the missive and thought. "I will write the baron and inform him of her request. We must keep the truth from her until we receive word from him."

Chapter 20

Lydia stood from her chair with her needlework in hand as the bedchamber door opened. Her lady seemed pleased. "Will Lord Filmore send it, my lady?"

Rhoslyn closed the door and sat on the window seat. "Yes, I hope to receive a reply from Father soon."

They embroidered while sharing their favorite stitches until the setting sun allowed shadows to creep into the room.

Lydia lit the tapers of the candelabra. She looked over her shoulder. "Perhaps it is time to dress you for the evening meal, my lady."

Rhoslyn held her embroidery at arms-length, admired the progress she had made on the pillow, and set it aside. Even though her fondest desire was to return home, she had to admit her present situation was tolerable and a vast improvement from the abbey.

Lydia laid the teal dress upon the bed, turned to see her mistress standing before her, and began untying the laces of her dress. "I can hardly wait to see you in that lovely gown." The bodice fell away. Lydia let it lay on the floor as she unfastened the skirt. It dropped to the floor. The servant kicked it aside as her lady stepped out of it.

Dressed only in her chemise, Rhoslyn waited while Lydia retrieved the skirt from the bed. She stepped into it and ran her hands over the material while it was fastened in the back. Next, she donned the bodice and held her breath while it was tightened. She looked down at her bulging bust spilling above the neckline.

"This is too revealing." She ran her fingertips along the neckline. "Even the lace of my chemise shows."

Tying the laces, Lydia stepped to face her mistress. "Let me see what can be done." She pulled the lace edge of the chemise upward increasing the length of the bodice hoping to give her mistress the modesty she preferred. "There. I think that should do it."

Rhoslyn looked down at her chest. She frowned.

Noticing her mistress's displeasure, Lydia retrieved the hand mirror and held it before her. "You look lovely and from this angle, you look well covered."

Rhoslyn looked in the mirror. *Not too revealing.* "Very well, I'll have to remember not to bend over." She shrugged her shoulder, her mouth half-smiled.

Lydia nodded. "Excellent, now let's pin your hair." She went to the wardrobe and looked for a matching ribbon. She searched the basket, but only found white.

Lydia unpinned, brushed, and pinned while weaving the ribbon into her mistress's hair. She handed the mirror to Rhoslyn for her inspection.

"Oh, very nice, Lydia." She touched the back of her head feeling the soft curls pinned in place.

"Thank you, my lady. Shall we go to the Great Hall?" Lydia smiled, confident her mistress would catch the attention of everyone in the room.

Rhoslyn pulled her chemise upward, but it was securely wedged between her body and the bodice. *I must remain upright.* She sighed. "Very well."

Lydia stepped to the bedchamber door, opened it, and allowed Rhoslyn to pass before closing it behind them. They descended the staircase to the Great Hall.

Conversations stilled while many stared at Rhoslyn as she stepped onto the stone floor of the room and leaned toward Lydia. "Must they stare so? I feel as if I'm on display."

"They are taken by your beauty, my lady."

They stopped before the High Table and curtsied. The Lord and Lady of Aldwinster smiled and nodded their head. Rhoslyn ignored the intense stare of Jayden, turned, and made her way to her seat next to Lady Myla, who looked toward her.

"You look lovely tonight, my dear."

"Thank you, my lady." Rhoslyn felt Lydia touch her right arm. She looked over her shoulder at her servant as she leaned toward her and whispered in her ear.

"Did you see the way Lord Jayden looked at you? His mouth fell open."

"No, I care little for what he thinks." She glanced at the end of the table as Lydia took her seat. Lady Carling was scowling.

Sir Darwin leaned toward the young lord. "I can't remember the last time my eyes witnessed such beauty. She's stunning."

"I agree. She is very beautiful, but with her beauty comes a sharp tongue." Jayden lifted his tankard from the table and drank.

Rhoslyn remained upright as possible throughout the meal. She avoided looking at the people in the room fearing many would be staring at her especially the men with lust in their eyes and the hatred and jealousy in the orbs of Lady Carling. As the tables were cleared and the music began to play, Lydia stood and excused herself.

"My lady, I shall see you in your bedchamber."

"Thank you. I intend to retire soon." Rhoslyn heard the scraping of chairs against the dais floor to her left and turned to see the Lord and Lady of Aldwinster leave the table for the first dance. Her eyes momentarily locked on Jayden, who was staring at her. She turned away to watch his parents dance.

Sir Darwin witnesses the exchange between his lord and the lovely lady. "Are you going to ask her to dance, or shall I?"

Jayden looked toward his knight. "She will refuse my offer."

"Then I shall ask for this dance and you ask Lady Carling." The knight bated snickering internally.

Jayden glanced toward Rhoslyn, staring at her profile. *She is lovely.* He hesitated, weighing the risk.

Lady Carling assumed the young lord was admiring her. She waved and smiled, but he looked away without acknowledgment. Her smile faded.

Jayden lifted his tankard from the table, drank it half-dry as if trying to work up the courage to do what he must. He confided in his knight. "If I dance with Lady Carling, I fear my offer will only lead her on."

Sir Darwin glanced at both women. "Ask Lady Carling. I will ask Lady Rhoslyn. We will switch partners during the dance. I will keep Lady Carling occupied for the remainder of the evening."

"Very well." He sighed as a new tune began. He rose from his chair and approached Lady Carling. The woman's eyes enlarged, she smiled foolishly and fussed with her hair. She looked at Rhoslyn, hoping to invoke jealousy.

Jayden bowed slightly and presented his open hand. "Lady Carling, may I have this dance."

The woman sprung from her seat like a jack-in-the-box. "Why certainly." She grabbed his arm and dragged him to the dancefloor.

The unpleasant expression on Jayden's face conveyed his repulsion toward his dance partner. Rhoslyn chuckled at the spectacle. *Oh, the sacrifices an attractive lord must make.*

"My lady."

She turned to see the knight standing beside her.

He bowed and presented his hand. "May I have this dance." His offer appeared sincere.

"You may."

They joined the other dancing couples. Rhoslyn discovered the knight was just short of Jayden's height as she reached to place her hand upon his shoulder. She tensed as his hand wrapped around her lower ribcage just above her waist.

Sir Darwin thought to put the woman at ease by engaging her in conversation. "May I say, my lady, you look stunning tonight."

"Thank you, it is a beautiful gown. A substantial change in attire from what I was forced to wear while at the abbey."

"I agree, but I believe the one who dons it is equally as beautiful. No, I misspoke. Exceeds its beauty."

"Thank you, you are too kind." She found the knight charming and handsome for a man of his age.

They took several turns around the room passing Jaydan and his dance partner, who clung to him like a fly on flypaper. He stared into the distance absentmindedly, while Lady Carling chattered on and on. His face was void of expression except for an occasional cringe as her foot stomped upon his.

Sir Darwin assumed his lord had endured enough of Lady Carling. "My lady, if you don't mind, it is my duty to rescue my lord from his current torment. I feel obligated to exchange partners. Would you mind terribly?"

She looked at Jayden. He did not attempt to camouflage his discontent with his dancing partner. Even though she preferred to dance with the knight, she understood his loyalty and duty to his lord. "Very well."

They stopped dancing. Sir Darwin bowed to her as she curtsied. He went to his lord and tapped him on the shoulder. The couple stopped dancing.

The knight looked toward Lady Carling and smiled. "My lord, may I have a turn with this lovely lady?"

Flattered, yet reluctant, Lady Carling looked at Jayden for his response.

"Sir Darwin, I dare not keep you from the experience." He released her and went to join Rhoslyn, who waited.

Lady Carling narrowed her eyes as Jayden left her side. She looked to the knight, forced a smile, and curtsied.

Rhoslyn wished to retire instead of being subjected to Jayden's boasting.

He stopped before her and bowed. She curtsied, refusing to make eye contact. Her hand reached for his shoulder. He was taller than his knight.

He ventured a topic of conversation as they began to dance. "Thank you for rescuing me."

She looked toward his face.

Gazing into her aqua eyes, he resisted the temptation to scan the mounds protruding from her bodice. She seemed vexed and such an action, he feared, would be perceived as impertinent. "My feet could no longer tolerate her abuse."

Rhoslyn spoke her mind. "You created your misery by asking her to dance."

"As Aldwinster's guest, I'm obligated to be a proper host."

"You could have been more selective, chosen otherwise. There are plenty of other women willing to be your dance partner." She looked at the flirtatious wench, who winked at Jayden as they passed her. Rhoslyn glared at him with an 'I told you so' expression.

"I cannot control how women act toward me."

"You encourage such behavior. In a way, it is cruel. You give them false hope." The music stopped and their feet stilled. "Plus, it makes you look like a rake."

Her words hit true, disturbing him, but why? Why did he care what she thought?

"Do you think so little of me?" He released her from his embrace.

"I do. You have yet to prove otherwise."

Everyone had cleared the floor. Rhoslyn glanced about realizing they stood alone in the center of the room with everyone watching them.

Her face felt hot and presumed it was flushed with embarrassment. "Thank you for the dance." Curtseying, she left the Great Hall and ascended the staircase.

Jayden watched her intently as the next tune began.

The Lord and Lady of Aldwinster observed the couple from the High Table.

Lady Myla looked at her husband for reassurance. "Oh, I do want him to be happy, but it looks as if they are still at odds."

"Happy or not, they are betrothed."

"When do you plan to tell them?"

"Tomorrow. They need to resolve their issues."

Chapter 21

Lydia closed the book she was reading with a snap and stood as the bedchamber door opened. "My lady, did you enjoy the dancing?"

"As well as can be expected." Rhoslyn pushed the door closed, but it failed to latch shut. "Lord Jayden asked Lady Carling to dance. It was amusing until Sir Darwin asked me to dance. Partway through the song, Sir Darwin said it was his duty to rescue his lord. Lady Carling kept stepping on his feet. It was quite funny until they switched forcing me to dance with Lord Jayden. If I didn't know better, I believe they had it planned from the start."

"My lady, Lord Jayden is so handsome."

"And full of himself." Roslyn presented her back to Lydia.

"Why would you say that?" Lydia began unfastening the bodice.

"His constant flirting with woman, his incessant topic of conversation about them while we traveled from the convent. He is so full of himself. I doubt he has any room left in his heart to love another."

"In all honesty, my lady, he sounds like a normal man to me. Most men brag about their conquests and exaggerate." Lydia removed the bodice and began unfastening the skirt.

Rhoslyn stepped out of the skirt. She waited while Lydia retrieved a robe and held it open for her to slip on. Tying the sash over her waist, she sat in the chair before the fireplace. Lydia stoked the embers and set another log on to take the chill from the air.

"I wish I had a book to read." Rhoslyn stared at the flickering flames.

"I have one you may borrow. I can finish it after you are done."

"That is kind of you Lydia, but I will ask Lord Filmore if I may borrow one from his library tomorrow."

~

Jayden emptied his tankard again. He lost count of the number of times he had done so. He peered through drooped eyelids at Sir Darwin, who continue to entertain Lady Carling, quite thankful to be rid of the woman. He looked at the staircase. *Lady Rhoslyn, you have befuddled my mind. Most women go out of their way for my attention, yet you oppose it. Am I that repulsive to you?* He exhaled. *Perhaps I should find out.* He staggered across the dais, climbed the staircase, and walked lethargically down the hallway. Shadow stood at the base of the staircase with his ears perked and his head tilted to one side.

Jayden widened his eyes as his vision blurred and tried to focus on the bedchamber doors to determine which one was her room. With the guidance of the flickering candelabras evenly spaced along the hallway, he went from door to door pressing his ear to each and listening. After trying several doors unsuccessfully, he pressed his ear against one and fell into the room.

The bedchamber door banged against the wall. Rhoslyn looked toward the noise to see Jayden face down on the floor.

He raised his head, looked toward her before rolling onto his back. "My lady, I'm sorry. Your door was unlatched."

Lydia rushed to the fallen lord. "My lord, are you well?" She pulled on his arm helping him to rise.

He looked at Rhoslyn as he struggled to his feet leaning heavily upon the servant. "I find you to be the most beautiful woman. Why don't you like me?" His speech was slurred.

Rhoslyn rose from her chair. "You're drunk, my lord."

He widened his eyes to clear his blurred vision. "You didn't answer my question."

"And I don't intend to do so." Rhoslyn went to the vacant side of Jayden and peered around his torso at Lydia. "Let's get him to his bedchamber."

"Yes, my lady."

"Here." Jayden placed an arm over each of the women's shoulders burdening them with his weight. The women put an arm around his waist and clasped the hand dangling over each of their shoulders. He glanced toward each woman. "Much better."

They exited the bedchamber.

Jayden pointed with his left hand. "My bedchamber is that way." He turned his face toward Rhoslyn. "Honestly, why don't you like me? I like you." He leaned toward her with his lips puckered.

Rhoslyn wrinkled her nose at the stench of his breath and pulled her face away from him before he could kiss her.

The women guided him down the hallway.

Lydia spied Shadow sitting before a closed door. "That must be his chamber, my lady."

Jayden looked left and right to see if they had the correct door. "Yes, that's it."

Rhoslyn unlatched the door and pushed it open with her foot. The bed was on the opposite side of the large room. She was tempted to let him sleep on the cold stone floor but guided the drunken lord to the side of his bed. "In you go, my lord."

They lifted his arms from their shoulders, pushed him forward into the bed, and lifted his legs to lay him out.

He rolled onto his side and patted the mattress. "Come join me, ladies."

Shadow mistook his master's signal, jumped onto the bed, and lay alongside him.

Lydia looked at her lady for her reaction to the inappropriate invitation and decided to wait in the hallway.

Rhoslyn scowled and shook her head. "Tempting, but no, my lord." She clasped the latch of the door. "Goodnight, my lord." She closed the door joining Lydia in the hallway. The women looked at each other and burst into laughter. They returned to their bedchamber and bolted the door securely.

Chapter 22

Raindrops splashing against the bedchamber window echoed louder than normal, or at least Jayden thought so as he opened his eyes lethargically, moaned, and sat on the edge of his bed. Supporting his aching head with his hands, he rested his elbows on his thighs. He thought of lying back down, but his stomach grumbled, and he knew there was food in the solar.

Shadow sat next to the bedchamber door waving his front paw in the air and thumping his tail on the stone floor.

Jayden stood a little too quickly. The room spun as he stepped toward the end of his bed and grabbed the bedpost to steady himself. He selected a clean tunic from his wardrobe and changed before leaving his bedchamber and stepping through the threshold of the solar.

Lady Myla finished her breakfast long ago. She sat in a chair near the window and looked up from her embroidery as her son entered the room. "Good morning."

Jayden cringed. "Not so loud, mother." He sat at the table and scanned the food.

"My, are we not feeling well?" She tried not to grin.

"As always, Mother, your perception is correct." He took a thick slice of bread and spread it with butter.

"You must have had a splendid time after we retired." She pulled her needle through the cloth.

"I don't recall much other than emptying my tankard." He bit into the soft bread. "Several times." The taste of sweet butter filled his mouth. *What did happen last night?*

"Lady Rhoslyn certainly caught everyone's attention last night. She's quite a beauty." Lady Myla poked her needle into the cloth and peeked at her son for his reaction.

"Yes, she is very pretty."

"When you are finishing eating, your father wants to see you in the library."

Jayden stopped chewing and looked to his mother. "What does he want?" He picked up his tankard of watered ale, scowled as he sniffed it, and returned it to the table.

"He wants to discuss a few things with you." She pulled her needle making another stitch and looked to the window noting the morning shower had stopped.

Thinking little of his father's request, Jayden ate hoping the food would help dissipate the fogginess in his mind as he tried to recall the past evening. After dancing with Lady Carling and then Rhoslyn, he was quite certain the remainder of his evening was spent at the High Table. He touched his chin and cringed at its tenderness. *Bruised?* Setting his plate of scraps on the floor for Shadow, he stood. "Have a good day, Mother." He kissed her forehead and exited the solar.

"You too." She raised her eyebrows, displayed an all-knowing smile, and continued to sew.

Jayden descended the staircase to the Great Hall and looked at the two women sitting before the fireplace. He watched as Rhoslyn leaned toward Lydia.

Rhoslyn snickered. "Finally, the dead has arisen." She brushed away a wrinkle on her midnight blue skirt before putting both of her hands in her lap.

Lydia turned to see Jayden. "He looks worse for wear."

They watched him cross the room and enter the hallway toward the library.

Hearing footsteps behind him, Jayden looked over his shoulder to see Rhoslyn following him. He stopped and turned toward her. "Did you need something?"

"Not from you. Your father wishes to see us both."

He motioned with his arm for her to precede him through the hallway and enter the library.

Lord Filmore looked up from the document he was reading at his desk and motioned for them to sit in the chairs before his desk. "Close the door please." He watched as his son did so and Rhoslyn seated herself. "Jayden, I trust you had an eventful night."

Jayden glanced at Rhoslyn, who covered her smile with the palm of her hand. He sat in the vacant chair. "You wanted to see us, Father."

He nodded to the missive in his hand. "I have before me an important document, legal and binding."

Rhoslyn sat forward in her chair. Her curiosity made it impossible to hold her tongue. "Is that from my father?"

"As a matter of fact, yes. I received it several weeks ago."

Rhoslyn sat back in her chair upon realizing it wasn't a reply to her missive.

Lord Filmore glanced from his son to Rhoslyn and then to the contract. "It is an offer from Lord Atherton, and I accepted the terms. The two of you are betrothed."

Jayden's mouth dropped open as he stared at his father. *Did I hear him correctly?*

Rhoslyn sprang from her chair, fisted her hands, and placed them on her hips. "My father would never agree to such a match."

Lord Filmore exhaled as he laid the contract on his desk and leaned back in his chair. "It was he who set the terms of the betrothal. Since this comes as a bit of a shock, I will allow the two of you to agree upon a date for the wedding. Until that time, I advise you to spend some time together and come to terms with the agreement."

Rhoslyn looked at Jayden, who stared at his father, transfixed. How could her father have betrothed her to such a cad? She snapped her head back to Lord Filmore, glaring. "Is that all, my lord?"

Lord Filmore ignored the venomous undertone of her voice. He kept his voice calm. "Yes."

She stomped to the door, flung it open, and exited the room nearly plowing over Shadow.

Jayden looked to his father, who sighed, rose from his desk, and shut the door. What he had to say was for his son's ears only. "There is more you must know."

Ignoring his father, Jaydon spoke his mind. "You have committed my soul, the remainder of my life, to an eternal hell. Father, she truly hates me."

Lord Filmore returned to his seat. "Then it will be up to you to change her mind. Spend some time with her. Let her see the person you truly are."

"You said there is more?"

Once again Lord Filmore took the contract in his hand. "Yes. Her father sent this missive in his time of desperation, possibly moments before the Lord and Lady of Bardenham were arrested for a crime against the baron. From what I understand, the charge is treason. I don't know the details, nor do I care to. Instead of facing a trial and an unpleasant death, Lord Atherton chose to ingest poison. He is dead. Lady Eugenia is being held in a tower at Somerville awaiting an investigation. If she is found guilty, she will be beheaded. I'm waiting for word from the baron on his ruling of her trial."

"Does she know about her parents, her father's death?"

"No. The Lord and Lady of Bardenham arranged for her lodging at the Sisters of Charity months before they were charged with the offense. I assume she is innocent of whatever treasonous act they may have committed. When the time comes, I want you to be the one to tell her."

"Me? Are you trying to get her to hate me even more?"

"On the contrary, I'm hoping the tragedy will have the opposite effect and pull you closer together."

"I highly doubt it, Father. She has mentioned her desire to return home."

"For the time being, she has no home to return to. Bardenham belongs to the baron. I assume it will become your kingdom to rule once you are wed."

Jayden nodded his head once in agreement.

Lord Filmore stood indicating the discussion was over. "Shall we announce your betrothal during the evening meal?"

"I think it would be wise to give my future wife time to adjust to the idea." He needed time to accept the arranged marriage as well. "But I will ask her just the same."

"Very well."

Chapter 23

Rhoslyn stormed across the Great Hall and up the staircase.

Lydia saw the blur of midnight blue pass by and stared as her mistress ran up the staircase taking two steps at a time. She raced after her mistress to see Rhoslyn run down the hallway and enter her bedchamber slamming the door behind her. The servant paused, wondering if she should give her a moment alone. Tiptoeing, she pressed her ear to the door and listened before opening it cautiously. "My lady? Is all well?"

Rhoslyn stopped pacing and looked toward Lydia as she closed the door. Tears cascaded down her cheeks, her hands balled into fists as she took a moment to catch her breath. "No, all is not well. My father betrothed my hand in marriage to Lord Jayden."

"What?"

"Lord Filmore accepted the contract terms."

"Oh my."

"He is allowing us to determine the wedding date."

"Have you set one?"

"Can you predict the day Hell freezes over because that is the date I choose."

Lydia sighed, uncertain of how to calm her mistress. "My lady, in all honesty, you do not know his true self. You have yet to converse with him on an intellectual level. Besides, staring at his face for the rest of your life wouldn't be all that bad." She smiled trying to make light of the situation.

Rhoslyn glared at Lydia. "You think of him as an intellectual?"

"I believe most men's brains are in their pants." Lydia giggled placing her hand over her mouth to regain control over her laughter. Her effort was unsuccessful.

Rhoslyn cracked a smile. The more Lydia laughed, the bigger her smile became until she began to laugh too.

Once Lydia regained her composure, she offered another perspective. "Perhaps he isn't thrilled with the betrothal either."

"I fear our marriage will be scandalous and humiliating. If he continues to chase skirts after we are wed, I will suffer the same miserable fate as my mother."

A knock sounded upon the door. Lydia stepped toward it and opened the portal to see Jayden and Shadow.

Rhoslyn was aware of the heat rising in her face as he looked toward her. *Good lord, did he overhear our conversation?*

Jayden hesitated, searching for the proper words to approach her without offending. "Lady Rhoslyn, may I have a moment of your time?" He motioned toward the hallway.

Rhoslyn marched into the hallway, crossing her arms over her chest, and she turned to face him.

He waited for Lydia to close the door, took a deep breath, and looked down into Rhoslyn's defiant eyes. "Would you be opposed to my father announcing our betrothal at the evening meal tonight?"

She uncrossed her arms and entwined her fingers while considering his question. "The contract is signed and binding, so let the truth be known."

He nodded in agreement. "I will inform Father." He stood before her as if searching for a topic of conversation. *Should I tell her about the fate of her parents?*

She looked to his face, unsmiling. "Is there something else?"

With the truth hinged on his lips, he chose to lie instead, heeding the advice of his father. "Do you know how to play chess?"

Rhoslyn scrunched her face into a disbelieving scowl. "What?"

"Chess, do you know how to play?"

"Yes."

"Would you care to join me in the Great Hall for a game. I believe my parents have a chessboard in the solar. We can retrieve it along the way."

Rhoslyn glanced at the closed bedchamber door. '*You do not know his true self. You have yet to converse with him on an intellectual level*' echoed within her mind. *I guess we shall see how intellectual you are, Lord Jayden.*

"Very well." She opened the bedchamber door and looked at Lydia. "Would you like to join us in the Great Hall?" She raised her eyebrows in a silent plea.

Lydia looked from her mistress to Jayden. "Yes, my lady. I shall sit by the fireplace and work on my needlework." The servant picked up the basket containing their embroidering projects before following the couple at a respectful distance so as not to overhear their conversation.

The women waited by the solar doorway while Jayden retrieved the chessboard and pieces. Once in the Great Hall, Lydia took her place next to the fireplace. She glanced in the direction of her mistress, who chose a bench at a table on the other side of the room, retrieved her needlework from the basket, and began to sew.

Jayden set the chessboard with its pieces on the table, and Shadow took his place beneath it.

Rhoslyn picked up the white queen and rotated it between her finger and thumb analyzing the intricately carved marble. "What a lovely chess set."

Jayden sat across from her. "It was a gift for my father. I believe a friend gave it to him. White moves first."

She set her queen on its square and pushed the pawn in front of her king forward two spaces. He moved his right knight up two and to his right one. She countered by moving her bishop diagonally toward his knight.

Jayden bent toward the chessboard and scowled. He moved his leftmost pawn forward two spaces.

She sighed. *This is too easy.* Rhoslyn moved her queen diagonally to the right two spaces.

He countered by moving another pawn.

She moved her queen forward to take his pawn. "Checkmate."

Jayden scowled as he reviewed their moves. He squared his shoulders as he sat up straight and conceded. "Well done. Is there anything you aren't good at?"

"Fighting with a sword."

"Then we will practice it on the field to improve your skill." He reset the chessboard. "Another game?"

She looked toward Lydia, who glanced at her as she pulled her needle through the material.

"Only one more. I have an embroidery project I would like to work on."

"So, you're skilled in needlework too?"

"I know many stitches, but I don't consider myself a master of the art of embroidery."

"And what is the urgency in this particular project?"

"It is a gift for the Sisters of Charity. I would like to finish it as soon as possible."

~

Lady Carling heard voices echoing from the Great Hall as she left her bedchamber and entered the hallway. One seemed familiar, very familiar. She went to the balcony, peeked over the railing, and saw the couple playing chess. Her eyes narrowed to mere slits. *Oh, no you don't you little vixen.* She descended the staircase and sauntered toward Jayden.

Rhoslyn glanced toward the woman who was sneaking up behind Jayden like a slithering snake eyeing her prey.

Lady Carling traced her finger from Jayden's shoulder to his hand. She tilted her head to look into his eyes. "May I play the winner?"

Rhoslyn displayed a Cheshire cat-like smile. "That would be me."

Lady Carling's smiled dissolved as she looked at the woman on the opposite side of the table.

Rhoslyn stood. "We have yet to begin this game. Why don't you take my seat?" She looked at her betrothed, who was scowling. "As I stated, I would like to work on my embroidery. Thank you for the entertaining game. I look forward to our next match."

He nodded as she left her seat to join Lydia.

Lady Carling plopped down in her vacated seat. "I have the first move, right?"

Lydia, who poked her needle into the cloth, looked at her. "Who won the game?"

"I did." Rhoslyn smirked.

"Was your conversation civil?"

"For the most part. Did you bring my embroidery with you?"

"Oh, yes." Lydia retrieved her pillow, thread, and handed it to her.

"Thank you." Rhoslyn removed the needle woven in the cloth and begin the next stitch.

Servants emerged from the kitchen carrying trays of food and pitchers of ale. They laid out the midday meal on a table.

Sir Darwin entered the room accompanied by several men. He noted the young lord entertaining Lady Carling and the two women near the fireplace. He paused before Jayden.

"So, this is why you weren't at practice? Too busy entertaining the lovely Lady Carling." Sir Darwin looked from Jayden to Lady Carling and winked at her. She smiled, thrilled by the compliment.

Jayden looked to his knight. "I need a moment of your time." He turned toward Lady Carling. "If you will excuse me for a moment. Please make your move while I am gone." He did not wait for her reply and stepped into the hallway toward the library with his knight in tow.

"I've been informed by Father that I'm betrothed to Lady Rhoslyn." He watched the knight's eyes enlarge. "Did you know of this arrangement?"

"No, my lord, but a lovely match I must say." The knight smiled.

Jayden ran his hand through his hair pulling it away from his eyes and back over his head as he went to rejoin his chess partner. He looked to the chessboard and moved his queen to a square. "Checkmate." He looked up to his knight, who studied the chessboard. "I was going to join you for practice this afternoon. Why aren't you on the field?"

Thunder resonated within the Great Hall. Conversations stopped. Many looked toward the ceiling as the windows rattled. A torrent of rain on the rooftop resonated throughout the room as if someone had turned on a faucet.

Sir Darwin nodded toward the ceiling. "That's why. We could see the wicked clouds in the distance and thought it best to call off the training until the storm subsided." The knight watched as Lady Carling laid her king on its side. "Lady Carling, would you like to join me for the midday meal?"

"Only if Lord Jayden joins us." She tilted her head to one side and batted her eyes.

~

Rhoslyn tied off the thread, cut it with the scissors, and set her embroidery aside. She recalled the toil and effort she put into the vegetable garden at the abbey. "I hope the heavy rain doesn't damage the crops too badly."

Lydia looked at Jayden as he passed by with Lady Carling's arms entwined through his. "I feel sorry for Lord Jayden. The woman is so forward."

Rhoslyn looked at her betrothed and Lady Carling as they approached the table laden with food.

"Persistent, isn't she? You'd think he would draw from his vast experience with women to curtail her obnoxious behavior and put her in her place." Rhoslyn sat back in her chair and waited for Lydia to finish her stitch. The unnerving cackle of Lady Carling resonated within the room drawing her attention. She watched as the annoying woman sat next to Jayden, rose from her seat, and went to the table to select something to eat. Lydia set her embroidery down quickly and followed.

As the thunderstorm rolled in and rain fell the remainder of the afternoon, Rhoslyn sewed the final stitch of the pillow. She held up her project to admire her handiwork while servants began setting up for the evening meal. "Lydia, perhaps we should retire to the bedchamber."

"Yes, and have you change into a gown for the evening." Lydia gathered the sewing materials and basket.

Jayden drew his attention away from the chessboard as the women crossed the room and ascended the staircase.

Lady Carling followed his line of vision. She placed her hand upon his arm. "I believe it is your move."

"Perhaps we should continue the game later. The servants are preparing the room for the evening meal."

"Just as well. I need to change my dress. Is there a particular color you wish me to wear?" Lady Carling raised her eyebrows teasingly and smiled.

"Wear whatever you wish." Jayden left the table. He had no intention of escorting Lady Carling to her bedchamber.

Chapter 24

A roaring fire in the Great Hall's fireplace crackled and popped with its heat drying the dampness from the room. Golden candlelight added a warmness to the atmosphere of the evening meal. All were seated with full tankards in hand as servants stood in the doorway of the kitchen waiting for the Lord of Aldwinster's signal to serve the food.

Lord Filmore stood before his seat on the dais with his arms raised signaling for silence. He waited while the room quieted. "It is with great pleasure that I announce the betrothal of my son, Lord Jayden to Lady Rhoslyn."

The room filled with murmurs.

Sir Darwin rose and lifted his tankard. "Huzzah!"

The guests in the hall stood and followed his lead. "Huzzah! Huzzah! Huzzah!"

Sitting next to her mistress, Lydia leaned forward to watch Lady Carling's reaction to the news. The woman raised her tankard but remained silent, unsmiling.

Lady Myla leaned toward her future daughter-in-law. "My dear, have you chosen a date to wed?"

"No. I assume my parents will want to host the wedding at Bardenham, so I will send a missive requesting they choose a date that is convenient for them."

Lady Myla nodded, picked up her goblet, and sipped her wine while making a mental note to tell her husband of Rhoslyn's intention.

Curious, Rhoslyn looked toward Lady Carling, who's head was downcast as she moved her food around her plate with her fork. *Perhaps she will discontinue bothering him now that the announcement has been made.*

Lady Carling looked up from her plate to find her nemesis staring at her. *Oh, future bride of my Jayden, I do not give up so easily.* She raised her tankard to Rhoslyn and forced a congratulatory grin on her face.

As the meal came to an end, tables were cleared and moved aside while the musicians took their place. Rhoslyn turned to Lydia. "Is there dancing every night?"

"Yes. The Lord and Lady of Aldwinster insist upon it. They enjoy dancing."

The attendants watch the traditional first dance by their lord and lady. It was followed by applause as a new tune began.

As his parents returned to their seats, Jayden rose and went to his future bride's side. "May I have this dance with the most beautiful woman in the room?" He smiled and presented his hand to help her rise from her chair.

Lady Myla looked at her son's hand and then to Rhoslyn, who appeared defiant.

Rhoslyn assumed her betrothed had used the well-rehearsed line many times before on his strumpets. She looked at his mother. "Does your son always tell such falsehoods?"

"My dear, all men and women tell falsehoods to some extent. Whatever preconceived assumption you have made of Jayden's character, I can assure you, in this case, he is telling the truth." She looked up to her son and smiled, a proud smile only a mother could convey.

Rhoslyn looked into the askance sky-blue eyes staring down at her. As a little girl, she imagined marrying a loyal, devoted husband, strong and handsome, and one she loved. Maybe the world had changed since she was a child, had she finally understood the reality of marriage or had a morality between right and wrong been instilled within her mind while at the abbey? Whichever it may be, she did not see any promising qualities in Jayden. Against her better judgment, she would do as her parents wished and marry him. She exhaled before putting her hand in the palm of her future husband and rose. He guided her toward the center of the floor as the musicians began the next song.

She refused to make eye contact with him as he pulled her close, placed his hand on the small of her back, and clasped her hand within his.

The tension between them was as thick as a stone wall, steadfast and solid. Unable to withstand the silence any longer, Jayden spoke his mind. "Why do you hate me so?"

Startled by his question, she glanced at his eyes before looking away. "I don't hate you. I hate what you do."

He scowled, puzzled by her comment. "And what do I do, exactly?"

She turned her head toward him ever so slowly, narrowing her aqua eyes as her anger flared. "I dislike the way you treat women. Your incessant flirting, lack of respect. It is as if they are nothing more to you than a conquest, a notch to your bedpost so to speak. I can only imagine how many skirts you've flipped."

Taken back by her accusation, his feet came to a halt, they stood at a standstill while couples continued to dance to the music. He stared down into her eyes. Even though her accusation was untrue, well, for the most part, he pried further. "How should that trouble you?"

"I don't want to be married to someone unfaithful. It's scandalous, embarrassing, especially when the other women…" She paused her face flushed with color as she recalled her mother's humiliation each time her father produced a bastard.

"Go on." He waited patiently.

She took a breath gathering her courage. "When they are pregnant with your child. I don't want to marry you especially if you continue to gallivant with women and be unfaithful like…"

"Like?"

She looked him squarely in the eye, her rage boiling. "My father."

He sighed understanding her aversion to him, to all men. "The contract is out of our hands. It is a fate we must accept. I've come to terms with the arrangement. You seem unwilling to do so."

"I plan to return home and have my father revoke the contract." She lifted her chin staring at him defiantly. "I will not be married to one such as you."

His nostrils flared, heartbeat quickened, for she was a stranger who knew very little about his true character. He glanced toward the High Table. Sir Darwin was staring at him. He stared down at his future bride. "Perhaps we should have this discussion in a less public place."

Rhoslyn clenched her teeth. "No, the discussion is closed." She turned toward the staircase and wove her way between the dancing couples leaving him dumbfounded and alone.

He was tired of her assumptions, her prejudice opinion. He looked to his knight, who nodded his head toward Rhoslyn to indicate he should follow her. He looked to the ceiling, clenched his teeth, and stepped forward in pursuit.

She heard his footsteps behind her as she climbed the staircase and looked over her shoulder. "Leave me alone!"

He took the stairs two at a time. His long stride allowed him to catch her midway of the staircase and walk beside her. "I need to tell you the truth."

"Why should I believe anything you say? All that seems to come out your mouth are lies." She reached the top of the stairs and quickened her steps to reach the safety of her bedchamber.

He grabbed her arm and turned her toward him. "Just listen to what I have to say. Please." He inhaled trying to catch his breath. "Let's go into the solar where we can talk in private." He motioned toward the open door hoping to encourage her to come with him, took a step forward, and waited.

She sighed before charging into the secluded room confident her trusty dirk attached to her calf was there if she needed it for defense.

Jayden closed the door and turned to see her standing with her arms crossed over her chest. He could hear her foot tapping on the stone floor.

Rhoslyn wasn't interested in what he had to say. She wanted to go home to Bardenham. The sooner she arrived home, the sooner her father could retract the contract. "Well?"

He motioned toward a chair indicating she should sit. She remained standing. He sat in a chair, crossed his right foot over his left thigh, and stared into her aqua orbs. "I have a feeling that no matter what I say, you will not believe me. So, ask me any question that burdens your mind. What do you want to know?" He waited patiently as she began to pace the floor gathering her thoughts.

Shadow scratched at the door. Jayden held up his index finger in a silent request to wait. He let the dog into the room, closed the door, and returned to his seat.

Rhoslyn had many questions running through her mind. She stopped pacing and faced him. "What is Lady Carling to you?"

A question he had not expected.

"A pain in my ass, annoying. Her husband died a year or two ago. She would like to become the next Lady of Aldwinster, my wife."

"So, you have no feelings for her whatsoever?"

"I can think of a few; repulsed, nauseated, and disdain."

The comment brought a slight smile to her face. "What about all of the women in the kingdom who you flirt with constantly?"

"Your perception is incorrect. They flirt with me."

"But you reciprocate and lead them on."

"I don't want to appear snobbish. After all, they are peasants who will be under my reign someday."

"What of the conversation between you and Sir Darwin during our journey from the abbey? Were you not bragging of the many women you had bedded?"

"That was just talking between men."

"Lies?"

"Exaggerations." He motioned with his hand in the air as if shooing away an insect. "Men talk about that topic all of the time. It is just men talk."

"I never heard my father talk of such."

"Not to you, but I can assure you he had such conversations with other men."

Rhoslyn looked to the ceiling before turning away from him.

He stood. "You don't believe me?"

"If you are so implied to 'exaggerate', how do I know you aren't exaggerating just to appease my curiosity?"

She has a point. He sighed as he ran his hand through his charcoal hair pulling it away from his eyes. "I will share with you something personal, private, and for your ears only. Promise me that you will not mention my secret to another."

She turned to face him with her fisted hands on each hip. "No exaggeration? Only the truth?"

"Yes, I promise, but you must promise not to laugh."

Her curiosity was piqued. She was reluctant but agreed. "I promise."

He exhaled and stared into her eyes wondering if he could trust her with his secret. After all, he had a reputation to uphold. "I've never, how did you say it, 'flipped a skirt'." He paused. "I've been forewarned of the consequence of such an act. As requested by my father, Sir Darwin is my guardian ensuring I remain virginal, so my offspring are legitimate." He dared not breathe as he waited for her reaction to his revelation.

Taken back by his admission, it explained Lydia's comment about his lack of bastards. As promised, she did not laugh or even smile. He trusted her to keep his secret and she would, but was he telling the truth?

A knock sounded upon the door. They looked toward it.

"My lady, is all well?" Lydia waited with her ear pressed to the solar door.

"All is well, Lydia. I shall join you momentarily in my bedchamber."

"Very well, my lady."

Rhoslyn looked at her betrothed.

Jayden wished to show his knight, as well as Lady Carling, that all was well between himself and his betrothed. "If it wouldn't be too much to ask, could you rejoin me in the Great Hall for a dance or maybe two?"

She crossed her arms over her chest and opened her mouth to reply.

He anticipated her refusal and extended the palm of his hand toward her. "Lady Rhoslyn, I beg you, let us present the perfect picture of a happy couple to dissuade Lady Carling and any other women who desire to become my wife."

She exhaled and looked to the ceiling before taking a step toward the door. "Very well."

"Thank you." He opened the door and motioned with his arm for her to exit.

Chapter 25

Lady Carling finished the spiced wine in her goblet, held out the empty vessel, and a nearby servant refilled it. She stared at the betrothed couple as they spun around the floor.

The Lord and Lady of Aldwinster and Sir Darwin kept a watchful eye on the woman at the end of the table as she consumed another tankard. Her state of intoxication exposed her revengeful tainted soul as she scowled at the betrothed couple.

Lord Filmore lifted his drink from the table and looked toward the knight. "Sir Darwin, we don't want to appear as a bad host. Perhaps you should stay close to Lady Carling."

"Yes, my lord, but it's not my company that she wants."

"Nevertheless, I would appreciate you monopolizing her time until she leaves Aldwinster."

"Do we know when that will be, my lord?"

"Unfortunately, no."

Sir Darwin downed his drink, wiped his mouth across his sleeve, and rose from his chair. He removed the tankard from Lady Carling's hand and set it on the table.

Jayden rotated to see Sir Darwin obtain Lady Carling's full attention. "Knowing my father, he has sent Sir Darwin to distract Lady Carling. Maybe she will stop staring at us now."

Rhoslyn glanced toward the High Table. "She can't help it. Sometimes one's heart directs the mind."

"You speak of compassion." He looked down into her eyes, questioning her logic.

"Perhaps I do. The world is not kind to women. Even though you find her annoying, I understand her actions to be one of desperation, not necessarily love."

Their dance was followed by a second, then a third. Jayden watched Sir Darwin lean toward Lady Carling, whisper in her ear, and caress her cheek with the back of his fingers. She was enjoying his undivided attention. The glow of happiness upon her face was genuine.

He looked down to see his future wife yawn. She had become comfortable and compliant in his arms. "I believe it is time for you to retire."

She looked up into his eyes, yawned again, and nodded in agreement.

Jayden placed his hand on the small of her back and directed his betrothed to the staircase. His faithful canine trotted ahead of him and waited by his bedchamber door. The young lord glanced back at his knight, who winked indicating all would be well. As he escorted Rhoslyn to her bedchamber, he posed an idea. "Weather permitting, would you like to join me on the practice field tomorrow?"

She put her hand on the door latch and looked back at him. "For?"

"You indicated you are weak with the sword. I thought you may want to practice it with me."

She nodded her head in agreement. "Until tomorrow, goodnight."

"Goodnight." He waited until she closed the bedchamber door and heard the latch click into place.

He went to his bedchamber and paused before his door as he heard giggling from the staircase. He saw Sir Darwin and Lady Carling with their faces close together. The knight had his arm around her shoulders and held his index finger across her lips as if trying to stifle her laughter. Jayden shook his head, allowed Shadow to precede him, and entered his bedchamber without being seen by the pair.

Chapter 26

"You want to wear what?" Lydia could hardly believe her ears. "You're going to be doing what?" She set the tray of breakfast food on the table before her lady.

"I believe you heard me correctly. I need something to wear like breeches, so I can move easily, be active. Lord Jayden has offered to help improve my skill with the sword."

"Hmmm…" Lydia turned toward the wardrobe. She mentally scanned the garments inside. *Maybe Pearson can help me find something for her to wear. Breeches?*

~

Shadow darted toward the solar as Jayden opened his bedchamber door. As he pulled his door closed, he heard another door down the hall close and looked to see Sir Darwin with a spring in his step and grinning.

"Good morning, Sir Darwin. I assume you made Lady Carling very happy last night."

"Good morning, my lord. Only the young boast about their conquests. At my age, we treasure them." He smiled as he walked with his lord to the solar door.

"I'll keep that in mind." Jayden smiled not wanting to know the details of the knight's evening.

"Not to pry, my lord, but did your evening go well with your betrothed?"

"I haven't won her over yet, not certain I want to. But we were civil toward each other."

"Give her time. Shall I see you on the practice field today?"

"Yes, but I will be practicing the sword with Lady Rhoslyn."

"Very well, my lord." Sir Darwin continued onto the Great Hall as Jayden entered the solar.

~

"My lady, Pearson and I searched for something appropriate for you to wear. This is the best we can do for you." Lydia held up a simple burgundy bodice and skirt. "You can wear your chemise beneath it and tie the bodice loosely."

"Perfect." Rhoslyn untied her robe. With Lydia's assistance, she put on the skirt, bodice, and slipped on a pair of leather boots found at the bottom of the wardrobe. They were a little too large for her feet but would do nicely for the day.

~

Having finished their breakfast, Lord Filmore and his son exited the solar and descended the staircase to the Great Hall.

Lady Carling closed the door of her bedchamber. Her heart fluttered as she recalled the events of the previous night, placed her toe on the top step of the staircase, and froze as she saw Lord Filmore and Jayden talking at the opposite end of the Great Hall. She retreated into the darkness of the hallway and listened to the echoing voices from below.

"Still no word from the baron?"

"No. I'm certain he will send word once the investigation of Lady Eugenia's alleged crime is complete. For Lady Rhoslyn's sake, I hope she is found innocent. As I have stated, use your discretion as to when to inform her of her father's death and the confinement of her mother. I would advise against telling her of his self-inflicted poisoning to avoid the charge of treason though."

"It is difficult to determine the right time to inform her of such bad news."

"The right time may never present itself. Nevertheless, it must be done."

Their voices faded as they entered the hallway to the library. Lady Carling stepped from the shadows. *Interesting.*

Chapter 27

Placing her foot on the seat of the chair, Rhoslyn strapped her dirk to her calf and let her skirt fall back in place. She sat and waited patiently while Lydia used extra pins to keep her hair out of her eyes and in place during her practice. As the servant stepped away indicating she had finished and handed her a mirror, Rhoslyn turned her head one way then the other to ensure her hair was presentable. "Are you certain you don't want a lesson as well?" She rose and set the mirror on the chair.

Lydia laughed at the suggestion and picked up the tray from the table. "No thank you, my lady. I have other tasks to occupy my time." Her mistress preceded her out of the bedchamber door.

Rhoslyn looked over her shoulder. "If you have time, could you find some material for the back of the pillow I made for the Sisters of Charity?" She stepped onto the floor of the Great Hall.

"Yes, my lady." Lydia continued toward the kitchen.

From the corner of her eye, Rhoslyn spied Lady Carling sitting at a table sipping from a glass of wine.

Lady Carling's vessel lowered. With an all-knowing smirk on her face, she blinked lethargically as she stared at the woman threatening to take her place as Jayden's wife.

Ignoring the woman, Rhoslyn turned into the hallway, exited the Keep, and went to the stable to see Beval saddled and tied to a post. She entered the stable and waited outside of Laila's stall while Jayden helped Kolby lift Laila's saddle onto the mare's back. "Good morning, my lord, Kolby."

The stableboy reached under Laila's stomach to retrieve the girth belt. "My lady, we are just finishing."

Jayden turned to face her. He patted Laila's rump as he stepped into the aisle. "Good morning. Shall we wait in the warmth of the sun while Kolby finishes?"

She nodded in agreement.

The bailey was abuzz with merchants displaying their trades. A woman passed carrying a chicken in a basket to be used as trade for a round of cheese or loaves of bread.

Assuming the peasant woman was staring at him for a moment of his attention, Jayden fought the urge to look toward the alewives.

Rhoslyn looked to the woodcarver's establishment. She hoped he retained the box she requested. Jayden followed her line of sight, reading her mind.

"She is ready, my lady." Kolby emerged from the stable with Laila in tow.

Shadow came around the side of the stable and looked at his master, anticipating a day out of the castle.

Rhoslyn climbed atop of her mare and took the reins in her hand. She noticed a leather bag attached to Jayden's saddle but said nothing as he mounted his warhorse and reined him toward the front gate. Rhoslyn brought Laila alongside Beval and Shadow trailed behind the pair.

They rode their horses over the drawbridge, through the village, and toward the practice field. Rhoslyn vowed to do her utmost best hoping not to embarrass herself, or worse, get hurt.

As if reading her mind, Jayden reached down and patted the bracers tied to his saddle. "I brought a pair to protect your arms while we practice."

They reined their horses on the fringe of the practice field. A page rushed forward taking the reins. With his nose to the ground, Shadow scampered off to hunt for a rabbit in a nearby field.

Jayden motioned to the bench. "Sit so I may put these on you." He loosened the lace on one of the bracers.

Rhoslyn sat and held up her right arm with her palm downward. He rotated her arm until her palm was upward, wrapped the piece of thick leather around her forearm, and placed her wrist between his thighs squeezing it slightly to hold it in place. She tensed as she looked at her hand trapped between his legs.

Jayden pulled the lace to tighten if from her elbow to her wrist. He looked toward her uneasy expression. "Is something amiss?"

She looked to his inquiring eyes. "No." She remained silent as she watched him finish lacing and tightened the bracer securely.

"There's one." He released her arm and reached for the other.

Rhoslyn made a fist and rotated her right arm testing the bracer. It was comfortable and did not impede her mobility. Her attention was drawn to her other hand as Jayden finished lacing it.

"There, now to select a weapon for you." He went to a pile of wooden swords, chose one, and tested the blade to ensure it was solid before handing it to her. "See how this one feels?"

She looked to him for clarification as she accepted the sword. "It feels like a sword."

"No, I mean is it too heavy, too light, the right length?" He selected a sword for himself and checked the sturdiness of the blade.

She held the hilt firmly and tilted the blade back and forth. "It seems fine to me."

"Then let's find a spot on the field." He motioned toward a vacant area among the men, allowing her to go before him.

As she reached the small clearing, she turned to face him, set her feet, and raised her sword. He nodded his head accepting her challenge and charged.

Rhoslyn fought like a banshee, drawing knowledge from years of practice with her father's knight. She lunged, countered, and parried his every move.

Men on the field gather around to watch the couple spar.

Jayden analyzed her technique, footwork, and impressive agility. He held up the palm of his hand for them to break as their chests rose and fell from the exertion. A page came forward with a bucket of water to quench their thirst. Jayden accepted the full ladle from the lad and offered it to his future bride, who accepted it and drank it dry. "I fail to see your difficulty with the sword. You're quite skilled. A few times you were off-balance, but overall, you're quite accomplished."

She gave the ladle back to the lad, who dipped it into the bucket and offered it to his lord.

"I've practiced with my father's knight over the years. He showed little mercy. My difficulty with the sword lies in the weight of a true sword." She lifted her practice sword easily. "A real one that is."

He looked to the wooden blade in her hand. "A real sword, you say?" He dropped the ladle in the bucket.

"Yes. I do not possess the strength to wield one. Most are too large. They are made for men, not for someone as small as me."

"I understand, but to give you a smaller sword would put you at a disadvantage during a fight."

"True, but sword or not, my arm is much smaller than a man's arm. They will always outreach me."

He could not argue with her logic as he scanned her small stature. "I agree."

"That's why I became accurate with a knife and arrow."

He recalled the knife she threw in the shop and her accuracy with the arrows. "Your aim is impressive. They're skills you have mastered indeed."

"Thank you."

He looked skyward to the midday sun and tapped the wooden sword on the end of his boot. "Do you wish to continue practicing, or shall we find a quiet spot to eat our midday meal."

"My lord…" She began to object.

"Jayden."

"I don't…what?"

"Since we are betrothed, please address me by my given name, Jayden." He hoped she would allow him to use her given name as well, but out of respect, he would wait until she gave her permission to do so.

She did not want to think of him as her betrothed, but she did as he wished. "Jayden, I don't want to monopolize your time."

"I have set my day aside to be with you. It's of no imposition whatsoever. In fact, I'm enjoying it thus far." He looked toward Sir Darwin, who had beads of sweat running down his reddened face, his tunic damp, and droplets dangling on the end of his curly sun-bleached hair. "Much better than spending it with my odorous knight." He grinned as he nodded his head toward his guardian.

Rhoslyn looked to the loyal knight, admiring his work ethic. She watched as he raised his sword to block an attack. "Very well, but I would like to return to the Keep after we eat so I may finish my gift for the Sisters of Charity." She dropped her sword onto the pile.

Jayden did the same. He reached for her arm and held it steady as he unlaced the bracer with one hand. She looked to his face as he focused on the kind gesture. He looked into her eyes and grinned as he reached for her other arm and did the same. The page brought their horses forward. Jayden tied the bracers to his saddle, climbed atop, and turned to see his betrothed in her saddle. He searched his mind for a secluded place to eat their midday meal and decided the large oak tree beside a winding river in the distance would be an enjoyable spot for conversation. He encouraged Beval into a trot.

Shadow lifted his head from his paws where he lay napping. He realized his master had finished practicing, rose, and ran after him.

Jayden reined his ebony warhorse beneath the ancient oak. He scanned its canopy's leafy branches, rigid in the gentle breeze. "I think this will do nicely." He dismounted and unfastened the leather bag from his saddle and waited for her to join him at the base of the tree. Letting their horses graze on the tall grass, they sat on the ground and leaned against the massive trunk facing the river.

Jayden unlaced the bag. "Let's see what Pearson has packed." He retrieved two corked bottles of watered ale and handed one to Rhoslyn. Cold meat pies, slices of buttered bread, and sweet cakes were each individually wrapped in linen.

Rhoslyn looked up into the branches of the large oak and presumed it to be quite old. The cascading water over several large boulders in the brook drew her attention. "It's very pretty here, peaceful."

He held the linen with meat pies before her.

She selected one. "Thank you."

An uneasiness settled within her stomach as she realized she was sitting too closely with her body touching his. She was unaccustomed to being alone with a man and being this close to him was inappropriate. She was compelled to scoot away, distance herself, yet she did not want to offend him. Maybe it was her imagination, but she thought he was uncomfortable, perhaps nervous too.

"Have you lived at Aldwinster all of your life?" Rhoslyn bit into the meat pie.

He looked toward her. "Yes."

"It's a lovely kingdom." She looked toward it in the distance.

"Tell me, what is your home like?"

"Very similar, a little smaller perhaps. Father keeps Bardenham in good order. The peasants are happy and well cared for with adequate housing. The fertile ground produces well."

He nodded his head in understanding while he ate.

She uncorked her bottle of ale and took a drink. "Do you know if there has been any word from my father?"

Jayden slowed his chewing while he thought of an appropriate response. "Not to my knowledge." He tossed Shadow a portion of his pie.

"I hoped to hear from him by now. I planned to ask him to retract his signature from our contract but know in my heart he will not do so. He must have paid your father a large dowry to be rid of me."

Jayden wanted to tell her the truth, that her father was dead but feared her reaction. They had been civil to each other thus far. Such news may put an end to it. "The messenger may have been delayed." It was the best excuse that came to his mind. "As far as the betrothal contract, it was a surprise to me as well. I do not know the terms of the agreement, but I would not consider you to be a burden." He looked toward her and smiled. "Maybe he paid a large sum to ensure you are well cared for?"

"Perhaps." She pinched a loose piece of meat from her pie and popped it into her mouth. "When is Lady Carling returning to her home?" Rhoslyn hoped it was soon. The woman made her skin crawl.

"When her husband died, she was forced to live with relatives. So, in truth, she has no home. Father insists we play the role of proper hosts. As far as when she is leaving, I do not know."

171

"I saw her on my way to the stable. She was in the Great Hall glaring at me. Her expression reminded me of a cat who had just eaten a mouse."

"Never a good sign when it comes to her. She is headstrong and determined to get what she wants. I'm thankful Sir Darwin has kept her occupied and away from me." Jayden raised his eyebrow as he picked up the linen with buttered bread and offered her a slice.

The remainder of their meal was accompanied by general conversation, shared secrets, and future dreams. Once their bottles of watered ale were empty and food was eaten, they repacked the bag and laced it tightly. Jayden presented his open hands to assist Rhoslyn to stand. She looked to his kind face, knew his offer to be genuine, and placed her hands within his. He pulled her upward with ease. They retrieved their horses and rode back to the castle.

Chapter 28

"How was your day, my lady?" Lydia hung a freshly washed gown in the wardrobe as her mistress entered the bedchamber.

Rhoslyn reflected on the time she spent with her betrothed. He had been patient, kind, attentive, and thoughtful. "In all honesty, pleasant."

"So, Lord Jayden isn't the cad you thought him to be?" The servant raised an eyebrow as she tilted her head to the side.

Rhoslyn thought for a moment as she sat in the chair next to the sewing basket. "I don't recall him giving his attention to anyone other than me. Unless the personality he displayed was false, he acted like a true gentleman." She peered into the sewing basket. "Were you able to find a cloth for the back of the pillow?"

"My apologies, my lady, I've been too busy with my duties thus far. Would you like me to do that now?"

"No, I think I would like to select the cloth myself. Can you direct me to the sewing room?"

"It's the tiny room beneath the staircase of the Great Hall."

Rhoslyn took her embroidered panel from the basket. She admired the green floss in the embroidery and hoped to find a material to match it. She descended the staircase and located the room.

Lady Carling stepped into the Great Hall with a full tankard of wine in her hand and watched Jayden's betrothed disappear through a doorway beneath the staircase.

A window on the far wall of the sewing room offered plenty of natural sunlight. Bolts of every imaginable cloth filled the shelves lining the walls. Baskets contained thread, lace, pins, needles, and scissors. A long wooden table in the center of the room with several chairs around it offered space for cutting material and laying out patterns. With her embroidered pillow in hand, she scanned the bolts of material looking for a suitable shade of green. The door to the chamber creaked open. She turned to see Lady Carling enter and close the door behind her. The woman's eyes drooped half-closed as she walked in a crooked line with a sneer upon her face.

"Well, I see we are alone." Lady Carling waved her nearly empty goblet in the air before placing it to her lips and finishing its contents. She set the tankard on the table's edge. It dropped to the floor. "Oops."

Rhoslyn redirected her attention to a bolt of material in the perfect shade of green to compliment the embroidery. From the woman's slurred words, it was obvious Lady Carling was drunk. "I assume you are here to choose material for a gown."

"Um, no. I came to talk to you."

"About?"

"Your father."

She looked at the intoxicated woman. "And what do you know about my father?"

"Only that he's dead. He was caught in a treasonous act against the baron and chose to take his life instead of facing the punishment for his crime. Your cowardly father drank poison."

Rhoslyn placed her fisted hands upon her hips. "My father is not a coward."

Lady Carling hiccupped. "The fact argues otherwise. Oh, the baron has confined your mother for trial. If she is found guilty, she will be beheaded."

Rhoslyn's eyes narrowed. "How do you know this?"

"I overheard Lord Filmore and your future husband talking. Your parents arranged your betrothal after they sent you away. The contract is nothing more than a plea for your protection once they are dead."

"You lie!"

Lady Carling waved her hand in the air as if to brush aside her accusation. "Unfortunately, I do not." She opened the door. "If you don't believe me, then go and ask them." She left the room to get another tankard of wine.

Rhoslyn stared at the open door with thoughts racing through her mind. Her father's order to leave Bardenham, her incarceration at the abbey, the chest Sir Cedric transported and presented to the abbess. Would her father have paid to ensure her protection? Did he arrange her marriage to secure her future? She needed answers. Exiting the room, she saw Lady Carling plop onto a bench, fall to the side, and upright herself before bursting with laughter.

Rhoslyn looked at the hallway leading to Lord Filmore's library and hoped the Lord of Aldwinster may bring light to Lady Carling's information. She marched to the library and opened the door without knocking.

Lord Filmore was alone in the room and looked up from his account book. "Is there something you need, Lady Rhoslyn?"

"Yes, the truth. Is my father dead and my mother being confined at Bardenham on charges of treason?"

Lord Filmore exhaled as he placed his quill in the inkwell. He wondered if his son had told her the news. "How did you hear of this information?"

"Your drunken guest, Lady Carling told me. She said she overheard you and your son talking. Is she telling the truth?"

"I was hoping Jayden would be the one to break the news to you."

Her eyebrows raised and her eyes enlarged at the revelation. "He knew!"

"I told him of their status after informing the two of you of your betrothal. We are awaiting word of the baron's decision of your mother's trial."

"So, everything she said is true?" Her bottom lip trembled. Her chest became heavy and she struggled to breathe.

He opened his mouth to explain further, but she darted from the room. He assumed she went to her bedchamber to shed her tears of grief in private.

Chapter 29

In a state of disbelief, Rhoslyn kept her tears in check as she crossed the Great Hall, exited the Keep, and headed toward the stable. She marched into the stable. "Kolby, saddle Laila!"

The stableboy noted the woman's agitated state. "Yes, my lady." He leaned a pitchfork against a wall and hastened to retrieve the bridle and saddle.

Rhoslyn stepped to the stable doorway and looked toward the sky. She would have several hours to travel before nightfall. *They must be lying. Mother would never be involved in any of Father's misdoings. Surely, the baron is aware of her innocence.* She imagined her mother safely confined to her bedchamber in Bardenham with guards posted outside of her door. She called over her shoulder. "I also need a cloak, a longbow, and quiver of arrows."

Kolby paused as he glanced in her direction. "Yes, my lady." He resumed buckling the bridle while planning to take the liberty of stopping in the kitchen to gather provisions for a journey he assumed she would be taking.

~

Jayden raised his practice sword to counter the attack by Sir Darwin. He rotated the sword trapping the knight's sword to the ground.

Sir Darwin grinned as a thought crossed his mind. "So, have you tamed your future wife?"

Jayden took a step backward releasing his knight's sword. "She is spirited, but I must admit, I admire such a quality. I would hate to 'tame' it, for it's who she is."

"So, your time together was civil?"

Jayden thought for a moment as a page came forward and handed him a ladle of water. "For the most part, yes. We spoke kindly to each other on various topics." He emptied the ladle and gave it back to the lad. "She's quite skilled with the knife and arrow. Her interest in the sword gives us a common ground. I hope to build a solid relationship with her, a marriage of trust, and perhaps we will love and appreciate each other someday."

"I assume she is back at the Keep." Sir Darwin accepted a ladle from the page.

"Yes, she mentioned something about sewing." Jayden watched as his knight gave the empty ladle to the page, he set his footing and raised his sword.

~

To remain inconspicuous, Rhoslyn reined Laila at a leisurely pace as she rode through the bailey, over the drawbridge, and through the village. She looked over her shoulder to ensure she was a good distance from the castle before touching her heals to her mare's belly encouraging her into a gallop. She planned to ride until nightfall and hoped to verify the truth once she arrived at Bardenham.

~

Lydia passed through the Great Hall with an armful of laundry. She realized servants were preparing the room for the evening meal and assumed her mistress may be waiting to be dressed. However, Rhoslyn was not in the bedchamber upon her arrival. *Perhaps she has lost track of time and is still in the sewing room selecting material for her pillow.* Lydia put the laundry away before going to fetch her mistress. As she stepped into the sewing room, her foot kicked something on the floor. *A goblet?* She picked it up, spotted the material with the embroidered cross embellished with lilies lying on the table, and went to the kitchen hoping the steward could help locate her mistress. Apprehensive to enter the room bustling with people, she searched for Pearson, dodged the busy staff, and tapped him on the shoulder.

The steward turned and looked down at Lydia. "Yes?"

"Pearson, have you seen Lady Rhoslyn?"

"She is with Lord Jayden. He was entertaining her on the practice field for the day." He looked over her head and scowled. "If you will excuse me, I must redirect a member of the staff."

Lydia's stomach twisted in a knot. Her lady had returned from the practice field in good spirits. Reentering to the Great Hall, she saw Sir Darwin step into the room. *Could she have gone back to the practice field?*

"Sir Darwin." She approached the knight. "Have you seen Lady Rhoslyn?"

"She was on the practice field with Lord Jayden. They left at midday."

"Where is he now?"

"He is talking with a few of the shopkeepers."

"He's shopping?"

"I didn't ask specifics. Maybe he is verifying the repairs to Lady Carling's carriage are finished."

"Thank you." She turned away from the knight, her fists on each hip, and took a deep breath. *Maybe our paths have crossed.* Heading back to the bedchamber, she looked down at each step to ensure she did not trip as she ran up the staircase. When she reached the top, she bumped into Lord Filmore, who caught her around the waist to prevent her from toppling backward and set her to one side.

Breathing deeply, her eyes widened as she stared at the Lord of Aldwinster. "Oh, I'm sorry, my lord. I should be more careful."

"That's quite all right." He descended the staircase followed by Lady Myla.

Lydia returned to the bedchamber, ran into the center of the room, and turned in a circle. Her lady was not there. *The garderobe!* She ran down the hall to the small chamber. She discovered it empty. *Where can she be?*

She leaned against the stone wall of the hallway, breathed deeply to catch her breath, and calm her pounding heart. She went back to the bedchamber, tossed the needlework in the basket, and laid out an evening gown for Rhoslyn to don once she joined her.

~

Rhoslyn dismounted and led her horse to a stream to drink. She disliked pushing Laila to near exhaustion, but her urgency to get home and discover the truth was paramount. Luckily, she knew the way to Bardenham and Laila's long stride made it possible to travel the distance rapidly.

Her stomach grumbled. She could shoot a rabbit and cook it, but that would take too much time. As she watched Laila munch the tender grass near the riverbank, she saw a leather bag on her saddle swing to one side as her horse stepped forward. Curious, she rose, retrieved the bag, and discovered provisions inside. *Kolby?*

~

Conversations echoed within the Great Hall as servants filled tankards with ale or wine and ensured every table had enough food for all to eat. Jayden leaned forward and looked at the vacant seat of his betrothed. Her servant was absent as well. He tilted his head toward Sir Darwin. "I wonder what is keeping Lady Rhoslyn?"

Sir Darwin looked toward the staircase to see Lydia descending, her face conveying distress. "I think you are about to find out." He nodded his head toward the servant.

Jayden watched as Lydia approached the High Table wringing her hands. She glanced at him before standing directly in front of Lord Filmore, who lowered his tankard.

"Yes, Lydia, what is it?" He leaned forward awaiting her response.

"My lord, I cannot find Lady Rhoslyn."

"She isn't in her bedchamber?"

"No, my lord. I have searched the Keep. No sign of her."

Lord Filmore turned toward his son. "When was the last time you saw her?"

"After we ate our midday meal together, she wished to finish her embroidery, so I escorted her back to the Keep before returning to the practice field."

Lydia took a step forward drawing everyone's attention. "Lady Rhoslyn went to the sewing chamber to select some material. I found her embroidery on the table and an empty tankard on the floor. However, she was not there."

Lord Filmore looked toward Lady Carling. The woman smirked, her eyes half-open. He redirected his attention to the servant. "Lydia, could you go to the stable and ask Kolby if her horse is in its stall?"

"Yes, my lord."

Jayden followed his father's line of thought. "You believe she has left Aldwinster?"

Noting the tone of concern in his son's voice, Lord Filmore remained calm. "I'm just eliminating the possibility."

Sir Darwin leaned toward the young lord hoping to reassure him that all was well. "Women are fickle. She's probably within the Keep. Maybe she got lost exploring its rooms or is preoccupied with reading a book."

"Perhaps." Jayden looked at the Great Hall doorway. For some reason, he doubted his knight's reasoning.

Time ticked by lethargically while everyone at the High Table waited for Lydia to return. Unable to wait a moment longer, Jayden began to rise from his seat when the sound of footsteps echoed from the hallway. Kolby preceded Lydia into the room. Both stood before the dais with their chests rising and falling as they tried to catch their breath.

Lord Filmore opened his mouth to speak.

Jayden leaned forward, interrupting his father. "Did you find her?"

Kolby looked from Jayden to Lord Filmore. "My lord, Lady Rhoslyn came to the stable earlier this afternoon requesting I saddle her horse, retrieve a bow and quiver of arrows, and a cloak. She was quite agitated. I assumed she would be gone for a good length of time, so I had Pearson ready a satchel of provisions. She has yet to return."

Lord Filmore scowled. "Did she say where she was going?"

"No, my lord."

Jayden rose from his seat. "Kolby, saddle my horse."

Sir Darwin stood. "And mine."

The stableboy nodded his head and left the room.

THE MOMENT OF TRUST

Lord Filmore stood and looked toward his son and knight. "I would like to see both of you in the library, immediately."

Chapter 30

Rhoslyn rode under the cover of the moonless night. Fully aware of highwaymen who could rob, or worse yet, rape her if she should come upon them, she pushed Laila thus far. No matter how determined she was to reach Bardenham, she would not risk her mare's life from an unseen rut in the road. Reining her horse, she slowed Laila's gait to a walk while looking for campfires where others may have bedded down for the night along the roadside. She brought her horse to a stop and listened. Silence met her ears.

"Perhaps we should rest for the night." She leaned forward and patted her horse's neck before scanning the thick forest on each side of the road. It appeared unoccupied. Rhoslyn dismounted and led her mare into the foliage.

~

"Before you two go riding off into the night, do you know where to search for Lady Rhoslyn?" Lord Filmore sat in his desk chair and waited for a reply.

Jayden and Sir Darwin looked to each other unable to answer. Shadow trotted into the room and cocked his head to one side as he listened.

"That's what I thought." The Lord of Aldwinster tapped the fingers of his right hand on the desktop gathering his thoughts. "We know she has taken her horse. She either remains within Aldwinster's border or she has crossed it. I think it would be wise to question some of the villagers. Maybe they saw the direction she traveled."

Jayden stared into the wise eyes of his father and nodded his head in agreement. "Very well, Father."

~

Nestled at the base of an old oak tree, Rhoslyn rested her head back against the trunk and closed her eyes. She listened as Laila ate the tender forest grass and hoped the reins, secured to her ankle, would remain tied. Vowing to doze for only a short time, she hoped to wake just before dawn and be on her way.

~

Jayden and Sir Darwin called on the assistance of the garrison, who went from dwelling to dwelling in the village searching for someone who may have seen Rhoslyn on horseback.

"Lord Jayden!"

Jayden turned to see one of the garrison striding toward him with a peasant man in tow. "Yes."

"I believe this man may have seen Lady Rhoslyn on horseback." The soldier pushed the man forward.

The peasant nodded to the young lord. "My lord, I was working in the field and saw a woman in a red dress on a dapple-gray horse. The horse was quite large. She kept her horse at a slow gait, looked behind her, and spurred it into a gallop taking the road out of the village."

"Do you know the approximate time of day you saw this woman?"

"About midafternoon, my lord."

"Thank you." Jayden looked to the soldier. "Please tell Sir Darwin to call off the search and return to the Keep."

"Yes, my lord."

With commanding strides, Jayden walked from the edge of the village to the Keep with Shadow in tow. As he passed the stable, Kolby emerged.

"My lord, the horses are ready."

"Thank you, Kolby. I'll be with you in a moment." He entered the Great Hall and looked at the High Table. His father's chair was empty. He headed toward the library assuming Lord Filmore had remained inside.

Lord Filmore stood with his arms crossed over his chest staring through the window. He suspected the news of her parents' situation from Lady Carling was the cause for Rhoslyn's flight. He would ensure Lady Carling paid dearly for her transgression. He heard the library door open, turned, and watched his son enter. "Well?"

"A peasant saw her leaving on the village road. She has left Aldwinster."

Lord Filmore began to pace. "She may have gone to Bardenham."

Jayden scratched his chin. "Why? She seemed to be settling in nicely here."

Lord Filmore stopped pacing and turned toward his son. "Rhoslyn entered the library earlier today. She claimed Lady Carling overheard us talking and relayed the status of her parents. She came to me for confirmation but stormed out of the library before I could explain her mother was being held at Somerville."

"Father!"

"I assumed you told her the truth."

Sir Darwin opened the door and stepped into the room. He looked from Lord Fillmore to Jayden. "Do we know where she has gone?"

Jayden headed toward the doorway. "It's Father's assumption she went to Bardenham." He left the room.

The knight caught Shadow by the collar. "My lord, it may be best for him to stay with you." He led the dog to Lord Filmore, who restrained the canine until the knight left the library closing the door behind him.

Chapter 31

Rhoslyn's muscles tensed. She remained perfectly still as she opened her eyes to the sound of something or someone rustling within the foliage near her. She lifted her skirt and pulled her dagger from its sheath. Laila's reins remained tied to her ankle. She looked to her mare, whose ears flapped back and forth like a loose shutter on a house on a windy day. The leaves on a bush to her right shook. Rhoslyn readied her knife to strike.

A rabbit hopped out from beneath the bush and froze in place as if staying perfectly still made it invisible.

Laila turned her head toward the rabbit and sniffed its fur before it scampered back under the bush.

Rhoslyn exhaled and returned her knife to its sheath. She rose from the ground, brushed off her skirt, and looked at her surroundings.

Even though the trees filtered the early morning sunlight, she knew it was time to be on her way. She untied the reins from her ankle and led Laila to the roadside. Pausing on the fringe of the forest, she glanced up and down the road to discover it vacant before climbing atop her horse and spurring her into a gallop.

~

As night turned into day, Jayden and his knight stood by a stream allowing their horses to rest while they ate the provisions provided by Pearson. They had ridden the entire night in hopes of finding Rhoslyn.

Jayden shook his head as guilt gnawed at his heart. "I should have told her the truth even though it would have hurt her deeply. But I was afraid she would hate me for doing so. Now, she may hate me for failing to do so."

Sir Darwin glanced at his young lord before placing his steady hand upon his shoulder. "You can't change the past and it wastes time to think of the possibilities if you had done so. All you can do is stand by and support her while she comes to terms with the loss." The knight let his hand drop as he walked to his horse and attached the satchel. "Shall we be on our way, my lord? Bardenham is a half day's ride from here. Let's pray she is there upon our arrival."

~

Exhausted and dusty after riding all day and well into the night, Rhoslyn stared at the glowing windows of Bardenham's village as she pushed her horse at a full gallop toward the gatehouse.

A call rang out as the rider approached and the drawbridge lowered while keeping the portcullis in place for the kingdom's protection.

A guard came forward from the gatehouse, recognized Rhoslyn as she reined Laila to a stop. "My lady, we did not expect you. My apologies." He called for the iron gate to be raised.

Rhoslyn watched the portcullis lifted skyward and urged her tired horse forward as she ducked under the spikes of the castle's enforcement.

Jamie, the stableboy, heard the approaching hoofbeats and limped to the stable doorway. His mouth dropped open as Rhoslyn came into view. "My lady." He scanned Laila whose sweaty coat was frothy with foam on various parts of her body. He patted the mare's nose, her nostrils flaring, as her rider dismounted.

Rhoslyn looked toward the Keep before glancing back at the toe-headed, blue-eyed stableboy. "It's good to see you again, Jamie." She patted Laila on the rump, took a deep breath, and hurried toward the Keep.

The Great Hall was eerily quiet. The evening meal finished some time ago. There was no music, no dancing, and only the flickering candles to accompany the few seated within the room, who stopped their conversations and looked toward her. She thought to race up the staircase to the solar, for where else would her mother be?

"My lady?"

She turned to see Bentley, Bardenham's steward. The elderly man's baby blue eyes were wide with surprise. His black hair had grayed above his ears since last she saw him.

"Bentley, is Mother in the solar?"

The steward became tongue-tied, not quite certain what to say.

Rhoslyn took a step forward. "Bentley?"

"No, my lady, she is not."

"Do you know where she is?"

"Yes."

Growing impatient, she took another step toward the steward. "Well?"

Bentley glanced at the watchful eyes upon him. Everyone waited for the truth he must convey. "The baron's men came to arrest your parents. Your father ingested poison and is dead. I ensured he was properly buried as requested by Lady Eugenia."

Rhoslyn's heart seemed to shrink within her chest. *It's true. Father is dead.* With a quivering bottom lip and her eyes welling with tears, she dared to ask her next question. "And my mother?"

The steward inhaled as if gathering strength to speak. "She was taken into custody and is currently at Somerville awaiting trial. I have not received word of the baron's ruling, so I assume she is still alive. I'm sorry, my lady."

Tears spilled from her eyes cascading down her cheeks. She could not speak. However unladylike it may be, she fell to her knees. Whether guilty or innocent, those taken into custody were usually tortured until they confessed to a crime and then executed. A heart-wrenching sob echoed within the room as she covered her face with her hands and wept.

Bentley outstretched his hand toward the distraught young lady as he gingerly began to kneel beside her. Hearing footsteps from the hallway, he looked to the Great Hall doorway and stood as two men enter the room. "May I be of service?"

Jayden glanced at the elderly man as he approached his betrothed, bent down, and gently lifted her into his arms. Rhoslyn turned toward his chest wrapping her arms around his neck. "Yes, you may. A room with privacy would be greatly appreciated."

Bentley lifted his chin. "And may I inquire as to who are you?"

"I am Lord Jayden of Aldwinster, Lady Rhoslyn's betrothed." He nodded toward his knight. "This is Sir Darwin, my knight."

Hearing footsteps, Bentley looked toward the doorway.

Sir Cedric charged into the room. "Bentley, I was alerted by the guard that Lady Rhoslyn has returned." The knight looked to the crumbled young lady in the stranger's arms.

Jayden scanned the broad-shouldered man with a sword at his side and assumed he was a knight. He turned back to the steward. "Bentley, a room? The four of us can discuss this matter in private."

"Very well, Lord Jayden." The steward went to the large fireplace and retrieved a taper from its mantel and touched the wick to the flickering flames setting it aglow. "This way please." He led them down a hallway, its walls decorated with portraits. At its end, he opened the door and disappeared into a dark room. The men stepped inside and watched as the steward lit additional candles casting the library in a golden glow.

Sir Darwin spied a chair against the wall and brought it forward for his lord to seat himself.

Jayden nodded in appreciation as he sat and looked down at his future wife, who tried to catch her breath between sobs.

The steward went to the door. "Is there anything you need before I leave you, Lord Jayden."

"Bentley, I need you to stay to help us put the pieces of this puzzle together. Please close the door." He waited for the steward to do as instructed before looking to the knight. "I'm Lord Jayden of Aldwinster, Lady Rhoslyn's betrothed." He nodded to his knight who stood by his side. "This is Sir Darwin."

Bardenham's knight took a step forward. "My name is Sir Cedric. I served Lord Atherton and have been ordered to remain here until a new lord arrives."

Jayden nodded. "Yes, to ensure the kingdom's security and safety." He glanced down at his future wife as she wiped the tears from her cheeks. He looked at Sir Cedric and Bentley. "It seems as if we have many unanswered questions. Can either of you tell us the details preceding the arrest of the Lord and Lady of Bardenham?"

Bentley looked to Sir Cedric as he spoke. "You must understand, Lord Jayden, our lord was an extremely private man. He was accused of treason against the baron, but we do not know the details. As he was being arrested, he ingested poison and died in the Great Hall. Lady Eugenia was taken into custody. However, since she was, how shall I say this, not close with her husband, there is doubt she was involved. Unfortunately, that makes little difference to Baron Roldan."

Rhoslyn lifted her head from her betrothed chest and stood.

Sir Cedric continued. "It is of my opinion that his lordship suspected the baron may discover his plot and arranged for Lady Rhoslyn to live with the Sisters of Charity to ensure her innocence. No one in the garrison nor myself was involved. I believe he conspired with another lord, or maybe more than one. Also, before he was taken into custody, he entrusted me to ensure a missive addressed to Lord Filmore of Aldwinster was delivered along with a chest of coins. I assume your father?"

"Yes. I recall my father holding a missive in his hand before he sent me and Sir Darwin to the Sisters of Charity to escort Lady Rhoslyn to Aldwinster. The betrothal was contained in the missive." He looked at Rhoslyn as she wiped away another tear.

She glared at him before addressing the knight and steward. "Is Mother still alive?"

Jayden stood placing his hand on the small of her back for support.

Rhoslyn took a step away from him. "Have you received any word from the baron?"

Sir Cedric shook his head as Bentley answered. "None."

Jayden sighed. "My father has yet to receive word of the verdict as well." He looked at Rhoslyn. "Perhaps she is still alive."

She refused to make eye contact with him, ignoring his comment. "Do you think it's possible to convince the baron of her innocence? I know in my heart she knew nothing of my father's misadventures. They rarely spoke to one another."

Sir Darwin crossed his arms over his chest. "If you are suggesting we travel to Somerville, then we need a good night's rest and so do our horses."

Bentley went to the door. "If you will excuse me, my lord, my lady, I'll have chambers prepared and a meal for everyone to enjoy."

Jayden nodded. "Thank you, Bentley."

"My lord." Sir Cedric drew Jayden's attention. "If I'm no longer needed, I must return to the gatehouse."

"Very well. Thank you." Jayden looked at his knight. "Perhaps you should check on the horses."

With a nod, Sir Darwin followed Sir Cedric out the door closing it behind him.

Jayden turned to see Rhoslyn with her hands fisted on her hips.

"You knew and you didn't tell me?" Her eyes were narrowed.

Jayden always had difficulty reading women's emotions. However, he was quite certain she was angry. "Father told me of your parent's circumstances after he informed us of our betrothal. I wanted to tell you, but in truth, I wasn't certain how to break the news to you. I knew my words would inflict pain. I didn't want to hurt you. I'm sorry."

She reined in her anger, putting herself in his position. "I would have rather heard the bad news from you than from Lady Carling."

He watched his betrothed walk to her father's desk, tracing her finger along the edge of the desktop.

"I didn't get to say good-bye." Tears began to fall anew as she looked toward Jayden.

Compelled to comfort her, he stepped before her, wrapped her in his arms, and kissed the top of her head. "Did you not say your farewells before you went to the abbey?"

Rhoslyn calmed in his secure embrace. She rested her head against him and listened to the sound of his heartbeat, felt the rise and fall of his chest. A tear trickled down her cheek and he brushed it away with his thumb. She sighed. "Yes, but I didn't know it would be for the last time. I never knew my father to be anything but truthful. Could he have been guilty of such wrongdoing?"

"His actions seem to justify so, but I can only draw that conclusion on what I've been told."

She thought out loud. "Can my mother truly be involved? Could Father have tricked her to be an accomplice?"

"You are asking me a question I cannot answer. Father said she is being held by the baron during the investigation. He will decide her fate based on the results."

She lifted her head and looked up into his eyes. "Do you think he will allow me to see her?"

"I don't know, but if she is still alive, we can make a formal request."

As he released her, she looked at the top of the desk. "Oh, the letter I wrote Father. It should have arrived."

"Knowing he had died, my father retained it." He blew out a taper. "I think we need to eat a good meal and get some rest, so we are ready to travel to Somerville in the morning." They blew out the remaining candles and headed toward the Great Hall.

Chapter 32

Bentley looked at the staircase as Jayden descended. "My lord, I hope you slept well." The steward motioned toward a bench for the young lord to seat himself as a servant woman set a tray of food on the table and scurried back to the kitchen. "Jamie has assured me your horses are receiving the best of care and are rested. Sir Darwin has joined him in the stable. Lady Rhoslyn has yet to rise."

Jayden sat and poured watered ale into a tankard. "Thank you, Bentley."

The steward nodded and went to the kitchen.

Alone in the room, Jayden scanned its architectural features and concluded it was similar in style to the Great Hall in Aldwinster only smaller. He assumed the portrait hanging above the fireplace was of Lord Atherton and noted the windows on the east wall illuminated the room with sunlight. Hearing footsteps, he looked toward the staircase to see his betrothed descend wearing a riding dress appropriate for traveling. Her rosy nose and crescent shadows beneath her eyes indicated a restless sleep, but he thought to politely inquire, nonetheless.

"Did you sleep well?" He waited as she sat across from him, lifted the pitcher, and filled the tankard before her.

"Off and on. Haunting images of my time spent with my parents kept me awake." She looked down at her empty plate as her bottom lip quivered.

He reached across the table and placed his hand on her forearm. "Good memories."

She nodded in agreement without making eye contact.

He thought it best to change the topic of conversation. "Bentley has provided a nice meal to eat before we depart for Somerville."

She selected some cold meat, cheese, an egg, and a wedge of bread placing them on her plate. "He is an excellent steward."

"From what I have seen, I agree." He chose his words carefully as a thought occurred to him. "If you don't mind me asking, why did you leave Aldwinster?"

Rhoslyn finished chewing what was in her mouth and washed it down with some ale. "I needed to discover the truth for myself."

Jayden wrestled with her logic but understood her reason. "I'm relieved you were able to arrive safely home. In the future, I would prefer you are always escorted whenever outside of the castle walls."

"But I'm perfectly capable of defending myself."

He raised his eyebrows and smiled teasingly. "Heaven help anyone who may cross your path when you are prepared for an attack. However, you could have been outnumbered or caught unaware."

"In all honesty, I wasn't thinking clearly."

"Understandable, indeed. Now, if you'll excuse me, I need to send a missive to my father to inform him of our journey to Somerville." He rose. "I will return shortly. Please gather whatever items you wish to bring with us."

She nodded as she bit into a piece of well-buttered bread.

Jayden went to the kitchen and scanned the room until he spotted the steward. "Bentley, where may I have materials to write a missive?"

"There should be paper, pen, and ink in Lord Atherton's desk in the library. I shall see that it is sent straight away, my lord."

"Thank you." He turned toward the door but looked back to the steward. "Did the baron's men take Lord Atherton's body with them?"

"No. I ensure he was properly buried in the cemetery on the hill to the west of the castle."

Rhoslyn watched with intrigue as Jayden nodded to her as he crossed the room and disappeared into the corridor. She popped the last bite of bread into her mouth, tiptoed behind him, and peeked around the corner to see him disappear into her father's library. Knowing he would want to travel soon she went to her bedchamber to pack.

~

Jayden glanced about the library as he walked toward the desk. Its empty chair sent a shiver up his spine as if the ghost of Lord Atherton was sitting in it. He shook off the eerie feeling, sat in the chair, and took a moment to view the library in the daylight. Maybe Lord Atherton knew the kingdom was his daughter's true dowry because once they were wed, Jayden would become the next Lord of Bardenham. He opened several drawers before finding the supplies he needed. Dipping the quill into the ink, he quickly jotted down a note entailing the next leg of their journey and its justification. Without a lit taper to light the red wax candle, he carried the folded missive and candle to the Great Hall, selected a rush from the floor, and touched it to the embers in the fireplace before lighting the candle and letting the wax drip onto the missive to seal it. Once the wax puddled, he blew out the candle. Even though he did not possess a signet ring, he pushed his index finger into the wax leaving his fingerprint. Going back to the kitchen, he gave the missive and candle to the steward.

"Thank you, Bentley. We will be leaving as soon as Lady Rhoslyn is ready."

"Very well, my lord. I have sent provisions to the stable for your journey. Godspeed."

"Good. Thank you, again, Bentley." As he entered the Great Hall, Rhoslyn descended the staircase with a satchel and a cloak over her arm. He motioned toward the exit. "Shall we?" Placing his hand on the small of her back, they joined Sir Darwin at the stable.

Jamie held Beval and Laila's bridles as he looked toward the approaching couple with his chest puffed out like a proud rooster. "My lord, the horses have been well fed and rested. I also checked their hooves to ensure any wayward stone won't cause them to become lame."

"Well done. Thank you." He took the satchel and cloak from Rhoslyn allowing her to climb atop her horse. He handed her the garment, which she laid across her lap. Sir Darwin stepped forward and attached the satchel to Laila's saddle.

With everyone atop of their horses, they rode toward the gatehouse to begin their journey to Somerville. Jayden looked over his shoulder at his betrothed hoping for her sake her mother was still alive, and they had the opportunity to plead Lady Eugenia's innocence.

~

The trio rode at a fast pace only stopping for a midday meal to allow their horses to rest. Sir Darwin kept a watchful eye on the threatening dark clouds rolling in from the west as they continued their journey to Somerville until night had set in and the sky opened allowing the rain to fall.

Jayden looked over his shoulder to his betrothed, who struggled to shelter herself with her cloak. He reined his horse and waited for his traveling companions to join him.

"Sir Darwin, do you recall the nearest town with an inn or tavern where we may take cover from this rain for the evening?"

The knight stared down the road while mentally traveling the remainder of the journey to Somerville. "There is one ahead, but at least a four, or five hours away."

Rhoslyn peeked out from beneath her cloak. "I would rather camp than stay in a tavern. Filthy things and the beds are usually crawling with lice and fleas."

Jayden sighed noting the attached rolled oilcloth bound with rope behind their saddles. "Very well."

Venturing further down the road, he reined Beval into a small clearing horseshoed by forest. With a pile of ash in its center and skeletal lean-to on opposite sides, it had been used as a stopping point by other travelers too.

Jayden dismounted, led his horse to a sapling, and secured the reins. He wiggled each lean-to to ensure their sturdiness. "They should hold for the night."

Sir Darwin secured the reins of the remaining two horses before untying the oilcloths from the saddles.

Rhoslyn looked from one lean-to to the other. "There are only two."

Reading her concern, Jayden paused from draping his unrolling oilcloth over the makeshift shelter. "Yes, you will sleep in one and Sir Darwin and I will sleep in the other."

She nodded once before watching the knight drape an oilcloth over the shelter and place another inside on the ground as a protective barrier from the dampness. He motioned for her to go inside while he retrieved the saddles and blankets and set them inside each lean-to.

Jayden squatted at the opening of her shelter. "Comfortable?"

"Yes, and much dryer."

"The satchel on the other side of your saddle has provisions. Have something to eat and get some rest. We will leave at daybreak." He glanced up at the cloudy sky. "This is if there is any sun. Goodnight."

"Goodnight." Rhoslyn retrieved the satchel of food and spread her horse blanket over her lap. Glancing across the campsite, she watched as Jayden joined his knight within their shelter. She listened to the pitter-patter of the raindrops on the oilcloth while she ate. Once having her fill, she lay down snuggling beneath her horse blanket, closed her eyes, and prayed her mother was still alive before drifting off to sleep.

Chapter 33

Rhoslyn's body rocked back and forth. She opened her eyes, looked to the hand touching her right shoulder, and followed the arm upward to see Jayden looking down at her.

"It's time we are on our way." He waited until she sat up before removing the saddle and gathering the horse blanket she had cast aside.

Rhoslyn stood at the base of her lean-to, she look toward the rising sun in the cloudless sky. She rubbed her hands over her sore rump and turned to see the men's horses saddled and Sir Darwin attaching the oilcloth from their temporary shelter.

Jayden tossed Laila's blanket onto her back, adjusted it in place, and added the saddle winching it tightly. His betrothed came beside him as he lowered the stirrup and looked at her. "Did you sleep well?"

"Like the dead." She glanced at the blue sky. "At least the weather is cooperating with us today."

He took a step backward. "Up you go."

Rhoslyn hoisted her foot into the stirrup, grabbed the horn, and pulled her petite body upward. As she swung her right leg over the saddle, Laila sidestepped causing her mistress's hands to slip off the horn and tumble backward.

Recognizing the impending fall, Jayden stepped forward, placed his hands on her back and bottom, and pushed her upward onto her horse before retrieving the reins from the sapling.

Surprised by the forwardness of her betrothed, she scowled as he handed her the reins displaying a not so innocent look on his face.

Jayden fought to control his threatening smile. "Well, I could have let you fall." He nodded at the muddy puddle at his feet.

She glanced down at the brown murky water beside her horse before lifting her chin. "Thank you."

He raised his eyebrows teasingly displaying his pearl-white teeth. "Anytime."

Rhoslyn looked skyward and exhaled withholding her comment on his flirtatious innuendo.

~

To make up for lost time, they rode their horses well past dark before setting up camp.

Rhoslyn plopped down on a fallen log while Sir Darwin started a campfire to ward of the chill in the air. Jayden retrieved their satchels of food. He placed one in her lap before sitting on the opposite end of the log.

She opened the bag and withdrew an apple. "When do we reach Somerville?" A resounding crunch sounded as her teeth pierced the skin of the juicy fruit.

Jayden looked toward her. "If the weather holds up, tomorrow afternoon, maybe early evening." He looked to his knight crouched near the fire. "Sir Darwin, do you agree?"

The knight looked to his young lord before glancing at Rhoslyn. "Yes, however, I have a concern, my lord." He added a log to the fire before sitting on the ground and leaning on the trunk of a tree.

Jayden drew his eyebrows together. "Which is?'

Rhoslyn stopped in midchew.

Sir Darwin glanced between the two sitting on the log. "What if the baron accuses her of being part of her father's treasonous plot?" He waited for a reply but received none. "It may be best if she remains outside of the castle until we know the fate of Lady Eugenia."

Rhoslyn swallowed. "What you're suggesting is there may be no reason for me to enter if my mother is dead."

Sir Darwin nodded. "My lady, I pray she is still alive, truly." He looked at Jayden. "Now that you are betrothed to her, what if they try to implicate you in the plot as well?"

Jayden shook his head. "You know I wasn't involved, nor was she. Why else would her father have sent her away?"

"Exactly, to ensure she wasn't accused, but in the baron's eyes, it could be the reason for her stay at the abbey. There is no proof she wasn't part of the plot." He paused, venturing a suggestion. "When we arrive, I will find a page or servant to tell us if Lady Eugenia is still alive before we put your lives at risk. We should proceed with caution. One never knows what temperamental mood the baron may be in on any given day."

~

They arrived on the outskirts of Somerville by midafternoon. As they rode through the village, peasants in the fields looked up from their work as they passed. They reined their horses to dodge the people walking on the road and children playing in the village. Once allowed to pass through the gatehouse, they left their horses at the stable, found the nearest pub, and seated themselves at a table in the corner of the room.

Jayden searched the faces of the strangers in the room. Rhoslyn sat in the adjacent chair wedged in the corner. Sir Darwin sat across from his lord bookending Rhoslyn between them.

The knight scanned the room. "The place hasn't changed much over the years."

Jayden looked to his knight. "I was here once before with Father, quite a few years ago."

They paused their conversation as a serving wench approached their table. Even though she was a full-bosomed woman, Jayden averted his eyes and looked toward his betrothed as a tankard was placed before him and filled with ale. He reached in his belt bag and laid coins upon the table. The wench took what was needed and helped herself to a tip before returning to the barkeeper.

Sir Darwin took a swig of his ale, slid a few of the coins from the center of the table into the palm of his hand, and stood. "Since I know my way around the kingdom, I'll see what I can find out."

Rhoslyn assumed they would be spending the night in an upstairs room. "Sir Darwin, could you retrieve my satchel from my saddle on your return?"

"Yes, my lady."

Jayden nodded his head as his knight departed. He waved the wench back to their table and ordered two bowls of stew and a loaf of bread.

Rhoslyn lowered her tankard to the table. "If my mother is alive, I would like to see her. It may be the last time I can do so."

"We will see what Sir Darwin uncovers." He sighed before choosing his words wisely. "Do you have any knowledge of what your father had done?"

"None whatsoever. But since he took poison instead of trying to clear his name, he must have been guilty of the charge."

"And your mother?"

"I can only assume she is innocent. My parents weren't the best of friends. They rarely spoke to each other. So, it's not difficult to imagine my father doing something my mother knew nothing about."

They looked toward the woman approaching them. She balanced a tray on her shoulder and lowered it to the table. She placed two wooden bowls of stew, a fresh loaf of bread, knife, and a crock of butter before them. Scanning the coins on the table, she selected payment and a generous tip before returning to the kitchen.

Jayden cut several thick slices of bread, buttered an inner slice, and presented it to Rhoslyn, who accepted the offering.

"Thank you." She bit into the hard-crusty bread, butter coating her upper lip like the foam of a stout ale. While she chewed, she dunked the edge of the bread into the steaming stew. Her mouth watered as she inhaled its delicious aroma of tender beef. She watched as Jayden took a bite of the stew, chewed with his mouth open while exhaling to dissipate its heat. He reached for his tankard and took a swig.

She lifted the sodden bread from her bowl to allow it to cool. "Is it good?"

He nodded his head in a silent reply before swallowing. "Yes, quite."

Trusting his opinion, she bit into the saturated bread. "Mmmm…"

Their conversation during their meal was pleasant. They talked about their childhood, their homes, and their parents while they waited for Sir Darwin to return.

The barkeeper stared at the young couple, who had finished their meal long ago. "Hey, are you two going to be needing a room for the night?"

Jayden glanced out the window and stared into the darkness of night. Scanning the room, several of the tables were empty. While deeply involved in a conversation with his betrothed, he failed to notice the late hour. "Yes, we will need a room." He turned to Rhoslyn keeping his voice at a whisper. "For you. I will sleep outside of your door."

"But what of Sir Darwin. What can be keeping him? Do you think he has run into trouble?"

Jayden raised an eyebrow and smiled. "Nah, no need to worry about him. He'll return soon." He winked before tilting his tankard upward and draining it dry.

Rhoslyn covered her mouth with the back of her hand trying to camouflage a yawn.

However, Jayden recognized her attempt. "It's been a long day. Let me escort you to your room."

The chair screeched on the floor as Sir Darwin sat with a big grin on his face.

Jayden leaned forward and whispered. "Well, what did you find out?"

Rhoslyn leaned forward in her chair, hoping for good news.

Sir Darwin leaned forward, speaking for their ears only. "She's alive." He watched as the news brought a sigh of relief and a smile to Rhoslyn's face. "She's being held in the dungeon. The baron is trying to pressure her to confess. I've arranged for us to visit her later tonight."

Jayden tilted his head to the side. "How did you manage that?"

"Oh, I can't tell you all of my secrets." The knight smiled. "Her trial is set for tomorrow. Unfortunately, I found no indication of its outcome. The baron is unpredictable."

~

Under the cover of darkness, Jayden, Rhoslyn, and Sir Darwin kept to the shadows of the buildings and darted through the candlelight cast by the windows onto the muddy street as they crept toward the entrance of the kitchen where a servant woman waited.

Sir Darwin knocked three times. The portal opened for the knight to enter. "Good evening, darling." He greeted as he squeezed through the partially open door with his lord and future lady following behind him.

The servant carried a single lit taper. She cupped her hand before the flame as she led them through several hallways and down spiral staircases to the lowest level of the castle. The air was heavy with dampness making it difficult to breathe. Rhoslyn covered her nose with the edge of her cloak hoping to filter the stench of sodden rushes, burnt skin, and overflowing buckets of excrement.

The servant paused before a doorway. "The guard should be asleep. I added something to his tankard to ensure so." She handed Sir Darwin the taper. "I'll wait here for you to return and keep watch."

"Thank you, darling. We won't be long."

The door creaked on its unoiled hinges as the three tiptoed into the dungeon. Rhoslyn gasped. Her feet froze in place refusing to take another step as she stared at the ghastly room. Several torches flickered on the walls, a legged cast-iron bucket containing two branding irons with their tips embedded in glowing ash-covered ambers, an empty cage large enough to fit a body hanging from the ceiling by a chain, a wooden chair with spikes on its surface bolted to the wall, a press that most likely lead to someone being squeezed until they confessed or died, and a guard, who sat on a stool leaning against the corner of the room. She peeked down into a hole in the floor covered with an iron grate and hoped her mother was not in the darkness of the forget-me-not.

Jayden grasped her arm. "We don't have much time. This way." He followed his knight, who held the taper before each cell only to find

213

them empty. Reaching the last cell, he discovered a woman lying on the damp floor with her back toward him and waved toward Jayden to come forward. He handed the candle to his lord.

The knight withdrew his dagger in case he needed to thump the guard on the head and put him back to sleep. "I'll watch the guard."

Rhoslyn peered into the cell. "Mother." She whispered. "Mother, it's me, Rhoslyn."

Lady Eugenia opened her eyes.

"Mother wake up. I don't have much time."

"Rhoslyn?" Lady Eugenia rolled over to see her daughter reaching through the iron grate of the cell. She crawled on her hands and knees and clasped her daughter's extended hands. Her emerald gown soiled, graying auburn hair disheveled, and her aqua eyes sunken with dark half-circles beneath them, yet she smiled. "It is you. How did you get in here?"

Sir Darwin looked toward the cell trying to recall the familiar voice.

Rhoslyn clasped her mother's cold hands. "It matters not. Tell me, what do you know of Father's misdoing?"

"I know nothing." She looked past her daughter to the man standing behind her. "Lord Jayden, it is good to see you again."

"Forgive me, my lady, but I must have been quite young the last time our paths crossed, for I do not remember you."

"Yes, nevertheless, I am comforted by my husband's foresight to know Rhoslyn will be well cared for no matter what the outcome of my trial may be."

Rhoslyn rubbed her mother's hands trying to warm them. She knew the answer to her question but wanted to ensure it was true. "Will the baron be holding your trial tomorrow?"

"Yes, all of the others have been tried, most of them were put to death."

The servant woman peeked into the room and looked toward Sir Darwin. "I cannot afford to give you any more time. The guards will be changing soon."

Sir Darwin nodded and relayed the message to Jayden, who put his hand on the small of Rhoslyn's back. "We've run out of time." He looked to the prisoner. "We will attend your trial and remain hidden in the audience, silent in our support. I don't want to risk Lady Rhoslyn being implicated."

Lady Eugenia nodded her appreciation before looking into the concerned eyes of her daughter. "Please remember, Rhoslyn, my love for you. If I am no longer able to see you again in this life, well, then perhaps the next."

"I love you too, Mother."

The trio left the room and joined the awaiting servant, who guided them through the Keep to the exiting doorway.

Jayden pressed several coins into the woman's hand. "Thank you." He nodded before passing through the open portal into the darkness.

The woman opened her hand and examined the coins. "Thank you, my lord." She closed and bolted the door.

Rhoslyn kept her head bowed and allowing her tears to fall as the trio made their way to the pub. She went directly to her room but paused in the doorway turning toward Jayden and his knight.

"Thank you both, for taking the risk and allowing me the opportunity to see my mother, perhaps for the last time."

"You're welcome, my lady." Sir Darwin lowered himself to the floor, leaned against the wall, and closed his eyes.

Jayden stood before her. "Do not give up hope. Her trial may result in a positive outcome."

She wiped the tears from her cheeks. "I pray it will. Goodnight." She closed the door.

Jayden sighed as he turned to his knight, who was already asleep. He sat beside her chamber door and leaned against the wall in doubt of finding much rest.

Chapter 34

Jayden and Sir Darwin woke at first morning's light. Standing guard outside the chamber, they looked toward the faint sound of footsteps, which grew louder as the barmaid approached them, knocked on the door, and entered to assist Rhoslyn to dress.

Jayden stared at the closed portal. An uneasiness stirred within his soul. He nudged his knight tilting his head toward the end of the hallway in a silent order to follow him so as not to be overheard by Rhoslyn.

Sir Darwin followed. "My lord?"

Jayden glanced at the chamber door. "You know as well as I do the normal outcome for such trials."

His knight scowled. "Innocent or not, the odds are stacked against Lady Eugenia."

"If a guilty verdict is reached, I fear Lady Rhoslyn may be incapable of controlling herself and reveal her connection to her mother."

"Yes, and be implicated in the scandal as well."

"I need you to remover her from the Great Hall before the announcement."

The creak of a door drew their attention. They watched as Rhoslyn stepped into the hallway with the barmaid following. Her brunette hair was pinned in place and she was dressed in a clean, although wrinkled, royal blue dress.

Rhoslyn's aqua orbs conveyed determination as she walked with her chin held high and stopped before them. "Do we know the time the trial will begin?"

The barmaid interrupted. "You will have time to enjoy breakfast. The baron prefers to sleep until midmorning."

Jayden looked over his shoulder and nodded. "Thank you."

They returned to the same table, sat, and ate what the barmaid served.

Sir Darwin pushed his empty plate aside and ventured a suggestion. "We can use the excuse of going to the stable to check on the care of our horses and ask the stableboy if he knows the time of the trial. Otherwise, we can find a page to inquire for a coin or two."

The trio stepped from the musty-ale tavern into the busy street. People scurried about with many heading toward the Keep. Jayden clutched his betrothed's elbow protectively as he wove his way to the stable. Sir Darwin went inside to make the inquiry.

Rhoslyn stood with her back against the stable wall, her arms crossed over her chest, aghast by the activity in Somerville. "Are all these people here to witness my mother's trial?"

Standing in front of her like a shield, Jayden turned to face the busy street. "Perhaps. It seems quite crowded for the morning hour."

Sir Darwin stepped from the shadowed darkness of the stable and went to his lord's side. "The trial begins within the hour. We may want to return to the pub and retrieve her cloak so she can conceal her face with its hood. With this many people about, it may be wise to go to the Keep now and remain in the back of the Great Hall before it is filled."

Jayden comprehended his knight's logical plan of remaining close to the doorway to removed Rhoslyn quickly when the time came. "I agree."

People crowded around the doorway of the Keep, forcing them to ease their way forward like a herd of cattle going through a tiny gate. They lined themselves against the back wall of the Great Hall and waited. Some of the people were seated while others stood hoping to catch a glimpse of the accused. A group of men placed wagers on the conviction and punishment given by the baron.

Rhoslyn raised onto her tiptoes, but her view was obstructed. She wanted her mother to know she was nearby, supporting her.

Conversations in the Great Hall quieted as Baron Roldan entered the room. Jayden lifted his chin and peered over the audience. He estimated the baron to be a decade older than his father. His bulbous stomach an indication of his wealth and a man who liked to eat and drink more than his fair share.

Baron Roldan stepped onto the dais, sat in his ornately carved chair, and leaned against its high back. A servant rushed forward with a full tankard on her tray and presented it with a curtsey. The baron drank nearly half of it before signaling to someone in the hallway. All heads turned as the prisoner was brought into the room. Lady Eugenia was shackled and forced to sit on a narrow wooden bench before the baron.

Jayden turned toward Rhoslyn to ask her a question, but she was no longer next to him. He leaned forward scanning the wall to his right and left before leaning toward his knight. "She's gone."

"Who?"

"Lady Rhoslyn. She's disappeared."

Sir Darwin leaned forward to verify the spot where she was standing was vacant. "Damn."

Rhoslyn managed to squeeze between the curious patrons and sit on a front bench. She lowered her hood. Lady Eugenia kept her head bowed respectfully at the baron and caught sight of her daughter while giving no indication of recognizing her.

The baron drained the remainder of his tankard and held it at arm's length. "So, Lady Eugenia, what shall become of you?" A servant rushed forward and refilled his tankard as he looked toward his prisoner.

Lady Eugenia remained silent. Her eyes downcast knowing her fate was in his hands.

"Your husband took the coward's way out, yet you sit before me, his possible accomplice." He leaned forward in his chair. "Those who were involved and convicted of treason have paid the highest price with their lives. If their involvement was minimal, their death was merciful. They were merely hung. Others who were greatly implicated were disemboweled, beheaded, drawn, and quartered. I find it interesting, however, not one person involved mentioned your name during their trial. They only stated your husband's guiltiness in the matter. What do you have to say in your defense?"

Lady Eugenia stood on shaky legs. She took a deep breath to calm her nerves and subdue her trembling. "Baron Roldan, I appreciate the opportunity to speak. My husband and I lived separate lives. We seldom spoke, ignored each other during evening meals, and after disappointing him by producing a daughter, we no longer shared a bed. I possess no knowledge of my husband's daily activities, business, or his involvement in this notorious plot. I can confirm he took poison before being arrested, thus leaving me to fend for myself for a crime he committed. I beg for your mercy and hope you can see my lack of involvement in this matter." She remained standing.

Jayden continued to scan the crowd in search of his betrothed. His knight did the same.

The baron pursed his lips as he looked to the ceiling in contemplation. "They always claim they're innocent." He opened his mouth for sentencing but was interrupted as Rhoslyn rushed to her mother's side.

"Baron Roldan, a moment to speak on this woman's behalf?"

Lady Eugenia's eyes became wide with fear. "Rhoslyn, no."

Sir Darwin leaned toward his lord. "Found her."

The baron, intrigued with curiosity, leaned forward. "Who are you?"

Rhoslyn took a step forward. "I am Lady Rhoslyn of Bardenham, her daughter."

"So, you are involved in this matter as well?"

"No, I have no knowledge of my father's affairs. I have been in residence at the Sisters of Charity. If you would like a confirmation, you may address a missive to Mother Margaret, the abbess."

"I can confirm her residency." Jayden stepped forward.

Baron Roldan placed his left hand on the arm of his chair, scooted to its edge, and lifted his tankard toward the young man who stepped into the center of the room. "And who are you?"

"I am Lord Jayden, son of Lord Filmore of Aldwinster."

"Well then, Lord Jayden, how do you know about her residency at the abbey?"

"My father sent me and my knight, Sir Darwin, to escort her from the abbey to Aldwinster."

"And why would he do that?"

"He received a missive from her father, who agreed to secure Lady Rhoslyn's future as my betrothed."

The baron's eyebrows rose, he bellowed a boisterous laugh and slapped his hand on his thigh. "I must say, you have your hands full with this lady as your future wife."

Jayden looked at his betrothed with a slight, proud smile on his face. "Ah, I admit she has a mind of her own, a handful no less, but I find it an admirable quality in a wife."

Rhoslyn returned his smile and nodded her head in appreciation.

The baron sat back in his chair. "Who else can collaborate this story?"

Sir Darwin stepped forward. "I can. I'm Sir Darwin. I serve Lord Filmore and Lord Jayden. I accompanied Lord Jayden to the abbey to escort Lady Rhoslyn." He looked at Lady Eugena. She was staring at him. As if recognizing an old acquaintance, he nodded politely.

Baron Roldan sighed. "Yes, well I believe we've established Lady Rhoslyn's innocence in this matter. However, that doesn't clear you, Lady Eugenia." He looked down his nose at the accused.

Rhoslyn looked at her mother in fear of the condemning decision the baron was about to make. However inappropriate to argue with him, she was compelled to sway his mind. "Baron, I can assure you of her innocence."

"How would you know? You were living with the nuns. I wager you have no proof of her innocence."

"I agree. Unfortunate, the dead cannot speak to clear her name." She tapped her chin with her forefinger as she began to pace. Looking toward the baron, she stopped. "Did you say, a wager?"

The baron narrowed his eyes. "You wish to gamble for your mother's life?" He looked to Jayden and his knight. "I assume in combat?"

"I like to call it a competition." She tilted her head to one side and raised an eyebrow.

The baron smiled. "Which man do you chose to represent you?"

"Neither. I shall represent myself."

Jayden stepped to her side clasping her upper arm. "Rhoslyn, what are you doing?"

Gasps echoed throughout the room as heads tilted toward one another in conversation.

"Yourself?" The baron scanned her petite body. "You cannot wield a sword."

"I agree, plus my size is a hindrance. Most men would be able to outreach the length of my sword. A clear disadvantage."

The baron waved his hand as he allowed her to choose. "Then what do you propose?"

She looked to her mother, her betrothed inquisitive sky-blue eyes, and back to the baron. "Even though I have heard acclaimed praise of your skilled bowmen, I choose the bow."

"The bow? Are you sure you can pull back the string?" The baron grinned as he looked about the room at the snickering attendants.

As murmurs of doubt filled the room, Rhoslyn ignored it. "I will do my best."

"Your mother's life depends on it." The baron thought a moment longer. "And since you have so much at stake, I will allow you to define the parameters."

Rhoslyn looked toward Sir Darwin and thought of Aldwinster's practice field. Most of the bowmen fire from stationary positions. "Select your finest bowman from your garrison. We shall fire at stationary targets while riding at a gallop on horseback."

Gasps echoed from those in attendance as their smiles faded.

Confident his best bowman surpassed the woman's skill, the baron smiled adding his parameter to the competition.

"I agree to your terms. If you win, your mother will not be put to death. But if you shall lose, you will join your mother at the gallows to be hung until you are both dead."

Chapter 35

The crowd parted as the baron led the way out of the Great Hall while barking an order for a page to retrieve his best bowman. With Jayden on her left and Sir Darwin on her right, she followed the baron toward the stable.

Jayden leaned toward her. "Rhoslyn, I know you are skilled with a bow, but on horseback?"

"It's a game I played often as a child. However, I've never played for such high stakes."

"A game? For god's sake, your life is at stake."

She stopped before the stable. "And my mother's life too."

Sir Darwin looked at the young couple. "I shall saddle your horse, my lady."

"No need. I'll ride her without a saddle and bridle."

The knight's mouth fell agape. "My lady?"

Jayden ran his hand through his hair pulling away from his eyes. "Are you blindly tempting fate?"

"Blindly, no. I plan to keep my eyes open." She sighed. "Did I have any other choice? He was going to sentence my mother to death." She lifted her chin upward, unsmiling as she stared up into his eyes.

Sir Darwin glanced toward the hulking soldier with bracers on his arms immerging from the gatehouse carrying a bow in his hand and a full quiver on his back. "I'll retrieve your weapon from your saddle and Laila."

Jayden did not hear the words spoken by his knight. He sighed as he stared into the defiant eyes of his betrothed. "I'll accompany you onto the field. I know you are more than capable of outshooting his best bowman. The baron doesn't like to lose, so let's hope he upholds the rules you have set forth."

Rhoslyn's mouth curled at each end as she nodded slightly. At the sound of hoofbeats, she turned to see the knight leading her horse with a rope around Laila's neck. "Thank you, Sir Darwin." She accepted the end of the rope and removed it from her mare's neck. Jayden presented his clasped hands hoping she accepted his assistance. She inserted her foot and was easily boosted atop her horse. He extended his hand toward his knight and accepted the quiver full of arrows and bow.

With her betrothed on one side of Laila and his knight on the other, they walked onto the field and took their position as onlookers gathered.

Jayden handed her the quiver. "Shall I string your bow?"

Rhoslyn's hands shook as she struggled to attach the full quiver to her body and glanced toward him. "Please." She looked at the distance targets on the field trying to focus on the challenge at hand. Something bumped against her shoulder drawing her attention. She turned to see the strung bow in Jayden's extended hand. As she grasped it, he placed his free hand over her hand and their eyes locked.

He gave a nodded of encouragement. "I've full confidence in your ability. Go and win for your mother and yourself."

Sir Darwin watched as the baron's chosen bowman climbed atop a warhorse and settled within the saddle. The man, a bit awkward, pulled an arrow from his quiver and practiced aiming it at a distant target. "My lady," he turned toward Rhoslyn, "I think you will do remarkably well. Never doubt yourself."

She smiled at the knight. "Thank you, Sir Darwin."

The trio's attention was drawn to the baron who stood in the center of the shooting line. "Everyone, step back, give them room. Competitors, come forward."

Jayden looked up to his betrothed. "Off you go. Good luck." He patted Laila on the neck.

Rhoslyn exhaled to calm her nerves. With a gentle touch of her heels, Laila walked forward and stopped before the baron, who waited for his bowman to join them before speaking.

"I must admit, this is an interesting contest, such high stakes too." Baron Roldan rocked back and forth on his toes with his hands clasped behind his back. "Rules. Yes, we must have rules. Riders shall make a single pass in the direction of their choice. The closest to the center of each of the six targets will be declared the winner of that target, with the total wins to determine the overall winner." He looked at Rhoslyn. "My dear, are you sure you want to ride without a saddle?"

"Yes, baron, quite sure."

"Very well, then. Who wants to go first?"

Rhoslyn looked at the bowman, who nodded toward her.

"Ladies first." He reined his horse to the starting point and waited for her to join him.

Pressure from her heel encouraged Laila to turn. Rhoslyn looked at her betrothed and his knight, their arms crossed over their chests and their feet shoulder-width apart. They both nodded their encouragement as she passed them and took her position at the end of the field. She was glad her mother was detained within the Keep. Seeing her would only increase her anxiety.

The baron nodded for her to begin her pass. She exhaled, drew the first arrow from her quiver and placed the nock firmly against the bowstring.

"Laila, years ago when I was a child, remember?" She focused on the nearest target. "Ha!" She touched her heels against her mare's belly and the horse darted forward. Pulling the string toward her chin, she aimed and let the arrow fly before reaching over her shoulder for another arrow and focusing on the next target. The arrow penetrated the innermost circle of the target, but it was not center. Her next four arrows struck true, dead center.

An Irish wolfhound mistook the competition as a game, ran to Laila's side, and nipped at her leg causing the horse to take a sudden sidestep away from the canine. Without the stirrups to help her stay astride her horse, she prematurely released the arrow to grab Laila's mane. The arrow went high into the air. Everyone followed its trajectory as it sailed upward in a large arch toward the target and landed in the ring surrounding the bullseye. Rhoslyn stared at the last embedded arrow as she brought her horse to a stop. Dread seeped into her heart as Laila tried to sidestep the dog before a soldier grabbed its collar and restrained it. Rhoslyn lowered her bow and turned her horse to find Jayden running toward her. He reached up with both arms to help her dismount.

Stunned by her failure, she fell into his open arms. "I missed."

He sighed as he ran his hand up and down her back while holding her against his chest. "Circumstances beyond your control are at fault. You did your best. All we can do now is see how the baron's bowman performs." He looked toward the bowman, his arrow ready to fire, as he kicked his horse into a forward charge. "And pray." He took the bow from her hand and unstrung it.

The bowman's first arrow hit the center of the target. Each of the following arrows was progressively off target. He reined his horse to a stop when finished.

A page went to the first target, measured with a stick, and removed the arrow of the winner holding it high above his head. Rhoslyn's arrow remained in the target. She bit her bottom lip as it began to quiver. The page moved to the next target. He hoisted her arrow into the air. She knew she did not win the last target. What if the contest ended in a tie?

The page moved to the next target, measured several times, and pulled her arrow for all to see. She looked up at Jayden, who looked at her and nodded his head confidently. The fourth and fifth arrows pulled for the targets declared Rhoslyn the winner. She removed her quiver and handed it to Jayden.

The baron resumed his position in the center of the shooting line and signaled the competitors to step forward.

Rhoslyn looked up at her betrothed as he placed his hand on the small of her back encouraging her forward. Sir Darwin strung the rope over Laila's neck and nodded his approval of her accomplishment.

The baron glared at his bowman, who kept his eyes downcast as he approached. "It appears that you have outshot my best bowman, Lady Rhoslyn. As was our agreement, your mother will not be put to death."

Rhoslyn exhaled unable to keep the grin from her face, relieved the worst was behind her. "So, she will be able to return home with me."

"No, the agreement is that she will not be put to death for her crime. She will remain here and serve her sentence."

She looked over her shoulder at Jayden, who was staring at Baron Roldan. The muscles in his chin flexing as he clenched his teeth. His line of vision shifted to her.

She looked back to the baron. "With all due respect, your lordship, my mother claims to have no knowledge of the crime, there is no proof she was involved."

"As of yet, that is true. There is also no proof of her innocence."

"How long do you intend to keep her locked in such horrid conditions?"

"Until she is proven innocent or until I feel she has served enough time."

"May I make a small request?"

The baron nodded.

"She is removed from the dungeon and given a proper chamber for a lady. It's the least that can be done for an innocent woman of royalty."

"Correction. The least that could be done is to leave her in the dungeon, but in recognition of your talented win, I shall honor your request." He raised his hand and dismissed his bowman before turning back to Rhoslyn. "Now I suggest you say your farewell to your mother and be on your way. If anything develops on her behalf, you will be notified."

Rhoslyn resisted the urge to argue any further. She curtsied, turned, and went to her horse and awaiting companions. They walked to the stable where they left Laila with the stableboy.

Jayden gave the stableboy the weapons before patting the mare's rump. "Have our horses saddled and ready."

"Yes, my lord."

Chapter 36

Lady Eugenia looked over her shoulder to see Baron Roldan enter the room with his daughter and her escorts following.

The baron signaled for the guard standing next to his prisoner to remove the iron shackles as he passed by, stepped onto the dais, and faced the people filtering into the room. "Lady Eugenia, your daughter's skill with the bow has spared your life. You will be retained within the walls of Somerville until your innocence can be proven or until I determine your sentence has been fulfilled. She has negotiated better accommodations for you during your captivity. I have given my permission for the two of you to say your farewells before she departs." He rose and left the room.

Lady Eugenia rubbed her raw wrists where the cold iron had chafed them. She looked to her daughter, who stepped forward and clasped her hands.

"Mother, I should learn to be a better negotiator. I won the challenge, but not your freedom. I'm sorry."

"In all honesty, I assumed my life would end here. Barron Roldan isn't interested in discovering the truth of my innocence. He only wants revenge for the transgression against him."

Jayden crossed his arms over his chest and inclined his head toward his knight. "On your way back to Aldwinster, divert to Bardenham and see if there is any evidence to prove her innocence."

"Yes, my lord. I shall seek the truth on their behalf." He looked at Rhoslyn and her mother, grinned and thought of his lord's future. "And yours." He watched as Jayden looked up to the ceiling, resisting the urge to smile at his insinuation. "I'll see to the horses, my lord." The knight dismissed himself.

With a farewell embrace, Rhoslyn held her mother at arm's length. "I will write often and pray evidence will confirm your innocence as soon as possible."

Her mother cupped her daughter's face with the palm of her hand, casting it to her memory.

Jayden stepped forward. "I promise to take good care of her, Lady Eugenia."

Lady Eugenia smiled at her future son-in-law. "I'm counting on it. Although by the sound of it, it looks as if she may be taking care of you."

"Yes, I do admire her skills with a bow and knife." He looked at her and grinned. "We look forward to your release in the near future."

"I pray it will be soon. Godspeed to you both."

Jayden motioned toward the doorway allowing his betrothed to precede him. He nodded his farewell to Lady Eugenia and followed.

The stableboy led Beval out of the stable. "My lord, the horses are ready."

"Thank you." Jayden accepted the reins and looked at his knight, who emerged from the stable with the two remaining horses saddled. Before he could offer his betrothed assistance onto her horse, Rhoslyn climbed atop Laila and encouraged her forward. He glanced at Sir Darwin, who shrugged his shoulders. They mounted their horses and followed her out of the gatehouse.

Unable to hold her emotions in check any longer, threatening tears cascaded down her cheeks. She was uncertain if her crying was the release of nervousness and pressure from the competition or relief her mother would live. Rhoslyn trusted her horse to follow the road, for she could not see it through her blurred vision. She lowered her head and adjusted the reins in her hands to avoid the inquisitive stares of the peasants as she rode through the village.

"My lord." Sir Darwin kept his voice a mere whisper so as not to be overheard. "She is upset over the loss of her mother."

Jayden watched as she brought her hand to her face to wipe away a tear. He looked at his knight, keeping his voice just above a whisper as he gave his order. "I will escort her to Aldwinster. Ride ahead to Bardenham and question every soul. There must be at least one person who can prove Lady Eugenia's innocence. Send word of any developments."

"Yes, my lord." Sir Darwin spurred his horse into a gallop as Jayden encouraged Beval forward alongside his betrothed. He remained silent. To save her from embarrassment, he stared into the distance.

Rhoslyn turned her head away from him as she dried her eyes and calmed herself. Confident enough to speak without her voice shaking, she looked toward him. "Where is Sir Darwin going?"

"On an errand." He returned her inquisitive stare and watched as she looked away, disappointment masking her face. He outstretched his left hand. "Give me your hand."

Rhoslyn looked at his hand reaching toward her, then to his sincere face. She placed her right hand within his palm.

His fingers entwined within hers, steadfast and strong. "Fear not, my dearest wife-to-be. All will work out for the best." He brought the back of her hand to his lips and placed a gentle kiss upon it. "You did well today and I'm very proud of you. I think the two of us make an impressive pair. Your bow and my sword. May Heaven help any man or woman who tries to step between us."

With her spirit lifted by his kind remarks, the glimmer of hope for their future happiness seemed possible. Her mother would not die at the hands of the baron. In time, perhaps evidence would prove her innocence. She grinned as he kissed her hand again before releasing it.

Keeping their horses at a steady pace, they rode until the sun dipped below the horizon and they set up camp next to a river for the night.

The campfire crackled and flames danced upward sending sparkling tiny embers toward the cloudless midnight blue sky. She glanced at Jayden as he handed her a piece of dried meat from the satchel and tilted her head to the side as a question burned in her mind.

He watched as her eyes looked toward him several times. Hesitant? Apprehensive? Scared? "Something on your mind?" He resumed rummaging through the items in the bag as he sat on a stump across from her.

She sighed. "Are you displeased about our betrothal?"

He cringed, a little surprised. "Displeased? I think the news of our betrothal was a surprise to both of us. It seems wrong not to have the choice in the pathway of your life. However, it's the way most marriages are decided." He watched as she nodded her head slowly in agreement. "If I may be honest?"

"Please."

"When I first saw you at the abbey, I was quite taken by your beauty. In truth, I still am. But there is more to you than beauty. For one can be the most beautiful person on the exterior, yet they may be rotten to the core on the interior. Over time, I have discovered you are as beautiful on the inside as you are on the outside. I admire your determination, confidence, and, I will admit, I am a bit envious with your skill with the bow and knife." He raised one eyebrow and smiled. "I'm honored to have you as my betrothed and someday my wife. Although your opinion of me is loathsome, I hope over time to change your mind and live up to your husbandly expectation."

She stared into his eyes, watching the firelight flicker within his orbs, searching her heart. Friendship? Love? She opened her mouth, but closed it, afraid of what she might confess.

Afraid to hear her reply, he looked away. "It's getting late and you've had a trying day. Perhaps you should get some sleep. I'll stoke the fire before I turn in." He rose from the stump and entered the woods in search of firewood.

A pang of guilt pierced her heart as he disappeared into the darkness of the forest. *He is kind, considerate, and supportive.* She looked skyward, almost embarrassed to admit to herself. *And quite handsome, tall, and strong. Yet, I'm conflicted, unsure of how I feel toward him.* She ate the last bite of meat as he emerged from the woods carrying an armful of firewood.

She watched as he took two thick sticks with their ends sheered off at an angle, shoved them into the ground near the fire and stacked some of the wood onto the sticks so the fire would feed itself as it burned each log.

He looked at her as he put the last log in place. "There, that should take the chill from the night air." He grinned, satisfied with a job well done. Her face was serious, unsmiling. His smile faded as he scowled. "What is it?"

"I have questions, concerns." She wrung her hands and bit her bottom lip.

"Very well." He sat on the log across from her, the fire blazing between them. "Ask."

"No lies."

"Rhoslyn, I hope to gain your trust. Lying will only destroy what little trust you have in me. I promise. No lies."

She nodded, took a deep breath, and exhaled. The heat of embarrassment rose in her face, she was blushing and thankful for the darkness of the night. "How many women have you had?"

Jayden scowled and his mouth dropped open. He closed his mouth and inhaled taking the time to choose his words carefully. "I assume you mean how many women have I bedded?"

"Yes."

"As I have stated before, none." He watched her mouth open to speak and held the palm of his hand toward her pleading for her to remain silent. "I confess. I'm not altogether innocent. Yes, I have kissed a few women, even fondled them, but bedded them? I have never bedded a woman. It would not please my mother and father to be a grandparent of an illegitimate child."

"What about all of the women who flirt with you?"

"They instigate the flirting. Afterall, wedded to a royal who will inherit a kingdom someday is an attractive prospect for any peasant woman who dreams of a better life. I will simply nod in acknowledgment from now on. I hope once we are married, their flirting will stop altogether."

"Many married men are unfaithful."

"That would be men who are unhappily married. Many married women are unfaithful as well."

She knew of many women who had affairs outside of their marriage. After all, they were forced to wed someone they didn't love. Who could blame them?

Jayden rose, went to the saddles, and picked up the blankets. He spread one on the ground before her feet and knelt before her. "Rhoslyn, I promise to be a loyal and faithful husband to you and, God willing, a devoted father to our children."

She looked at her lap as his hand entwined with hers. *So strong, yet gentle.* Looking into his sky-blue eyes she nodded slightly.

Releasing her hand, he stood. "Lay down and let me cover you with this blanket."

She lay upon the horse blanket and rolled toward the fire as the blanket was placed upon her.

He knelt and touched her cheek with the palm of his hand. "Try and get some sleep."

Chapter 37

The temperature dropped throughout the night. An incessant clicking sound pulled Jayden from his sleep. Rolling over to look behind him, the fire had reduced to ash. The noise came from beyond it. He stood, stoked the embers, pulled the stick from the ground, and adding them to the fire. Realizing the resonating sound was Rhoslyn's teeth chattering, he lifted the top blanket and lay beside her pulling her near. She snuggled into his chest tucking her head beneath his chin.

Their closeness seemed natural, comfortable with her body molding against his. He closed his eyes and drifted back to sleep.

~

He opened his eyes as she stirred within his arms and looked to the horizon to see the sun announcing the start of the day. *Will she be angry to discover me lying next to her?* To hold her a few moments longer, it was a risk he was willing to take. He remained still as she stretched, snuggled closer to his body, and opened her eyes lethargically. He watched her eyes rotated upward to meet his. *An explanation may be in order.*

"Your teeth were chattering so loudly that it woke me during the night."

She sat up taking the blanket with her and looked over her shoulder as he sat up as well. She could feel the heat rising in her face. "Oh, I'm sorry."

"No apology necessary. You did nothing wrong."

Rhoslyn threw the blanket aside, stood, and turned away from him allowing the flushness in her face to cool.

He gathered the blankets and began saddling the horses.

"You know I can do that myself."

He looked over his shoulder to see Rhoslyn with her arms crossed over her chest. She was grinning.

"I know you can." He unfastened a satchel from the saddle. "Here, see if there is anything left inside for us to eat while I finish."

She accepted the leather bag, sat on the log, and discovered three apples, a few pieces of dried jerky, a half-filled flask of wine, and a stale portion of bread.

Jayden joined her on the log. "Anything edible?"

"Enough to get us by." Using her knife, she cut the bread into equal halves and saturated them with wine to soften the hard crust. They split the jerky and apples between them with Rhoslyn cutting the remaining apple in half for the horses to share.

With their simple meal consumed, they mounted and headed for Aldwinster.

~

Shadow lay in his usual spot beneath the High Table. The Lord and Lady of Aldwinster rose to take to the floor for the first dance when they looked to the doorway to see their son and his future wife enter the room.

Slumped in her seat, Lady Carling straightened her back, lifted her chin, and displayed a gushing grin. She winked at Jayden and wiggled her fingers in a flirtatious wave.

Ignoring Aldwinster's obnoxious guest, Jayden locked his line of vision on his parents as he placed his hand on the small of Rhoslyn's back and guided her to stand before the High Table. The betrothed couple bowed and curtsied respectfully.

Upon seeing then enter the room, Pearson ordered two plates of food and tankards for the late arrivals to the evening meal.

Lord Filmore nodded to his son. "It's good to see you both. Please join us." He motioned to his left as he and his wife returned to their chairs.

Jayden guided Rhoslyn to the opposite end of the dais away from Lady Carling. She passed behind the Lord and Lady of Aldwinster and sat next to Lady Myla, who turned toward her and grasped her hand. "It's good to have you home, my dear."

"Hello, my lady." A voice greeted to Rhoslyn's right. She turned toward Lydia whose big brown eyes sparkled with delight.

"Hello, Lydia." Her eyes shifted to another who leaned forward with a not-so-pleasant expression on her face. *Lady Carling*. She looked back at Lydia. "I hope you've kept busy during my absence."

"I have, but I'm glad you've returned safely."

A servant placed a plate nearly overflowing with food before Rhoslyn while another filled a tankard with wine and set it by her plate.

Lord Filmore turned to his son and watched as he shoveled a mouthful of food into his mouth. "I received the message of your journey to Somerville. When you find a moment to take a breath, I would appreciate an update. We can talk privately in the library."

Jayden nodded his head as he chewed.

With the Lord and Lady of Aldwinster preoccupied in conversation, people lingered in the room. The musicians waited for their cue. Conversations stilled. Silence blanketed the room drawing Lady Myla's attention. She leaned toward her husband and touched his arm. "Dear, we are neglecting our duties."

Lord Filmore glanced about the room. People sat patiently looking at him in anticipation of the first dance. "An astute observation. Shall we?" He stood and took a moment to lean toward his son. "We'll continue this conversation upon my return." He went to his wife's chair to assist her to stand and motioned for Pearson instructing him to have the couple's plates and drinks taken to the library before leading his wife to the dance floor.

Rhoslyn picked up her fork to stab a chunk of pork. Her mouth dropped open as she watched as her plate rise from the table and stared

243

into the eyes of a servant. A wisp of her hair tickled her cheek as her betrothed whispered in her ear.

"Father would like to speak to us in the library. We are to finish our meal there."

She looked over her shoulder and into her betrothed's sky-blue eyes, nodded once before her chair was pulled away from the table, and placed her hand into his outstretched palm.

Lady Carling glared at the couple as they crossed the room and disappeared into the hallway. She slammed her empty tankard onto the table. "More wine!"

~

Rhoslyn stood silently watching Pearce light the candles to illuminate the room. He took the small table before the fireplace, placed it in the center of the room, and added four chairs around it. He signaled for the servants to place the meals on the table before ushering them out of the room and closing the door behind him.

Jayden stepped to a chair and presented it. "Shall we, before our meal becomes cold?"

Sitting in the offered chair, she waited for him to sit at her left. "What does your father want to talk about?" She feared he may pressure them into setting a wedding date but preferred to delay the ceremony until her mother could be present.

"I assume he would like to know about our adventure." He dabbed a piece of bread into a puddle of gravy and took a large bite.

Her stomach knotted. "You mean 'my adventure' don't you?"

He stopped in mid-chew and looked to the worried expression on her face. He chewed quickly, swallowed, and washed it down with a gulp from his tankard. "Father likes to get to the bottom of matters. He will ask questions, but there's nothing to worry about. Simply be truthful."

She glanced down at her plate and moved the food about with her fork.

The library door opened allowing laughter and merriment to filter into the room before growing silent once again. Rhoslyn's heart skipped a beat as the Lord and Lady of Aldwinster took their places at the table. Lord Filmore sat forward in his chair staring at her with an intensity sparkling in his sapphire eyes. He brought his elbows to rest on the table and steepled his index fingers beneath his chin.

"So, Rhoslyn, you left Aldwinster rather abruptly. I'm interested to know the reason why."

Searching for a moment to gather her thoughts, she set her fork upon the table and looked to Jayden, who answered her pleading eyes with a nod of encouragement.

Rhoslyn looked at her future father-in-law. "I went to Bradenham to discover the truth for myself."

Lord Filmore sat back in his chair shaking his head. He looked to the ceiling vowing to deal with Lady Carling later. He lowered his line of vision to Rhoslyn once again. "Why didn't you believe me when I confirmed her information?"

Jayden looked at his father. "Whose information?"

"I have been kept in the dark ever since I've arrived in Aldwinster. If you knew the state of my father and mother before I arrived, then why didn't you tell me?"

"You didn't answer my question."

"Nor you mine."

Jayden raised his voice. "Whose information?"

Rhoslyn looked to her betrothed. "Lady Carling overheard you and your father talking. She was the one who told me of my father's death and my mother's incarceration."

Jayden's eyes narrowed as he looked to his father. "I want that bitch gone. Tonight."

Lord Filmore scowled. "We will address Lady Carling's situation later."

Lady Myla reached under the table and patted her husband on his thigh to calm his temper. She held up the palm of her hand toward her son putting his comment on hold before addressing Rhoslyn.

"We were appointed by your father to care for you until you are wed. We take that responsibility seriously. However, it doesn't make our job very easy when you leave the kingdom without us knowing when or where you are traveling. Furthermore, it isn't safe for you to travel by yourself."

Rhoslyn lifted her chin. "I'm perfectly capable of traveling alone and defending myself."

Jayden smirked. "That she is."

His mother glared at her son.

A look of innocence masked his face. "What? Trust me, she is more than capable of defending herself."

Rhoslyn glanced at her betrothed. "Thank you."

"You're welcome." He winked.

"Getting back to the subject at hand." Lady Myla sighed trying to regain control of the conversation. "Rhoslyn, do I need to assign someone to remain with you at all times, and I mean AT ALL TIMES, to ensure you do not leave again?"

"No, that won't be necessary."

"Do you promise to stay within the castle walls and not leave without our permission?"

Rhoslyn glanced at Lord Filmore who had crossed his arms over his chest and glared at her as if looking from beneath his eyebrows. "I promise."

"Good." Lady Myla turned to her husband.

Lord Filmore sat forward once again to continue his inquisition. "Did you make it all of the way to Bardenham on your own?"

"Yes."

He looked to his son. "When did you catch up with her?"

"I arrived at Bardenham shortly after she did. She was determined to go to Somerville and verify if her mother was still alive. So, the three of us traveled there the next morning."

It dawned on Lord Filmore that he had yet to see his knight. "Sir Darwin did not return with you."

"He is on an errand."

"I see. And how is Lady Eugenia? Since I have not received word of her trial, I assume she is still alive."

"Yes." Rhoslyn confirmed.

Jayden set his tankard on the table. "Rhoslyn went against the baron's best bowman and competed for her mother's life. The baron has conceded to let her live."

Lord Filmore's eyebrows raised. "A competition? Of what?"

"Longbow." Jayden boasted.

"Really?" Lord Filmore looked to his future daughter-in-law. "How did you come by your skill?"

"Practice."

~

Lady Carling's vision blurred. She squinted her eyes as she watched two serving women approach her with their pitchers of wine. Or was there only one? She looked to the entrance of the hallways where Jayden had disappeared as she lowered her tankard for a refill. "I wonder how the four of them are getting along."

The servant assumed the comment was directed toward her. "My lady?"

Lady Carling wrinkled her top lip and scowled. "Not you. Go away." She waved her hand dismissing the woman, who curtsied and left.

Chapter 38

Empty plates remained on the small table as the conversation of their adventures to Bardenham and Somerville continued well into the night.

Jayden recognized Rhoslyn's attempt to disguise a yawn. "Father, it's late. Perhaps we can continue this discussion tomorrow."

Lord Filmore looked to his future daughter-in-law's sleepy eyes. "Yes, yes indeed. Until tomorrow then. Goodnight to you both."

The betrothed couple left the library and entered the silent, darkened Great Hall. Many of its candles were extinguished leaving only a few sputtering tapers to light their way across the room.

"Thank you." Rhoslyn dodged a wayward tankard on the floor.

Jayden's eyebrows squeezed together. "For what?"

"For excusing us from our conversation with your parents."

"You're welcome, but I share your sentiments as well. After the past few days, I'm looking forward to a good night's rest."

They climbed the staircase and stopped before her bedchamber door. Jayden opened it and motioned for her to enter. "I bid you goodnight."

"Goodnight." She closed the door behind her with a gentle click.

Candles on the nightstand and fireplace mantle remained lit, and a fire flickered in the fireplace to warm the bedchamber. Rhoslyn scanned the room. Lydia had retired for the night. As exhaustion overtook her body, she longed to climb into bed and close her eyes but needed to take off the uncomfortable bodice before doing so. After several attempts, she realized the task of untying the laces on her back was impossible. She looked to the door. *Would I appear too forward if I asked for his assistance?*

~

Jayden stared at the closed portal fighting his desire to hold her within his arms. He wondered if she would grow to care for him the way he cared and admired her. Entering his bedchamber, he removed his weapons placing them on the trunk at the end of his bed before lifting his tunic over his head and tossing it onto the back of a chair. He added a log to the fire and kicked off his boots. He loosened the laces on his breeches and turned to see something move in the crumbled covers of his bed. Tiptoeing, he peeked over the shoulder of whoever was asleep in his bed. A rather robust snore resembling the snort of a pig emanated from the passed-out woman as she rolled onto her back flinging her left arm over the edge of the bed and grazed his groin.

Jayden placed his fisted hands on his hips and clenched his teeth. A subtle tapping on his door drew his attention. He opened the portal to see Rhoslyn standing before him.

She inhaled as she stared into his muscular chest. Self-conscious of her rude behavior, she forced herself to look to his face and exhaled slowly.

He noticed the pinkish hue rise to her cheeks. "Are you well?"

She opened her mouth to speak, but only silence came forth. She cleared her throat hoping to regain her voice. "Yes, I, ah, find myself in a dilemma and wonder if you would be so kind as to help me."

"Certainly. However, I find myself faced with an unwelcome dilemma as well." He motioned toward Lady Carling passed out in his bed. "It appears she lost her way to her chamber or had an ulterior motive by placing herself in my bed."

Rhoslyn peeked at the woman with drool dripping from her mouth. "I have a feeling it's the latter of the two."

"Either way, I need to remove her from by bed before I can retire." He sighed. "So, how can I help you?"

"You see Lydia has gone to bed. I'm unable to unfasten my bodice and may have difficulty with the skirts as well. Could you undo the fastenings for me?"

Is she asking me to undress her? He looked at the dress. *It shouldn't be all that difficult of a task.* "I shall do my best."

She took a step into the room and turned her back toward him. She lifted her long brunette tresses from her shoulders revealing her slender neck, twisted the silky strands before pulling her hair over one shoulder and placed her hand on the front of the bodice to hold it in place.

Jayden examined the closure trying to determine which end to begin. "I must admit, this is a little out of my element, so be patient."

She smiled and waited.

Jayden discovered the bodice was unattached to the skirt as he felt along the bottom in search of the end of the lacing. He gently tugged a wayward string. The bow unraveled. Pulling one loop at a time, he watched as the bodice opened exposing a nearly transparent chemise made of the finest material. When he reached the top of the bodice, he pulled the laces free from the gromets to expose a plunging neckline of her undergarment revealing the soft, flawless skin of her back. His hands stilled; his pulse quickened.

Rhoslyn held the bodice in place to retain her modesty. She looked over her shoulder. "The skirt shouldn't be as difficult."

He blinked his eyes at the sound of her voice, unaware he was staring. He looked at the waistband of her skirt. *Such a tiny waist.* He untied the lacing and loosened it unsure how far she wanted it undone. There was a muslin skirt beneath it. "Do you want the second skirt unfastened as well?"

"Please." She reached for the waistbands to hold them in place while he unfastened the underskirt.

He pulled the drawstring. The opening in the skirt parted and drooped allowing him a glimpse of the shadowed gape of her bottom beneath her chemise and the curves of her shapely figure.

She looked over her shoulder as he leaned toward her face. "Finished?" She held onto her garments in fear of them falling to the floor.

"Yes."

She turned toward him. "Thank you."

He nodded his head. "I'm glad to be of service, my lady." He gave a slight bow.

She looked to the snoring woman in his bed. "How do you plan to remove her from your bed?"

Jayden looked at Lady Carling and sighed. "I doubt I'm able to throw her over my shoulder and carry her to her chamber. I mean, every man has his limit as to how much he can carry."

Rhoslyn grinned knowing the overweight woman would be a challenge for any man to carry. "Let me change into my robe. I can carry her feet while you carry her from under her arms."

Jayden crossed his arms over his chest and nodded his head. "Very well."

He untangled the covers from Lady Carling's body and glanced toward the doorway as he heard shuffling footsteps.

Rhoslyn went to the bed and grabbed the bedpost as she stared at his uninvited guest.

He smiled as he pointed at the bedpost. "See, no notches."

Rhoslyn ran her hand up and down the wooden post, smiled, and looked toward the ceiling at his jest.

He scratched his head considering the best way to remove the woman from his bed.

"Let me get her upper body off the bed and then you grab her feet before they hit the floor."

She nodded as they stepped to the side of the bed.

Grabbing the drunken woman beneath her arms, he turned his face away from Lady Carling's open mouth as she exhaled. "Good lord."

Rhoslyn chuckled. "I'm glad you have that end of her."

As Jayden scooted the chubby woman's body from the bed, Rhoslyn grabbed each ankle and placed her body between them. The couple stepped into the hallway in search of Lady Carling's bedchamber.

Rhoslyn glanced over her shoulder down the hallway. "Do you know which chamber is hers?"

"No, so just find one that is unlocked, and we will put her inside."

After trying several doors, one opened and Lady Carling was placed in the vacant bed.

Jayden escorted his betrothed to her room. "I think we managed quite well. Thank you."

"I agree and thank you as well. It would have been difficult to sleep in my corset."

They stopped before her open bedchamber door. He brushed aside a tress of hair from her shoulder. The sight of her dainty neck etched in his mind. "Rhoslyn, if you will indulge my attention for a moment, then I shall dream of our future with pleasant thoughts."

Fearing his intention, she searched his pleading eyes that echoed agony. "I intend to wait to lay with you after we are wed."

"I wouldn't have it any other way."

Daring to trust him at his word, she nodded her head once.

"Please turn around."

She hesitated but did so cautiously and waited. His hands touched her elbows and inched upward to her shoulders, her neck, lifting her hair, and placing it aside over one shoulder. His breath, so near and warm at the base of her neck preceded a gentle kiss that sent a shiver down her spine. He rotated his face placing his cheek against her rose petal-soft skin, traced it to her hairline, and placed a gentle kiss behind her ear. She closed her eyes, surrendering, and instinctively tilted her head to the side allowing him to continue.

He looked at her profile in the golden glow of the candlelight and touched his nose along her skin nuzzling her neck. She was compliant. He turned her face to meet his and gently kissed her lips. "Goodnight, Rhoslyn," he whispered against her lips.

Her eyes remained closed as a strange fluttering settled within her heart. She smiled. "Mmmm…goodnight."

He placed his hand on the small of her back and guided her forward into her bedchamber before closing the door behind her.

Chapter 39

Lydia entered Rhoslyn's bedchamber carrying her morning meal on a tray. It was midmorning and her mistress had yet to rise. She set the tray on the table near the window, set the place setting, and filled the tankard with watered ale from the small pitcher. Even though she tried to be as quiet as possible, Rhoslyn stirred, rolled toward her, and squinted, shielding her eyes from the brightness of the morning sun.

"Morning already? Lydia, I feel as if I have just gone to bed." Rhoslyn rolled onto her back and stared at the ceiling.

"Morning? My lady, it's midmorning." Lydia shuffled through several gowns in the armoire. "Any preference in what you wish to wear today?"

Rhoslyn tossed her covers aside, swung her feet to the floor, and sat on the edge of the bed. She took a deep breath giving her mind a moment to clear. In truth, she did not care which dress she wore.

"Any of them is fine. You decide." She picked up her robe from the end of her bed, slipping it on, and kicked aside her discarded dress on the floor as she crossed the room. She plopped into the chair, inserted her spoon into the bowl of porridge, and stirred as she gazed out the window. Was she falling in love or just falling prey to Jayden's way with women? She looked at the servant. "Lydia, have you ever been in love?"

The servant straightened the skirt of an emerald gown that lay upon the bed. "Very few women are ever given the chance to experience it, my lady."

Receiving an indirect answer, Rhoslyn pursued her initial question. "But have you ever experienced it?"

"Me?" Lydia looked at her mistress as she pointed to the center of her chest.

"Yes, you."

"It's difficult for me to say one way or the other. The line between love and lust can become blurred. Those who believe they are in love may also be blinded by it. But I believe love, true love endures the test of time."

Rhoslyn knew all too well her parent's loveless marriage was a failure. She had, or at least she believed to have witnessed true love between Lord Filmore and Lady Myla through their respect for each other, the way he stares and admires her, much like the way she caught Jayden looking at her.

Lydia selected a pair of matching slippers from the wardrobe, turned, and stared at her mistress, who was lost in thought. "When in love, you accept each other's faults. I think it boils down to a matter of tolerance despite each other's shortcomings."

Rhoslyn nodded. "Do you believe Lord Jayden loves me?"

"My lady, I don't know what's in his heart, but I do recognize the passion in his eyes when he looks at you. There is a longing, yet also a fear that you will push him away. I believe he would defend your honor and life even if it cost him his own. Ignore the rumors and trust him to remain loyal and faithful to you, for there isn't a finer man."

"For some reason, I still have my doubts."

"Perhaps you have yet to give him your heart because you fear he will break it? Is that it?"

Rhoslyn stared at her servant whose insight to her internal struggle seemed valid. "Perhaps. With so many women throwing themselves at him, how am I to know he will remain true unto me?"

"One never knows, my lady. It is a risk each of us must take." She placed the slippers near the foot of the bed. "Dare one never love, never know the heart swelling with joy, because of fear? Of never taking the risk?"

Rhoslyn sighed.

"My lady, take the risk, experience the love he has to offer, and trust him. You must open your heart to know his true character."

Rhoslyn rested her spoon on the edge of the bowl. "I fear I may end up like my mother and have a husband who takes a different woman in his bed every night."

"But your marriage may be one of love." Lydia sat in the seat across from her mistress. "The choice to marry him has been made by your father. But it is up to you to put forth the effort, ensure your marriage is a happy one, filled with love. It rests upon your shoulders. In my heart, I believe Lord Jayden is a good man."

Rhoslyn grinned. "I must admit, he is easy on the eyes."

"Yes, my lady, and tall, and handsome." The servant giggled as she teased.

Rhoslyn chuckled, for what her servant stated was true. "Thank you, Lydia, for your advice."

"You're welcome. Now, let's get you dressed. Then I with fetch several bolts of material for you to choose from to finish your gift for the Sisters of Charity." Lydia stood motioning toward the bed where the gown lay.

~

Her soft skin, thick auburn tresses, and aqua eyes haunting his mind with each attack of his sword. Jayden's growing fondness for Rhoslyn was becoming difficult to control, yet he must gain her trust to win her heart. Initially angry that his choice for a bride had been made for him, he was pleased to have her as his wife and looked to the future with the possibility of happiness.

He refused to look at the bedraggled woman who sat on a nearby bench cheering every clang of his wooden sword. The puffy bags under her eyes and her ashen face was a telltale sign of her previous evening's indulgence of wine.

"Well, done Lord Jayden!" Lady Carling clapped her hands.

He clenched his teeth and wished the next strike of his blade was over the annoying woman's head. His blade collided with his sparring partner's arm.

The soldier turned away rubbing his arm. He looked to Lady Carling and back to Jayden. "Ah, my lord. Don't let the woman get to you." The soldier raised his sword to continue.

"My apologies."

"Though I can't blame you for your frustration. Just don't take it out on me." The soldier chuckled and looked in the distance as a rider approached the practice field. "I believe you have a visitor, my lord."

Jayden turned to see Rhoslyn atop Laila. He lowered his sword.

Lady Carling traced the line of his sight. She scowled, looked back to her heart's desire, and ran toward him flinging her arms around his head, pulling it toward her, and kissing him on the lips. "Jayden, it's such a pleasure to watch you practice."

Rhoslyn reined Laila to a halt, stared at the spectacle, and watched as Jayden looked into the eyes of his admirer. *Was he just toying with me last night, pretending to blame Lady Carling after getting caught with her in his room?* Her chin jutted upward. Her heartbeat quickened. *I'm such a fool.* She yanked the reins directing her mare into a gallop back to the stable.

Jayden pushed his admirer an arm's length away. "I'm sorry, Lady Carling, but my heart belongs to another. If you'll excuse me." He tossed his practice sword to his sparring partner, ran to Beval, and pulled himself onto the saddle. He glared at Lady Carling before reining his warhorse and chasing after his betrothed.

Shadow lifted his head as he awoke from his nap, looked to the retreating figure of his master, and followed.

Rhoslyn heard her name called. She lowered her body closer to Laila's neck and spurred her mare to go faster.

"Rhoslyn!"

She ignored him as she galloped her horse through the gatehouse, dismounted at the stable, and ran to the Keep.

Jayden entered the bailey in time to see her disappear through the portal. He slowed his horse before the stable and hurried his steps toward the Keep.

Lady Myla emerged from the kitchen into the Great Hall to see Rhoslyn run past her and up the staircase. Footsteps echoed from the hallway as she looked to see her son.

"Mother." He hurried past her with his canine at his heels.

"Jayden, what's going on?"

"I don't quite know, but I'm determined to find out." He took the stairs two at a time as the sound of a door being slammed shut echoed in the hallway.

~

The bedchamber door slammed shut causing Lydia to squeal and drop the laundry from her arms. She turned to see her mistress bolt the door. "My lady! You're back so soon." She stooped to retrieve the clean clothes.

"I'm so naive!" Rhoslyn crossed her arms over her chest and paced.

"My lady?" Lydia set the laundry on the bed and stepped forward.

"Oh, I'm so mad! How can I be such a dimwit?"

Lydia held out a chair. "My lady, please sit. You are making me dizzy pacing back and forth."

Rhoslyn plopped into the chair.

Lydia stepped to her side to see her face. "You are not a dimwit. What happened?"

A hesitant knock sounded upon the door. Both women looked toward the portal.

"Rhoslyn?" Jayden tried to open the door but discovered it locked.

Lydia peered at her mistress, who remained silent with a scowl upon her face. If looks could kill, she feared Jayden would be dead.

Jayden kept his voice calm. "Rhoslyn, I need to speak with you."

"Go away!" Rhoslyn stood and began pacing again.

Lydia dared to intervene. "My lady, at least hear what he has to say."

She turned to her servant with her hands fisted tightly at her sides. "No, I know what I saw. He was kissing Lady Carling."

"Maybe you misinterpreted what you saw. Perhaps she was kissing him? At least hear him out."

Rhoslyn exhaled, crossed her arms over her chest, and shook her head before turning away from her servant and staring out the window.

Lydia tiptoed to the door, unbolted, and opened it to see Jayden run his hand through his hair in frustration. She put her index finger to her lips, allowed him to enter, and exited the room while grasping Shadow's collar and closing the door behind her.

Jayden paused, uncertain of how to handle the situation. Rhoslyn was angry, but how best to resolve the issue without escalating her temper was perplexing. He waited, staring at her defiant back.

"Honestly, I don't know how my mother tolerated my father's unfaithfulness. Am I to endure the same ill-gotten fate in my marriage?"

Jayden sighed as her insecurity was revealed. It was time to set her mind at ease. "No."

She turned to face him. "What are you doing here? How did you get in?" She scanned the room to discover Lydia was missing and pointed to the door. "Get out!"

"I'm not going anywhere until we settle this matter between us." He waited for her reaction to his statement. He heard the tapping of Shadows toenails on the stone floor and imagined Lydia's struggle to keep the large canine in check.

"Then I'll leave." Rhoslyn headed for the door.

Jayden placed his hand on the latch as she reached for it. "Please, just a moment of your time is all I ask." He spoke calmly, his eyes pleading with her venomous aqua orbs. She exhaled, crossed the room, and returned to her chair refusing to look at him.

He pulled the other chair from the table and placed it before her. Sitting, he rested his forearms on his thighs and leaned toward her wishing he could touch her. "What troubles you?"

She remained silent.

"From what I overheard, you believe I have been unfaithful and fear once we are wed, I will continue to do so. Am I correct?"

Pursing her lips, she glared at him with her arms crossed over her chest.

"I'll take that as a yes." He sighed. "Rhoslyn, I have been truthful with you from the very start. Yes, women do turn my head, they flirt, and in-kind, I do the same. It is harmless. But since learning of my betrothal to you, I have curtailed my behavior, as have others, because I understand it is hurtful to you."

She wanted to pace the floor, but he had ensured she would remain seated by placing his knee on each side of her legs. "What did I just witness on the practice field?"

"Lady Carling saw you approaching and purposefully flung herself at me just to make you angry."

"How can I not be angry? She is beautiful."

"Only on the outside. Inside, she is vindictive, spiteful, and greedy. The only thing she wants is a husband with a title." *A husband.* He would speak to his father of a suitable contender that came to mind. "I only want you, as my wife. In my eyes, you are the most attractive woman alive. From the moment I saw you at the abbey, my heart stopped. Inside, you possess a spark that shines brightly; such confidence, and determination. Do you have any idea how proud I was of you when you challenged the baron's best bowman?"

The expression on her face softened.

"Many marriages are arranged, loveless, thus encouraging the parties involved to seek love elsewhere." He pushed his chair backward as he knelt upon one knee, gently untangled one of her hands, and taking it in his. "On this day, I promise to always be faithful to you and only you. If I am not, please strike me dead, but be certain I am truly guilty of the charge before doing so. With your accuracy, I know your aim will be true." He reached behind him pulling his chair forward and sat.

Her eyes welled with tears and her bottom lip quivered. Stone by stone, the protective wall around her heart began to crumble. As each one turned to dust, a tear cascaded down her cheek.

Jayden's eyebrows raised, and his mouth dropped open. "Did what I say not please you?"

She shook her back and forth.

"Then why the tears?"

"I...don't...know." She sobbed, unable to catch her breath.

He reached for her elbow encouraging her to stand, rotated her body and guided her to sit in his lap. He leaned her against his chest and wrapped his arms around her holding her close. "Shhhh...." He ran the palm of his hand up and down her back while allowing her to cry. Whatever had been held within her heart needed to be released. He listened to her wrenching sobs wishing they would come to an end.

The final stone crumbled setting her heart free. Rhoslyn reached her arms upward and around his neck. "And I promise to be faithful only unto you."

He turned his head to stare into her bloodshot eyes, brushed away the trail of tears from her cheeks, and touched his lips to hers.

Shadow barked.

The betrothed couple's lips parted before their foreheads touched ensuring their pact to each other.

Jayden sighed. "Let Shadow in, Lydia."

The bedchamber door opened, and the large canine bounded to his master. Lydia closed the door allowing the couple additional time to be alone.

Chapter 40

After instructing Lydia to retrieve cold compresses to alleviate Rhoslyn's swollen, puffy eyes, Jayden went straight to the library and knocked on the closed door. Lord Filmore sat at his desk penning a reply to a missive. "Enter."

"Father, has there been any word from Sir Darwin?" He placed both hands on the front edge of the desk, leaned forward, and waited for his reply.

Lord Filmore shuffled through the small pile of sealed missives on his left. "I don't see his handwriting on any of these."

Jayden hit both fisted hands on the desk before sitting in the chair before his father.

His father scowled. "Jayden, what are you expecting from him?"

"Sir Darwin is to send word once he discovers evidence to prove Lady Eugenia's innocence."

"There's no guarantee he will find any. However, I imagine someone within Bardenham will have been entrusted with Lord Atherton's wrongdoing. A messenger perhaps?"

Jayden nodded his head in agreement. "On another issue, Lady Carling needs to leave."

"As a widow, she has nowhere to go."

"Then maybe we should find her a new husband."

Lord Filmore nodded. "Someone of a lower rank. We wouldn't want to give her any authority over us."

"Agreed." Jayden paced, stopped short, and looked to his father with a wicked grin on his face. "I have the perfect person in mind."

They composed a missive to the baron asking for his blessing, or rather mandate, for the unsuspecting couple to be wed.

With his plan in motion, Jayden delivered the missive to Pearce and requested a bath before the evening meal.

~

Lydia knocked on the door with her foot while juggling a basin of cold water and several linens draped over her arm.

"Enter."

The servant nudged the latch upward with her elbow, placed her backside on the door, and pushed it open.

"Lord Jayden wanted me to bring you cold compresses for your...oh my." The servant froze in place.

Rhoslyn raised her eyebrows quizzically. "That bad? I have yet to look in the mirror."

"The compresses will surely help, my lady." Lydia set the basin on the nightstand and submerged the linens.

"Let me get these clothes out of the way so you may lay on the bed." She picked up the laundry she previously abandoned and set the pile in the wardrobe. When she turned around, her mistress lay upon the bed with her head supported by the pillow.

"My lady, I want to apologize for allowing Lord Jayden into your bedchamber." She wrung the cloth of excess water and placed it over Rhoslyn's closed eyes.

"Even though it was against my wishes, it was the right thing to do. Thank you."

"You're welcome, my lady."

"Oh, and Lydia."

"Yes."

"I think we need to begin designing my wedding dress."

Lydia smiled. "Yes, my lady."

~

Rhoslyn turned clockwise for a final inspection by her servant.

Lydia had taken special care in dressing and styling her mistress's hair for the evening meal. She chose a lovely cranberry gown with pearl embellishments and added pearls and ribbons to her hair. "You're stunning, my lady."

"Thank you."

"I'll wait for you in the Great Hall." Lydia stepped into the hallway as Jayden exited his bedchamber and looked toward the servant.

"Lydia, is Lady Rhoslyn ready?"

"Yes, my lord. If you will excuse me." She headed toward the staircase.

Jayden stepped to the closed bedchamber door and knocked lightly. He took a step backward and straightened his sapphire tunic trimmed with silver thread.

Rhoslyn opened the door and curtsied.

Jayden bowed and presented his crooked right arm. She smiled sweetly as she threaded her arm through his and he placed the palm of his hand over hers. "You are a picture of beauty, my dear."

"Thank you. I find you equally as handsome."

"I hope you're well-rested because I plan to twirl you about the floor and dance nearly every song so that I may hold you in my arms most of the night." He winked and grinned.

They descended the staircase with many in the Great Hall admiring the happy couple. Jayden escorted his future wife to her seat at the High Table before sitting next to his father.

Lady Myla leaned toward her future daughter-in-law. "I understand from Lydia that you wish to begin designing your wedding gown."

"Yes, and I would appreciate your advice in its design."

"Shall we begin tomorrow?"

"I look forward to doing so, but I must finish the pillow for the Sisters of Charity first."

Lady Myla reached for her tankard, leaned back in her chair, and sipped her wine while the evening meal was brought forth from the kitchen. With Lord Filmore sitting back in his chair as well, Rhoslyn looked toward her betrothed to find Jayden staring at her. He raised his tankard toward her and nodded his head in respect. She nodded her head in a silent reply and smiled.

Lady Carling watched the exchange as she glared over the rim of her tankard.

~

Late one sunny afternoon as Shadow lay beneath a nearby tree while his master practiced his sword with a sparring partner, the canine lifted his head as a page came running onto the field. The young lord breathed heavily as he lowered his sword to accept a ladle full of water.

The page interrupted. "My lord, your father wishes to see you."

Jayden turned to see the lad awaiting his reply. "I will be there shortly."

"Yes, my lord." The lad hurried back to the castle.

Jayden looked in the direction of the Keep, curious as to what his father wanted. He handed his practice sword to his sparring partner. "Well, I believe our practice is done for today." He whistled. "Shadow!"

The loyal dog stood, shook his body from his head to the tip of his tail, and trotted toward his master, who climbed atop Beval and set his horse at a leisurely pace toward the Keep.

Jayden scanned the village with its many dwellings, the majestic castle, and fertile fields which produced enough crops to meet the demand of the kingdom and imagined ruling a kingdom with his wife by his side. He reined his horse at the stable and went to the library, assuming it was where he would find his father.

Lord Filmore looked up from the missive in his hand as his son stepped into the room. "Close the door."

Jayden halted, shut the door, and sat in the chair before his father's desk.

Lord Filmore put the missive on his desk. "I received a reply from Baron Roldan."

"And…"

"He approves of our chosen husband for Lady Carling and is sending his man of the cloth to perform the ceremony."

"Good, that's good news."

"There is more. Once you wed Lady Rhoslyn, he is appointing you to oversee Bardenham as its lord."

"As anticipated."

"I will send a missive to the groom and inform him that his bride is eager to wed. For now, we must keep this information to ourselves. Agreed?"

"Yes, Father. Agreed."

~

Rhoslyn waited patiently as Lydia placed the final pin in her hair. It seemed mundane to dress for the evening meal.

"Finished, my lady." Once her mistress stood, she pulled the bottom of the skirt to straighten the pleats and wrinkles.

Both women looked toward the door as a knock sounded upon it. It had become routine for Jayden to escort Rhoslyn to the Great Hall.

Lydia opened the portal to see Jayden standing in the hallway. The servant curtsied. "She's ready, my lord."

"Thank you, Lydia." Jayden allowed the servant to pass before looking to his future bride. "You look lovely this evening."

"Thank you."

He offered his arm as she exited the bedchamber. "Were you able to finish your wedding dress today?"

"Yes, it's sewn. We are adding the embellishments and should be done within a day or two."

"Good." He patted her hand as they descended the staircase to the Great Hall.

Rhoslyn stared at the cheeky grin on his face as he escorted her to her chair. "What are you up to, Jayden?" She sat in her chair.

"Nothing, my dear. I look forward to becoming your husband, that's all." He sat in his place at the High Table.

Rhoslyn suspected her betrothed wasn't as innocent as he claimed.

Chapter 41

Lydia stopped short in the bedchamber doorway surprised to see Rhoslyn sitting on the window seat dressed only in her chemise while sewing embellishments on her wedding dress.

"My lady, you've risen early." She nudged the door with her foot to close it before setting the tray of food upon the table.

"I rose at morning's first light." Rhoslyn pulled the thread through the teal garment adding another pearl while her servant filled a tankard of watered ale.

Lydia set the full vessel on the table. "You appeared to enjoy being in your betrothed arms and the countless turns about the floor last night."

Rhoslyn set her sewing on the window seat as she stood and selected a hardboiled egg and a thick slice of bread as she sat at the table.

"Have you overheard any plans Lord Jayden may have made? I sense he is up to something." She buttered the bread and set it on her plate.

Lydia looked to the unmade bed. "None that I know of." She pulled its covers to straighten them and fluffed the pillows. "Shall I make inquiries?" She glanced at Rhoslyn.

"No. I think all will be revealed in good time." She selected a small piece of meat pie from a plate.

The servant gathered the discarded garments from the floor and placed them next to the door. "What would you like to wear, my lady?" Lydia opened the wardrobe and began filing through the gowns.

"Don't fuss too much. Something simple. I plan to remain in my bedchamber today and hope to finish my dress."

"Very well." Lydia selected a rather plain forest green gown, laid it on the bed, and picked up the soiled clothing to take to the laundry. "I shall return shortly, my lady."

Rhoslyn added several pork crisps to her plate as she bit into the meat pie.

As Lydia exited the bedchamber, she nearly bumped into Jayden, who was about to knock on the door. "Oh, my lord, you startled me." She curtsied.

"Has Lady Rhoslyn risen?"

"Yes, but she has yet to dress."

"Could you make her presentable so I may speak with her?"

"Yes, my lord." Lydia dropped the armful of clothes on the hallway floor and reentered the bedchamber. "My lady, Lord Jayden wishes to speak with you. Let me get your robe." Lydia opened the wardrobe and withdrew a blue brocade robe from the hook on the door.

She held it open for her mistress to slide her arms into its sleeves, fold the sides over her body, and tie the sash to ensure it stayed closed. "There, my lady." Lydia opened the bedchamber door and nodded to Jayden as he entered, and she exited.

Rhoslyn looked toward her visitor. "Good morning." She motioned toward the chair at the opposite side of the table. "Have you eaten?"

"Long ago." He sat. "I came to tell you I will be occupied with my father today."

"Oh, anything in particular." She bit into the buttered bread with an all-knowing grin.

"We are discussing the operations of Aldwinster and making arrangements."

"Arrangements?" She raised an eyebrow tilting her head to one side.

"Yes." He stood.

She picked up her tankard. *A rather vague reply.* "You aren't going to elaborate?" She took a sip before returning it to the table and looking at him for a reply.

He leaned close to her ear and whispered. "It's a secret."

She looked into his eyes as he stood erect. "I see."

"What are your plans for today?" He helped himself to a pork crisp from her plate.

"I hope to finish my wedding dress, so I will remain here until I do so."

"If I'm able to get away from Father, I'll return to see if you're available for a game of chess. Until then." He lowered his lips and pressed them gently to her forehead causing her eyes to momentarily close. He squeezed her forearm slightly as he popped the crisp into his mouth, smiled, and left the bedchamber.

She watched the door close. *Something tells me I need to finish my dress quickly.*

Chapter 42

He went directly to the library. Closing the door to ensure their plan was not breached, two other men stood from their chairs as he turned toward them, one in which he was previously acquainted.

Lord Filmore looked toward his son. "Jayden, may I introduce to you Father Truman, the baron's priest, who has provided a missive to justify our cause." He motioned toward the priest. "I'm certain you remember this gentleman."

"Nice to meet you Father Truman, and good to see you again sir." He shook each man's hand.

Lord Filmore clapped his hands together. "Shall we get started?"

~

Rhoslyn examined her throbbing, red fingertips while her hair was pinned in place. She had worked diligently sewing as many of the pearls as possible, yet a good portion of the skirt still needed embellishing.

"There you go, my lady." Lydia handed her mistress the mirror and waited.

"It looks lovely. Thank you." Rhoslyn rose and brushed the imaginary wrinkles from her burgundy gown and straightened the lace on the sleeve.

Time seemed to tick by lethargically as Rhoslyn went to the window and looked to the kingdom below. The knock upon her door to escort her to the Grand Hall never came.

Lydia sighed. "Shall I escort you to the evening meal, my lady."

Rhoslyn imagined Jayden was still engaged with his father. She turned toward her servant. "I think that would be best."

The chattering from conversations echoed within the Great Hall as the aroma of the food brought forward from the kitchen tantalized everyone's tongue. Rhoslyn scanned the crowded room, not an empty seat at any bench. She glanced toward the High Table. Only Lady Myla and Lady Carling were seated.

Rhoslyn looked over her shoulder to Lydia, who was a step behind. "Is there something special planned for tonight? There are so many in attendance." Her attention was drawn to the hallway where Lord Filmore, Jayden, a priest, and another man entered the room.

Jayden hurried to the staircase meeting her at the bottom step and taking her hand within his. "I apologize for keeping you waiting." He pressed his lips to the back of her hand.

"You have been in a meeting the entire day?"

"Unfortunately, but for a good cause. You'll soon see. Shall we take our place at the High Table?" He placed the palm of his hand on the small of her back and motioned toward her seat.

The meal commenced as usual with ample food and drink for all. Lady Carling, in a particularly sour mood, glared at the priest, to Jayden, and back again as she consumed more than her fair share of wine. She scowled at the servant, who removed an empty tray from the High Table.

Sweetcakes carried forth from the kitchen announced the conclusion of the meal and were placed in the center of each table.

Lord Filmore stood. He withdrew a missive from his tunic and waited for the conversations in the room to quiet. "I have received an order from Baron Roldan. As you can see, his priest, Father Truman, and Lord Thornton are joining us this evening." He opened the missive for all to see and looked past his wife toward the end of the table. "Lady Carling, per the baron's order, in my opinion, he is being quite lenient despite the charge."

Everyone in the room looked toward the accused, curious of her crime.

Lady Carling's eyes widened as her face reddened. "What charge? I've done nothing wrong."

Lord Filmore held the missive before him and read. "Lady Carling is charged with obstruction, a most grievous crime. Since I, Baron Roldan, am in a generous mood, she may choose to either spend the remainder of her life in prison, be hanged, disemboweled, drawn and quartered, or marry Lord Thornton."

Rhoslyn's mouth dropped open as she leaned forward. Jayden winked while trying to contain his smile.

Lady Carling slammed her tankard on the table. "Obstruction? Of what?" She stood and crossed her arms over her chest. "I'm innocent!"

Lord Filmore continued. "Nevertheless, that is the charge of the transgression. What do you choose?"

Lady Carling looked to the disgusting man who licked his lips wetting them with spit before smiling at her. "There is only one choice truly available and that is to marry, or shall I say be forced to marry, Lord Thornton."

"An excellent choice." Lord Filmore turned to the priest. "Father you may begin the ceremony." He looked to those in the room. "I believe we have enough witnesses present."

Many smiled while others snickered filling the room with merriment.

Lady Carling could hardly believe her ears. "Now? I'm to marry him now!"

"Yes, and you will spend the night in wedded bliss and journey with your husband to Pembroke at sunrise. Unless you wish to change your mind for one of the other options."

Lady Carling looked to her future husband. A shiver ran up her spine. "No."

"Then we shall proceed with the wedding." Lord Filmore turned to the priest and groom. "Lord Thornton, if you will take your place before the High Table. Father, in front of him." He turned to Lady

Carling. "And if you will join your future husband so we may all witness the blessed nuptials."

With his book in hand, Father Truman stood in front of the High Table facing those in attendance. The groom rubbed his hands together, his smile from ear to ear as he stood on the right of the priest. Lady Carling took her place opposite the groom.

Father Truman opened his book. "Lord Thornton, do you take this woman to be your wife?"

Lord Filmore tilted his head toward his wife. "I've never seen Thornton so happy."

Lady Myla smiled. "Nor Lady Carling so miserable."

Lord Thornton reached for Lady Carling's hands and clasped them within his clammy palms. "Yes, yes, I do."

"And Lady Carling, do you accept this man as your husband?"

She hesitated to reply, questioning if the letter Lord Filmore received was genuine. She knew of no crime she was guilty of committing, but then again, many innocent people have gone to the gallows for worse. She sighed. "I do, not that I have a choice."

"By the grace of God, you are now husband and wife." Father Truman turned to the back of his book, brought forth a small inkwell and quill and had the couple sign it to record their marriage.

Lord Filmore stood and raised his tankard. "Here's to the happy couple. May they enjoy many years of happiness together."

A rather unenthusiastic cheer resounded in the room.

He motioned for the musicians to play. "The Lord and Lady of Pembroke shall have the honor of the first dance tonight."

Servants hurried to clear the floor for the couple's first dance as husband and wife.

A queasiness settled within Lady Carling's stomach as her husband reveled in the opportunity to hold her in his arms. She glanced at the people around her as she fought off Lord Thornton's roving hands while twirling her enthusiastically around the room.

Lord Filmore stood. "Come, my dear wife, let's join them." He led his wife to the floor to dance.

Jayden went to Rhoslyn. "Shall we join in the festivities?"

She nodded in agreement and placed her hand within his.

Chapter 43

A merry undertone buzzed throughout Aldwinster as staff packed and loaded Lady Carling's carriage at the break of dawn. Lord Filmore and his wife waited in the Great Hall for the newlyweds to emerge from their wedded night of bliss.

Lord Thornton wrapped his wife's arm within the crook of his arm proudly displaying his conquest as the couple descended the staircase. The Lord of Pembroke's belly shifting from side to side with each step as he stared at his wife while she looked straight ahead, unsmiling.

"Good morning, Lord Thornton, Lady Carling. I hope you had an eventful evening as husband and wife." Lord Filmore motioned toward a table set with the morning meal.

Lord Thornton bubbled with satisfaction. "Oh yes, my wife is quite the lover. She nearly wore me out." He turned to his wife. "Didn't you dear?"

Lady Carling's looked to the ceiling as her face turned a shade of red.

"Oh my, I have embarrassed my beloved." Lord Thornton patted her hand before releasing her arm for her to sit at the High Table. "Don't worry, my dear. I will make it up to you sooner than you know." He raised his eyebrows suggestively.

Lady Myla turned to her husband. "Has Jayden made himself scarce?"

"I have sent him to inspect the crops."

"An excellent idea." She sat in her chair as he pushed it toward the table.

Lord Thornton dominated the breakfast conversation with inappropriate details of his wedding night, encouraging everyone to complete their meal quickly, that is if they had not lost their appetite.

The Lord and Lady of Aldwinster escorted the couple to their awaiting carriages. Lady Carling assumed she would enjoy a quiet and peaceful ride to her new home. However, Lord Thornton climbed into the carriage with his wife. His empty carriage followed behind them.

As the small caravan departed, Lady Myla grabbed her husband's arm and burst out laughing as she saw a flurry of the woman's skirt flinging upward and Lord Thornton claiming his husbandly right before they reached the gatehouse.

~

Shadow preceded his master to the stable as Jayden looked to the midday sun before dismounting. Jayden went to the kitchen hoping the steward had time for his request. Not wanting to disturb the organized chaos of the cook staff, he stood in the doorway hoping for a moment of the steward's time.

"Pearson."

Upon hearing his name, the steward joined the young lord at the doorway. "Yes, my lord."

"Would it be too much trouble to set up our midday meal on a small table in the flower garden? Lady Rhoslyn has yet to enjoy its beauty."

"Certainly, my lord."

Shadow scampered toward a servant waving a wooden bowl of scraps as a tasty treat for the canine.

With a spring in his step, Jayden climbed the staircase. He combed his fingers through his hair pulling it away from his eyes, knocked on the bedchamber door, and was greeted by Lydia.

"Good day, my lord." She curtsied.

He looked past the servant to his betrothed. "Please inform Lady Rhoslyn her midday meal is being served in the flower garden."

Rhoslyn smiled as she recognized her betrothed's voice. She placed a ribbon in the book she was reading before closing it and looking toward the door.

The servant grinned, turned to look at her mistress.

"My lady, I have been informed your midday meal is being served in the flower garden."

Rhoslyn went to Jayden, who presented his bent arm. She threaded her arm through his.

"I thought you may enjoy the splendor of my mother's garden while we eat. It's her pride and joy and a sanctuary where she isolates herself in solitude when life becomes hectic. I think you will like it." Jayden led her out of the Keep and stopped before a stone wall containing a wooden door. A pair of stone statues stood guard on each side of the door. He reached behind one of the statues and withdrew a key as large as his hand, inserted it into the lock of the door, and turned it until he heard a rusty click. Returning the key, he pushed open the door hoping he had given Pearson enough time to have their meal in place.

Rhoslyn stepped into the garden. Her mouth dropped open as she looked about. Various plants were in full bloom with their fragrances filling the air. "Jayden, it's beautiful. There are so many colors."

They strolled the garden's flagstone pathways admiring each plant. At its center was a tree that offered plenty of shade. Beneath its canopy, a small table was set for two with a pitcher of warm spiced red wine, a plate of various meats and vegetables, bread with butter, and sweet cakes.

Jayden presented a chair for his future bride to sit, filled her goblet with wine, and handed it to her. "Did you finish your wedding gown?"

"Yes, I added the last of its embellishments this morning. Since it has taken precedence, I have neglected to write a letter of appreciation and send my gift to the Sisters of Charity. I would like to send it tomorrow if possible." She selected several items from the platter and placed them on her plate.

"I'm sure it can be arranged." Jayden waited for her to finish before making his selection. "Father insisted I tour and inspect the crops this morning. The kingdom should have a good harvest come autumn."

She ventured a question. "Has there been any word from Baron Roland?"

"None that I am aware of. I'm certain Father will let us know when a missive arrives." He watched as she looked down at her plate. "As they say, no news is good news."

She tried to smile.

A servant approached the dining couple. "My lord, is there anything you need?"

Jordan glanced at Rhoslyn before looking to the servant. "Can you help locate a box for Lydia to pack a gift for the Sisters of Charity? She is familiar with the size needed. Oh, and materials to write a letter as well."

"Yes, my lord."

~

Lydia entered the bedchamber carrying a wooden box with brass fittings on each corner and a piece of muslin she cut from a bolt in the sewing room. She set the box upon the bed and opened its lid to discover its key. So as not to lose it, she inserted it into the brass lock and lined the box with the cloth, folded the embroidered pillow neatly, and placed it inside.

Rhoslyn entered the bedchamber after spending several hours eating and conversing with Jayden.

Lydia looked to her mistress, who seemed aglow with happiness. "My lady, I assume you had a pleasant meal with Lord Jayden."

"Pleasant? Yes, it was quite pleasant." She peeked inside the wooden box.

"I have set out a quill, ink, and paper on the table for you to compose your letter to the Sisters of Charity."

"Thank you, Lydia" Rhoslyn sat at the table, dipped the quill in the black ink, and paused with the pen in midair. Her thoughts were scattered as she reflected on her time spent in the company of her betrothed.

"I've arranged for a messenger to take your gift to the abbess once you have finished." Lydia folded the cloth over the pillow hoping it would remain free of dust while being transported.

Rhoslyn looked to her servant, nodded, and tried to find the proper words to express her gratitude. She reflected on the nuns' way of life, their modesty, hard labor, and prayer. The eight masses per day were excessive in her opinion, but she had learned to respect the reverence, adoration, and passion in which they prayed. The months she spent in their company, living amongst them, enlightened her with a servant's perspective, especially peasants who labored in the fields. Putting the tip of the quill to the paper, she scratched a heartfelt note, fanned the missive with her hand to ensure the ink was dry, and folding it.

"Finished." Rhoslyn handed the note to her servant who, set it atop the gift, closed the lid, and turned the key to lock it securely. With the key in hand, Lydia picked up the wooden box and set out to deliver it to the messenger.

~

Shadow emerged from the Keep, saw his master enter the blacksmith shop, and lumbered toward him.

"Your sword is finished, my lord. It is made to your specifications." The blacksmith handed it to him hilt first. "I used a technique that ensures the iron is light in weight, yet strong."

Grasping its handle, Jayden twisted his wrist to estimate its weight. He placed his fingers near the hilt to check its balance. He held it up to his eye and looked down the length of the blade to ensure its straightness before examining the engraving upon it and its decorative handle.

"Perfect. Well done. And I will also take the dagger." He pointed to the weapon before reaching into his belt bag and extracting the necessary coin.

"Thank you kindly, my lord." He encased both items in their leather sheaths and proudly handed them to his lord in exchange for the payment.

Jayden reached down and petted Shadow's head as he crossed the bailey to the woodcarver's shop.

The crafter set aside his work and rose from his seat. "My lord, how may I be of service?"

"There is a wooden box you have set aside for Lady Rhoslyn. I would like to purchase it."

"Yes, indeed." He retrieved the item and presented it for his lord's inspection. The wooden box lid was carved in a lovely design and trimmed in brass.

Jayden lifted the lid to discover its interior lined with a soft black cloth and its key safely inside. "It is lovely."

"Thank you, my lord." The woodcarver wrapped the box in an oilcloth securing it with a leather strap to ensure it was well protected.

Jayden extracted the coins from his belt bag and paid the woodcarver.

"Thank you again, my lord." The crafter accepted the payment with a slight bow.

Jayden stepped over the threshold of the Keep, peeked into the Great Hall hoping to avoid his betrothed, he went to the staircase. He stepped aside as Lydia descended.

"My lord." She curtsied quickly and left.

"Lydia." He nodded as he tiptoed up the staircase hoping to remain undetected even though Shadow's toenails clicked on the stone floor indicated his location and entered his bedchamber. He placed the items he purchased in the chest at the foot of his bed before stopping by the solar to see if his father had received any news from Sir Darwin.

Lady Myla looked up from her embroidery as her son entered. "You must have read my mind. I was going to send for you." She retrieved a folded missive from the table. "Your father and I think it may be a good idea for you to retain the baron's letter as proof of your lordship of Bardenham."

He nodded and slipped it into his belt bag with the intention of storing it in the chest as well.

"And I thought you may need this." She went to the mantel and picked up a small brass box, opened it to reveal a ruby ring, her ring. "I thought your bride may need this on her wedding day."

291

Jayden glanced at the ring and then to her face. "Thank you, Mother."

She closed the box and handed it to him in exchange for a kiss on the cheek from her son.

He went to his bedchamber and placed it in the safety of the trunk at the foot of his bed.

Chapter 44

In the days that followed, Rhoslyn was either reading in her room, embroidering with Lydia, or on the practice field with her betrothed.

It became Jayden's habit to ask his father daily if there was any word from Sir Darwin. His father would simply shake his head.

~

A clap of thunder drew Rhoslyn's attention away from the chessboard.

"I believe it is your move." Jayden lifted his tankard from the table, sipped the warm wine, and scrutinized the board trying to anticipate her move.

Without giving it much thought, she slid her queen to a square. "Checkmate."

He stared in disbelief. "Well done."

"Thank you. I must admit, your skill is improving." Rhoslyn watched as servants entered the Great Hall in preparation for the evening meal. "If you will excuse me, I need to dress. I'm certain Lydia has my gown laid out and is pacing the floor."

"I'll go with you since I need to return this to the solar." Jayden picked up the chessboard and pieces.

The rain continued to fall into the night. Those in attendance for the evening meal enjoyed good food, a warm cozy atmosphere, and the security of the Keep.

Toward the end of the meal, a sodden messenger entered the room and bowed to Lord Filmore, who waved him forward. The messenger handed him a missive and waited for a reply. The Lord of Aldwinster broke the wax seal, unfolded the paper, and read the message before handing it to his son.

Jayden looked at the creased paper with Sir Darwin's signature at the bottom and back to his father before accepting the missive. As he read the message, a smile grew upon his face.

Lord Filmore leaned toward his son. "I assume you will leave for Bardenham at morning's first light?"

"Yes, as long as the weather clears. I would like you and mother to be there when we take our vows."

"Only death could stop me from attending." Lord Filmore clasped his son's shoulder and gave it a shake.

Jayden folded the missive and tucked it within his tunic as he glanced toward his future wife admiring her profile throughout the remainder of the meal.

As the musicians tuned their instruments, Lord Filmore and his wife took to the floor for the first dance and was joined by their son and his betrothed.

Jayden looked down into his betrothed aqua orbs. "My dear, I trust your wedding dress is finished."

"Yes." Rhoslyn scowled. She had informed him of its status over a week ago.

"Then have Lydia pack it and whatever else you wish to take with us, for we begin our trip to our new kingdom tomorrow."

"Tomorrow? Is Lydia to join us?"

"Yes, we leave at dawn for Bardenham where we shall be wed."

"Bardenham?"

"Yes, the baron has approved my lordship over the kingdom." He watched as her eyes widened and she smiled. "Does this please you?"

"Very much so."

~

Lydia set her packed bag and cloak on the floor in the hallway outside of Rhoslyn's bedchamber. She knocked lightly and entered without permission.

Rhoslyn turned to see who had stepped into the room.

"My lady, let's get you packed and ready to travel."

Several trunks lay open in the center of the room.

295

Rhoslyn glanced at the numerous open trunks in the room. "I don't understand why Pearson had all of these brought into the room. None of the dresses in the wardrobe belong to me and I only have a few items in my bag when I arrived." She held up her packed bag.

"Maybe Lady Myla is suggesting you take the dresses in the wardrobe with you?"

"I don't feel right doing so. They aren't mine."

"Well, my lady, you will need one trunk to pack your wedding dress. If it sets your mind at ease, I will ask Lady Myla." Lydia left the room.

~

Jayden returned the quill to the inkwell and folded the missive. He stood in his bedchamber staring at the open trunks. Tucking the missive in his tunic, he opened his wardrobe and packed his clothing inside the trunk as neatly as possible. Glancing around his bedchamber, one he had slept in his entire life, for anything he may have forgotten to pack. He took a deep breath knowing he would be sleeping in the lord's bedchamber in Bardenham with the kingdom's responsibility upon his shoulders. He closed the lid of the trunk, latching its leather straps. A page would take it to an awaiting wagon in the bailey. He looked around the room one final time and exited passing Lydia in the hallway.

"Is she ready?" He pulled the missive from his tunic.

"Nearly, my lord. We will join you as soon as she changes." Lydia hurried to Rhoslyn's bedchamber. She glanced in his direction to see Jayden disappear down the staircase before passing through the doorway.

"My lady, Lord Jayden asks if you are ready."

"I'm sure he is eager to get underway, as am I." Rhoslyn lifted her arms as a simple riding gown was pulled over her head. She was fitted with a half-corset. Her body jerked backward with each pull of its lacing hugging her body snugly. With her hair quickly pinned away from her eyes, she was ready.

Lydia picked up her bag from the hallway as she exited the room confident the trunks would be loaded with her supervision.

Rhoslyn draped her cloak over her arm, took her satchel in hand, and joined Lord Filmore, Lady Myla, Jayden, and Shadow in the Great Hall. She observed Pearson supervising the staff as they carried the trunks and provisions to the awaiting wagons and horses. She stepped before the steward. "Pearson, thank you for your hospitality and kindness during my stay."

"You are more than welcome, my lady. I hope you will return for a visit soon."

"I hope to do so as well."

"Safe journey, my lady."

"Thank you, Pearson."

The steward stepped to Jayden, remembering the day he was born and the joys of watching him grow into the competent man. "My lord, keep a watchful eye over this one." He nodded toward Rhoslyn.

"You know I will." He handed him the folded missive. "Please send this to Sir Darwin at Bardenham. It forewarns of our arrival."

"Certainly. Godspeed, Lord Jayden."

"Thank you." Jayden smiled as he bid him farewell.

The last of the trunks were loaded onto the wagons and protective oilcloths strapped down over them. Several garrison men were mounted, armed, and ready to escort and protect the members of the party. Lydia waited patiently astride a gentle mare letting her imagination dream of Bardenham's magnificence.

Shadow went to Beval's side and sat. He watched as the foursome exited the Keep and went to their awaiting mounts. Laila pawed the ground eager to be on her way. She looked toward her mistress as Rhoslyn put her foot in the stirrup and hoisted herself onto the saddle.

Jayden climbed atop Beval. He looked toward the Keep's door to see Pearson. He lifted his fisted hand as a final salute before reining his horse toward the gatehouse.

~

The long caravan traveled by pairs. The Lord of Aldwinster rode next to his son, Lady Myla beside Rhoslyn, Lydia accompanied by a soldier, and the wagons followed them in single file. The garrison resembled bookends as they began and ended the procession protectively.

Jayden glanced over his shoulder at his betrothed. She appeared in good spirits and was engaged in conversation with his mother.

They set a steady pace to accommodate the slower moving wagons with their heavy loads. The journey would take a day longer than the normal two days.

They traveled through the afternoon and into the early evening before stopping by the roadside and setting up camp. With the horses unsaddled for the night, a fire was built with everyone gathering nearby and sharing a meal.

Rhoslyn leaned toward Lydia. "I will return shortly." She stepped into the woods.

Jayden saw her disappear and followed with Shadow by his side.

She heard footsteps behind her and turned to see who it was. "What do you think you are doing?" She placed her hands upon her hips.

"Ensuring your safety, my lady. The last time you entered the woods alone, you were attacked by a wild boar." He reminded her.

"And as I stated then, I can fend for myself. As always, I have my dirk attached to my leg."

"Nevertheless, I'm accompanying you." He took a step toward her.

"I would appreciate a few minutes of privacy, please."

"And I shall give you what is necessary."

Unable to ignore her bladder's urgency, she exhaled in disgust, turned, and walked further into the woods. She found a large tree and stopped. "You stay on this side and I shall use that side."

"Fine." He stood with his back to the tree as she went around to the other side.

Shadow glance from his master to Rhoslyn and back again.

She lifted her skirt, tried to relieve herself but could not relax enough to do so. "You need to sing."

He scowled and smirked at the idea. "Sing? Why?"

"Because I can't, you know, when you can hear me."

299

He shook his head and stifled a laugh. "Come now, everyone relieves themselves. What difference does it make if I hear you?"

"I can't go unless I know you aren't listening."

"I can't sing." He admitted. "Would it help if I went at the same time as you did?"

"No! I don't want to hear you relieve yourself."

"How about if I whistle?"

"Fine." She waited for him to begin.

He inhaled, puckered his lips, and whistled.

Rhoslyn emptied her bladder and walked past him as he continued to whistle. "Thank you."

Shadow led the way back to the camp.

The campfire crackled and popped as they ate their tasty meal, talked quietly, and bedded down for the night.

The next morning, they rose early, saddled their horses, and continued their journey. They stopped at midday near a stream to allow the horses to rest while they ate a meal. Jayden had hoped to reach Bardenham by nightfall, but it was necessary to camp an additional night.

Lydia sat gingerly upon the ground next to her mistress. "I must admit, I feel a little stiff. I'm unaccustomed to being in the saddle for such lengths of time."

Rhoslyn held the palms of her hands toward the campfire to warm them. "We should arrive tomorrow." Bardenham would seem empty without her mother there. She sighed knowing she had done her best to save her mother's life but wondered if it would have been better for her to face death instead of rotting away in a chamber for the rest of her life. Something touched the back of her hand drawing her attention from her thoughts. She saw Jayden's hand clasping hers and looked to his face.

"I promise you, all will be well." He reassured reading her mind.

She acknowledged his statement with a nod.

Chapter 45

Sunlight announced their final day of travel. The camp was dismantled, horses saddled, and the caravan returned to the dirt road. Lord Filmore motioned for Jayden and Rhoslyn to ride ahead of him and his wife leading the way to their new kingdom.

At midday, they crested a hill and viewed Bardenham in the distance. Laila, acutely aware of her surroundings, turned her body sideways as she pranced anticipating her destination. Rhoslyn reined her mare back in line.

Jayden glanced toward his betrothed. "Shall we let our horses stretch their legs?" He raised his eyebrows in a silent challenge.

Rhoslyn displayed a devilish smile of pearl-white teeth, allowed slack in the reins, and touched her heel to her mare's belly. Laila bolted into a full gallop parting the garrison before them. Jayden laughed and encouraged Beval to follow. Fearful of being left behind, Shadow darted after his master.

Their horses kicked up a trail of dust as they approached the village. Slowing their horses to a leisurely gait, they entered the village passing peasants along the street with many waving and greeted Rhoslyn and acknowledging Jayden respectfully. The couple rode over the drawbridge, into the bailey, and reined their horses in front of the stable.

Jamie limped forward to grasp the bridles. "Lady Rhoslyn, Lord Jayden, we've been expecting you."

"Expecting us?" Rhoslyn tilted her head to the side as she looked to Jayden.

"I sent word ahead of our arrival." He confessed.

"Ah." She looked at the stableboy and smiled. "It's good to be home again, Jamie."

Lagging, Shadow joined his master, who petted his shoulder with an affectionate pat as the dog leaned against his leg. Jayden watched the lad lead the horses into the stable. He assumed his leg had been injured when he was younger. More than likely, it failed to heal properly. He looked toward the gatehouse as the thunder of hooves became silent and the garrison dismounted. His parents and Lydia continued toward the stable.

Lord Filmore helped his wife dismount as the stableboy hurried to take their horses.

Rhoslyn stepped forward. "My lord, my lady, this is Jamie, Bardenham's stableboy. He is very good with our horses and will see they are well cared for."

The Lord and Lady of Aldwinster nodded their heads toward the toe-headed lad, who nodded. Lydia stood behind her mistress with her bag in hand and scanned the shops along the castle wall.

Shadow was first through the Keep's door as his master and the others followed.

Alerted by a page, Bentley straightened his tunic as footsteps echoed from the hallway. "My lady, welcome back." He bowed as Rhoslyn entered the Great Hall.

"Thank you. Bentley, may I introduce to you the Lord and Lady of Aldwinster."

"Welcome. It is nice to meet you both and a pleasure to see you again, Lord Jayden." The steward bowed.

"Bentley." Jayden nodded.

"I received your correspondence and have readied your bedchamber, my lord. My lady, I have moved your belongings to the Lady of Bardenham's chamber and moved our permanent resident to your bedchamber."

Rhoslyn's eyebrows drew together as she looked to the steward. "A permanent resident? Who is it?"

"It's me."

Rhoslyn's attention was drawn to the top of the staircase where her mother stood smiling. "Mother!" She ran up the stairs as Lady Eugenia descended. They met halfway wrapping their arms around each other.

"If you will excuse me, my lord." Bentley nodded to Jayden and went to the kitchen to oversee the midday meal.

After kissing her daughter on the cheek, Lady Eugenia looked to Jayden's smiling face. She whispered to her daughter. "You look well, and quite happy."

Rhoslyn looked over her shoulder at her betrothed. "Yes, I am. Come, let me introduce you." They descended the staircase. "Mother, you remember Lord Jayden."

"Lady Eugenia, it is nice to see you again. I'm eager to hear the details of your release from Somerville." He motioned toward his parents. "May I introduce to you my parents, Lord Filmore and Lady Myla."

Lady Eugena nodded to the guests. "It is a pleasure to meet you both." She glanced at the hallway as servants began the parade of carrying trunks. Since she ate a late breakfast, she turned to her daughter. "Rhoslyn, I'll ensure each trunk is placed in the proper bedchamber." She glanced at the High Table as the midday meal was being served. "Please, your meal awaits." She motioned toward the dais.

"Thank you, Mother." Rhoslyn turned to her guests. "This way, please."

Jayden turned toward the sound of heavy footsteps echoing from the hallway.

"So, I understand our new lord and his betrothal have arrived." With a spring in his step, Sir Darwin grinned as he marched into the Great Hall with Sir Cedric a step behind him. Their left hands resting on the hilt of his sword.

Jayden went to his knight, embracing him with a slap on the back. "It's good to see you again. I assume you are in good health."

"As always, my lord." He looked to the top of the staircase as Lady Eugena disappeared into the hallway.

Jayden released his knight. "Sir Cedric, I hope you have familiarized Sir Darwin with the garrison and the castle's defense."

"Absolutely, my lord." The knight extended his hand and Jayden clasped it.

"Good, I will rely on you both for an orientation."

Lydia stood near the door of the hallway gazing about the room.

Rhoslyn noticed her servant and went to her side. "Lydia, leave your bag on the staircase. It will be taken to your bedchamber. Come and sit."

"Yes, my lady."

Rhoslyn stepped onto the dais and stood beside her mother's chair. She scanned the Great Hall and exhaled as she accepted the role of the kingdom's lady and sat. She looked at Jayden as he sat to her left, placed his hand upon hers, and gave it a gentle squeeze bringing a smile to her face.

~

At the conclusion of their meal, Bentley escorted Rhoslyn and her guests upstairs to ensure their rooms were to their satisfaction.

Lady Eugenia emerged from a chamber and met her daughter in the hallway. "My dear, I have taken the privilege of having a bath drawn for you."

"Mother, you read my mind." Rhoslyn laced her arm around her mother's and looked over her shoulder to ensure Lydia followed as she entered the bedchamber. Memories flooded her mind recalling the countless times she slept with her mother when she was ill or scared of a thunderstorm. The full-length mirror was still in the corner of the room. As a little girl, she would stand before it in her new dresses and admire how they made her feel special. She looked at the ever-bolted door to the solar and imagined it would remain unbolted once she was married.

"Of course, you may change and redecorate it as you like. It's yours now." Lady Eugenia turned to face her daughter.

"It will remain as is, Mother, filled with memories of us spending time together."

Lady Eugenia smiled as she turned and clasped her daughter's hands.

Rhoslyn tilted her head to the side and returned her mother's expression. "You seem happy, Mother."

"Oh, I'm very happy. I have much to be thankful for; my freedom, you, my future son-in-law, and a man who has returned to me after so many years."

Rhoslyn's eyebrows drew together. "Who?"

Lady Eugenia looked to Lydia, who stood by silently waiting to assist her mistress. She sighed. "I will update you on the details later. For now, I will leave you to your bath." She embraced her daughter.

Lydia curtsied to the matriarch as she exited and closed the bedchamber door. "My lady, I find Bardenham most delightful." She unlaced the bodice of her mistress, stripped her down, and held her hand as she climbed into the tub. "Shall I let you soak for a bit?"

Rhoslyn exhaled as the warm water enveloped her body. "Oh, this is heavenly. Yes."

Lydia opened the trunks and began hanging the gowns in the empty wardrobe. She withdrew the teal wedding dress, placed in on a hanger, and hung it on the door of the cabinet. "Do you know when you and Lord Jayden will wed?" She brushed the wrinkles from the skirt.

"We have yet to discuss the matter. I imagine it will depend on when a man of the cloth is available. My father sent our friar away years ago over a discussion of his infidelity."

~

Jayden remained in the Great Hall with the knights. "Has he arrived?"

Sir Darwin lifted his tankard to his lips and paused to answer the young lord's question. "My lord, I escorted him with Lady Eugenia on my return from Aldwinster. He is in residence in the chapel."

"What evidence did you present to the baron to convince him of her innocence."

"Bentley helped identify the messenger who transported missives to the conspirators. I took him to the baron. He stated the parties involved and ensured Lady Eugenia was not involved in any way."

Jayden leaned over the table to see the knight. "Sir Cedric, the status of the garrison?"

"Strong and ready when called upon, my lord."

"I look forward to inspecting their skill on the practice field." He spied Bentley passing through the room. "If you will excuse me, gentlemen." Jayden followed the steward into the kitchen. Shadow rose from beneath the table and trailed after his master.

"Bentley." Jayden stepped into the doorway of the room as the steward turned toward him.

"Yes, my lord."

Jayden watched servants rush about the room like organized chaos. "Is everything in place for tomorrow?"

"Yes, my lord. What time do you wish to wed?"

Jayden stared at the steward blankly.

"My lord, would you like a private wedding in the chapel or before everyone in the Great Hall? Will you need a midday or evening celebration?"

Jayden opened his mouth to reply and snapped it shut in contemplation. He held up an index finger. "I'll return shortly."

~

Lydia finished combing her mistress's damp auburn hair. With Rhoslyn fully bathed, she added a pitcher of hot water to the tub allowing her to soak a few minutes longer.

A knock sounded on the door. The servant went to the door and opened it a mere crack. "My lord."

Rhoslyn looked over her shoulder at the doorway.

"I need to talk to Lady Rhoslyn."

"I'm sorry, my lord, she is taking a bath."

"It's important."

Rhoslyn stood, reached for several large towels on the chair and covered the front of her body quite confident she was presentable. "Let him in."

Lydia looked to her mistress to see her current state of dress and reluctantly opened the door.

Jayden stepped within a few feet from his betrothed. "I'm sorry to interrupt, but I need you to choose the time of day you wish to be wed tomorrow."

Her eyes widened with surprise. "Tomorrow? How? We do not have a man of the cloth to perform the ceremony."

"Father Truman is in residence in the chapel. He accompanied Sir Darwin and your mother from Sommerville. Bentley wants to know when and where you would like to be wed." A movement caught his attention as Rhoslyn shifted her weight from one leg to the other. Jayden looked at the full-length mirror framing a reflection of her bare backside.

"I don't know. What would you prefer?"

He stared at the curvature of her bottom as he recalled an evening wedding in the glow of candlelight. "I would prefer a simple ceremony in the chapel followed by a grand celebration in the Great Hall."

Rhoslyn nodded and grinned. "Sounds lovely."

He stepped close enough to whisper into her ear. "Do you know what else I find lovely?"

"What?" She held the towel closer to her chest as she grinned at his teasing undertone.

"The reflection of your perfect bottom in the mirror." He grasped her chin between his index finger and thumb and slowly turned her head toward it. As her mouth dropped open, he kissed her cheek before leaving the room.

~

Bentley stood before a bedchamber and looked at Jayden as he stepped into the hallway. "My lord, this is your bedchamber." The steward opened the door allowing his lord to enter before him. "It is connected through that door," he motioned toward the portal, "to the solar which joins Lady Rhoslyn's bedchamber. Her door is currently locked."

Jayden toured the room. The bed was spacious, the fireplace large enough to warm the room with two highbacked chairs before the hearth and a small table between them. A large empty wardrobe was against a wall. His trunk next to it on the floor. The room was neat and clean.

"Very nice, Bentley." He looked out the window to see the bailey below. Hoping Rhoslyn would spend much of her time within his bedchamber, he made a request. "I need a table with two chairs and a chessboard brought into my room. We would like our breakfast served in the solar each morning."

"Yes, my lord."

"Lady Rhoslyn wishes a small evening wedding ceremony in the chapel followed by a grand celebration in the Great Hall. Can that be arranged by tomorrow?"

"Yes, my lord. I shall do my best. Is there anything else?

"Yes, musicians for tonight's meal."

"Very well." Bentley glanced at the trunk. "My lord, would you like me to unpack your trunk before I return to the kitchen?"

"No, thank you. I want to do it myself."

With a nod of his head, the steward left the bedchamber closing the door behind him.

Jayden opened his trunk to ensure his wedding gifts remained unscathed. Placed them in the bottom of the wardrobe. He glanced at the door to the solar as a plan formed within his mind.

~

Bentley observed with pride the proficiency of the staff as the evening meal was ending. He managed to find musicians and watched as they went to the corner of the room and gathered their instruments. With one remaining detail for tomorrow's evening meal, he approached the High Table. "My lady?"

"Yes." Lady Eugenia, Lady Myla, and Rhoslyn answered the steward simultaneity. They looked at each other and giggled.

"I apologize, my dear." Lady Myla blushed as she looked at Rhoslyn.

"I as well. Habit, I guess." Lady Eugenia motioned for her daughter to reply. "Proceed, my dear."

Rhoslyn turned to the steward. "Yes, Bentley."

"Would you like to request a specific dessert for your wedding celebration tomorrow?"

"Something to make the occasion special. However, I have no preference, so you decide."

"Yes, my lady."

Jayden rose from his seat and presented the palm of his hand. "May I have this dance."

She grinned as she placed her hand within his. "Yes, you may."

Chapter 46

Jayden stripped down to his breeches and glanced at the door to the solar. The hour was late when he escorted Rhoslyn to her bedchamber. He hoped he had allowed Lydia enough time to dress his future wife for bed.

Shadow lay on a rug near the warmth of the fireplace. Jayden assumed the dog was asleep for the night. Gathering his wedding gifts from the bottom of the wardrobe, he entered the solar and knocked gently on the adjoining door. "Rhoslyn, may I speak with you?"

She looked to the door as she held the edge of her covers in her hand with the intention of pulling them over her body and snuggling in bed for the night. Flipping the covers aside, she picked up the lit taper from her nightstand and went to the door. She looked down at her thin chemise, set the candle on the mantle, and retrieved her robe. Returning to the door, she tried to release the bolt. It would not budge.

"I can't open the door. I think it's rusted."

Jayden left his room, went into the hallway, and knocked on her bedchamber door. He placed his gifts behind his back.

The door opened the width of her body. He stared down into her askance aqua eyes.

"Did you need something?" Her eyes drifted down to his muscular chest before looking to his kind face.

"Just a moment of your time. May I come in?"

Rhoslyn peeked her head out the door and glanced toward each end of the hallway to ensure he was not seen. She opened the door wider to allow him to enter and closed it quickly.

Other than the single lit taper, the only other light in the room was the glow of the fireplace. Jayden grasped her hand and led her to the hearth to a single chair. He took the taper, placed it on the mantel, and guided her onto his lap as he sat.

"I wanted to give you these." He revealed his gifts hidden by the arm of the chair and placed them in her lap. "My wedding gifts."

Rhoslyn stared at the oilcloth covered items within her arms. "But I don't have anything for you." She looked into his eyes unsmiling.

He raised his eyebrows up and down teasingly. "We can resolve that later." He displayed a devilish smile.

She smiled.

"Open them." He encouraged.

"Which one first?"

"The small one."

She laid the longer gift in her lap as she unwrapped the other. "Oh." She inhaled. "The box from the woodcarver."

"The key is inside. There's something else inside too." He was delighted to see the surprised expression on her face as she opened the lid.

"A dagger?" She lifted it from the box and examined its handle. "Is this the one I threw at the target on the wall in the bladesmith's shop?"

"The very same. Now, open the last one."

She returned the dagger to the box. He removed it from her lap and set it upon the floor.

Rhoslyn removed the oilcloth and discovered her gift to be a sword protected by a beautiful leather sheath. "A sword?"

"Not just any sword. I had the blacksmith make it with a lighter, yet very strong metal."

She stood from his lap, unsheathed the weapon, and examined it by the light of the fire. "It's beautiful." Rhoslyn tested its balance and weight. She swung it in several directions as if sparing with an imaginary opponent. "It's wonderful, Jayden. Thank you." She returned it to its sheath and stood before him.

Jayden took the sword, laid it with the wooden box, and reached for her hand encouraging her to sit upon his lap.

She cupped the palm of her hands on each side of his face and placed a kiss upon his lips before wrapping her arms around his neck and resting against his chest. He placed his arms around her hips drawing her near and sighed.

They watched the flickering flames for several hours before her rhythmic breathing indicated she was asleep. He carried her to bed, tucked her within, and placed a kiss upon her forehead. He unbolted the door to the solar before returning to his bedchamber for the night.

~

Jayden awoke early the next morning to the aroma of pork crisps, eggs and sweet cakes wafting from the solar. Shadow's toenails tapped on the stone floor encouraging his master to rise. Sitting on the edge of his bed, he wondered if Rhoslyn was awake. Passing through the solar, he entered her bedchamber. She was still in bed.

"Good morning, my lady." He brushed her hair away from her eyes. "Breakfast is served in the solar. Would you care to join me?"

Rhoslyn opened her eyes a mere crack to see Jayden's smiling face. She yawned and stretched her arms. "Good morning. Yes, it smells delicious." Still wearing her robe, she reached down and petted Shadow before followed her betrothed to the solar. He held her chair for her as she sat and pushed her toward the table before sitting across from her.

Jayden glanced at his bride as he placed food on his plate. "How are you going to spend your day until this evening?"

"I'm certain my mother, your mother, and Lydia will keep me busy throughout the day. I may speak with Bentley and Father Truman to ensure everything is ready." She buttered a wedge of bread and placed the knife on the edge of her plate. "And how are you going to spend your day?"

"I need to familiarize myself with the account books, take a tour of the practice fields with Sir Darwin, Sir Cedric, and my father, and inspect the crops in the fields." Jayden handed Shadow a pork crisp as he glanced at Rhoslyn. *Even though she is high spirited, she has calmed her temperament as of lately.* Has she accepted him as a spouse? He watched her dainty hands tear apart the bread into a bitesize piece and reached for her hand as a nagging question entered his mind. "Do you think of me as you once did or has your opinion of my character changed?"

Her chewing paused as she looked to his inquisitive eyes. She resumed chewing as she thought and stared at the handsome, strong man genuinely seeking her opinion. Her first impression of her betrothed was an egotistical royal who thought highly of himself, but perhaps her opinion of him was tainted by her father's unfaithfulness to her mother. She looked to his hand upon hers and entwined her fingers within his. "My first impression of you was influenced by my father's behavior. I assumed all men behave as such and their wives suffer in silence as my mother did. It was easy to make that assumption of you through your interaction with others. The true affection your parents display for each other gives me hope that our marriage may be the same. Since our announced betrothal, I have witnessed a different side of you. I find you a man of your word, you are kind and thoughtful, and I look to the future with promise."

He exhaled as if lifting a great weight from his shoulders. "I must admit, I was not pleased about our betrothal, but I truly have affection for you. Is it love? I would like to think so. I know it will grow with time. I'm entering into our marriage willingly and am proud to have you as my wife, to share our lives together."

She smiled, released his hand as she rose from her chair, and went to his side. He rotated his chair allowing her to sit on his lap. She entwined her fingers in his charcoal hair and ran her index down the side of his face and along his jaw. "I find you quite handsome and I too am entering this marriage willingly. More than anything, I anticipate the day we practice with my new sword on the practice field." She giggled.

He laughed before kissing her on the lips and hugging her dearly.

Chapter 47

A knock sounded upon the bedchamber door.

"My lady, have you risen?" Lydia waited outside Rhoslyn's room.

"Enter." She called from the solar.

The servant peeked through the door to the solar to see Rhoslyn and Jayden eating their breakfast. "I'm sorry, my lady. I thought you may be ready to dress for the day."

"Good morning, Lydia." She looked over her shoulder at her servant.

"Good morning, Lydia." Jordan greeted.

"Good morning, my lord, my lady." Lydia busied herself with making the bed, gathering laundry, and setting out clothing for her mistress to wear.

Jayden rose from his chair. "I shall see you later tonight, my dear." He kissed Rhoslyn, dressed quickly, and left his bedchamber with Shadow in tow.

Rhoslyn pushed her chair back from the table and entered her bedchamber.

"Today is your wedding day, my lady. Are you excited?" Lydia held the hem of the skirt of the wedding dress as she admired the beauty of the gown.

Rhoslyn went to the bedroom window and looked to the bailey below. She was home, her mother was alive, and today she would be married. Her future husband…the thought of him brought a smile to her face. He was tall, handsome, thoughtful, kind, loyal, and she trusted him with her heart.

"Yes, Lydia. I am very excited."

~

Lord Filmore entered the library. "Jayden, my son, are you ready to wed today?" He carried a chest.

"Yes, father." He glanced up from the account book at the chest. "What's in the chest?"

"It's Rhoslyn's dowry. I thought you should have it for Bardenham's expenses."

"That's very kind of you, Father." He turned the ledger page. "Do you have any idea what this says? I'm having difficulty deciphering the handwriting." He pointed to an entry.

Between father and son, they spent most of the day reading through the accounts.

~

Rhoslyn stared out her bedchamber window at a distant hill while biting her bottom lip. Still dressed in her chemise and robe, she paced like a caged animal as memories weighed heavily on her mind. "I think I would like to take Laila to stretch her legs. Lydia, can you get..." Rhoslyn turned to her servant.

"Got it." Lydia pulled a riding gown from the wardrobe.

Rhoslyn threw off her robe tossing it onto the bed. She lifted her arms inserting them into the sleeves as the gown was pulled over her head and down her body. The corset was wrapped around her chest.

"My lady, shall I ride with you?" Lydia pulled the laces tightly.

"I prefer to go alone."

"Shall I pin your hair?" Lydia picked up the brush from the nightstand.

"Not today." Rhoslyn left the bedchamber and went to the kitchen.

The servants paused in their duties to curtsy or bow. Noticing the disruption in his staff, Bentley turned to see who had entered the room. "My lady, is there something you need?"

"If you don't mind, I will help myself, thank you." She cut a loaf of bread and sliced a wedge of cheese for a quick midday meal and wrapped it in linen before going to the stable.

Jamie looked up from the bridle he was cleaning as Rhoslyn entered the stable. "My lady, shall I saddle Laila for you?"

"Please."

The proficient stableboy had the large mare saddled in record time, led Laila out of the stable, and held her bridle as Rhoslyn climbed atop.

"Thank you, Jamie." She rode through the bailey, over the drawbridge, and pulled her horse to a stop on the fringe of the village as an internal struggle of emotions pulled at opposite sides of her heart.

On a distant hill were hundreds of mounds bearing crosses and swords amongst the tall field grass. She encouraged Laila toward the graveyard scanning it in search of recently overturned ground. There were several. Dismounting, she ran her hand over the tops of the wildflowers before gathering a small bouquet and entering the cemetery searching for her father's sword among the many. She looked at each grass-covered mound as she passed. Each sword marked the resting place of a member of the garrison. Some graves were simply donned with a wooden cross or remained bare. She looked for the hilt she had known so well, held many times within her hand.

As if Lord Atherton reached out to his daughter, the hilt of his sword reflected the sun drawing her attention. She went to the grave and stood before it. New grass was beginning to grow on the mound of dirt. Placing the wildflowers next to the blade of the sword, she sat upon the ground.

"I'm conflicted between anger and love, Father. My blood boils from your cowardly choice to take your life. I can only assume your guilt in the crime. Perhaps your infidelity to Mother was justified, in your mind, to an unwanted marriage. Maybe you wished to wed another. When I was little, your love for me was apparent. I assume your choice of Jayden was also made of your love for me. Whatever you did or why doesn't matter now. I wish you could be here to share in my joy and happiness on my wedding day."

She wiped a tear from her cheek as she looked at the hilt of his sword and a cardinal landed on the rounded end. It tilted its head to the left and then to the right as if trying to look at her with one eye at a time. She watched as it flew to a nearby tree and landed on a branch. She watched the wildflowers dancing in the breeze as she remained in the quiet solitude by his gravesite for hours recalling moments they shared, his laugh, his smile, and his patience.

~

Bentley stood in the open doorway of the library. "My lord."

Jayden looked to the steward. "Yes, Bentley."

"There are several peasants wishing a moment of your attention."

"My attention?"

"Yes, you and Lady Rhoslyn's attention to rule on matters of disagreement." The steward glanced at Lord Filmore before looking back to Jayden. "The hearings are conducted daily or at least they were before Lord Atherton's death."

Jayden opened his mouth to speak, closed it, and nodded once accepting this new responsibility. "Where is Lady Rhoslyn?"

"My lord, she left the Keep several hours ago."

"Alone?"

"I did not see anyone accompanying her."

"Did she say where she was going?"

"No, my lord."

Jayden glanced at his father as he shut the account book. "If you don't mind, I'd like to continue this another time?"

"Very well." Lord Filmore watched Shadow raised his head from where he lay. The canine set off after his master.

"Jamie!" Jayden called halfway to the stable.

The lad stepped from the stable. "Yes, my lord."

"My horse!" Jayden hurried into the stable and noted Laila's empty stall. He grabbed the bridle from a nail on the wall and forced the bit into Beval's mouth while Jamie laid the blanket upon the destrier's back and hoisted the saddle atop. "Did Lady Rhoslyn say where she was going?"

"No, my lord."

Pulling the strap securing the girth belt, Jayden climbed atop his horse ducking his head as he rode through the doorway and exited the castle. Once over the drawbridge, he entered the village scanning every alleyway and between buildings. He reined his horse before the well and looked at a field to see peasants tending the crops.

"My lord?"

He looked down at a woman carrying a bucket of water.

"Can I help you?"

He doubted she could but thought to inquire anyway. "Lady Rhoslyn left the castle a few hours ago. Have you seen her?"

"No, my lord, but her gray mare is on the hill." The woman pointed to where Laila grazed.

"Thank you." He spurred his horse into a gallop.

Rhoslyn heard the approaching hoofbeats and rose from the ground to see Jayden riding toward her.

He reined his horse to a skidding stop, jumped to the ground, and went to her side. "What are you doing out here alone?" He scrutinized her face. It was apparent she had been crying. "Are you well?" It was then he noticed the mounds around him with their protruding swords.

"Yes, I'm well." She motioned to the grave beside her. "My father's grave." Feeling the need to explain, she sighed. "I just needed to think some things through and be alone while I did so." She reached for his hand.

Jayden placed her hand upon his waist as he drew her into his arms. "And have you come to terms with your thoughts?" He tucked her head under his chin giving her a moment to respond.

She tilted her head back and looked up into his blue eyes, smiled, and nodded.

"If you're finished, we are needed in the Great Hall." He ran his hand up and down her spine reassuring her that all was well and released her.

"We're needed for what?" She assumed Bentley needed a decision on a detail of the wedding.

"Our obligation to settle disputes between the citizens of Bardenham. Since you know more about the kingdom than I do, I would appreciate your advice while we hear complaints and requests from the peasants."

She looked to her father's grave in a silent farewell, back to her future husband, and nodded.

As they entered the Great Hall, they were met by a small crowd who awaited their arrival. They stepped onto the dais, sat in their chairs, and spent several hours choosing the best course of action for each complaint.

With the last conflict settled, Jayden looked at his bride. "Well, my dear, shall we ready ourselves to become husband and wife?"

"Yes," she smiled, "I would like nothing more."

Chapter 48

A steaming bath awaited Rhoslyn in her bedchamber. With the help of Lydia, she was soon bathed, dried, and dressed in her teal wedding gown. The bodice was beautifully embellished with beads, pearls, and trimmed in lace. The skirt was the fullest she had ever had the pleasure of wearing. Lydia took special care when doing her hair.

"You take my breath away, my lady." Lydia smiled

"Thank you." Rhoslyn ran her fingertips over the beading of the bodice. "The dress is all I imagined it to be."

A meek knock sounded upon her bedchamber door. Lydia opened it to see Lady Eugenia. The servant stepped aside allowing the woman to enter. "My lady, I will step into the hallway to allow you some time with Lady Eugena."

"Thank you, Lydia."

Lady Eugena glowed with pride. "My dear, you are stunning."

Rhoslyn blushed. "Thank you, Mother." She brushed her hands over the skirt. "Now that we have a moment alone, my curiosity has been piqued. Who is this gentleman who has reentered your life?"

Unsure of how her daughter would react to her admission, Lady Eugena tried to hold back her smile but was unsuccessful. "Years before my betrothal to your father, I fell in love with a young man. He was kind, loyal, and strong, very strong. He was my heart's desire, my true love, but my parents refused to allow the match. I was astonished when I first saw him in Somerville. As expected, he worked diligently to free me from captivity. After all these years, Sir Darwin and I have found each other once again."

"Sir Darwin. Oh, Mother, I'm happy to see you so happy."

"Thank you. Well, it is nearly time for the ceremony. I'll join the others in the chapel."

Lydia entered the bedchamber after stepping aside for Lady Eugenia to exit.

~

Freshly bathed and dressed in a black tunic with gold embroidering, Jayden strapped on his sword, dirk, and belt bag. He opened the trunk at the foot of his bed, took out the small brass box, and slipped his mother's ruby ring onto his pinky finger. He looked down at Shadow who sat staring up at him. "What do you think? Do I look ready to take a wife?"

The dog tilted his head from one side to the other. He seemed to smile as he stood on all fours wagging his tail.

"I'm glad you agree." He went into the hallway and knocked on the bedchamber door.

Lydia opened the portal and smiled. "My lord, may I present your bride." She stepped aside swinging the portal fully open.

Rhoslyn curtsied before looking at Jayden to see if she met his expectations.

He bowed, smiled, and held out his hand for her to come forward. She placed her hand within his as he held her at a distance to take in her beauty. "I've never see you look so beautiful, my dear."

"Thank you, my lord. You look quite handsome yourself."

He placed her hand within the crook of his arm and led her to the top of the staircase. Pausing, they scanned the capacity filled room. Rhoslyn stomach fluttered as she exhaled and looked at her future husband.

Jayden lifted his chin as they descended the staircase, passed through the Great Hall, and went to the chapel with Shadow trailing behind them.

The chapel was aglow with flickering candelabras lining its walls. A pair of candles, protected by red glass cylinders, illuminated the crucifix hanging over the altar. Father Truman waited before the altar with his prayer book open in his hands. The Lord and Lady of Aldwinster, Lady Eugenia, Sir Darwin, and Sir Cedric looked toward the back of the room as the soon to be Lord and Lady of Bardenham appeared in the doorway.

Lydia grabbed Shadow's collar before the dog could follow his master and stood at the back of the room.

Rhoslyn's heart pounded within her chest as they walked toward the altar. She looked at her mother, who smiled and brushed a tear away from her cheek. Sir Darwin's hand rested on her mother's waist for reassurance and support. Rhoslyn nodded to him approvingly before looking at Jayden's profile. He appeared confident, calm. She wondered if he was nervous too. They stopped before Father Truman, who chattered on about something in Latin, but his words failed to resonate within her mind.

Jayden turned to his bride taking both of her hands within his. "From this day and forevermore, my heart will always belong to you and only you. I promise to care and protect you until my death." He removed the ruby ring from his little finger, held it before Father Truman, who blessed it and placed it on his wife's ring finger.

Rhoslyn looked at the ring and glanced at Lady Myla, who smiled with a single nod of her head. She looked at Jayden and smiled. "My heart belongs to you and only you, my lord. And I promise to care and protect you until my death."

Father Truman raised his chin. "My lords, ladies, and knights, I present to you the Lord and Lady of Bardenham."

The witnesses clapped their hands in celebration. Lydia could no longer hold Shadow and he darted toward his master.

Jayden cupped his wife's face within his hands and touched his lips to hers. Rhoslyn threading her arms around his neck pulling him toward her and deepening the kiss. After they were congratulated by those in the room, Father Truman instructed the couple to sign the registry while everyone else adjourned to the Great Hall.

The newlyweds emerged from the hallway and were greeted with congratulatory cheers from those in the crowded room. They took their place at the High Table and kissed for all to see. Jayden took their tankards from the table, handed one to his wife, and waited for the room to quiet.

"I would like to thank everyone for attending our celebration. We especially appreciate my parents, the Lord and Lady of Aldwinster, for enduring the journey to witness our marriage." He lifted his tankard toward them. They did so in return. "By the grace of God, Lady Eugenia is with us to celebrate our happiness." Jayden looked at the people in attendance. "And with our loyal knights," he looked at them raising his tankard again, "we promise to rule fairly and justly, to keep our kingdom strong and its citizens protected."

The people cheered.

Jayden looked at the steward, who stood in the doorway of the kitchen. "Pearson, bring forth our meal." He helped his wife to sit in her chair, lifted her hand to his lips, and kissed it gently before sitting next to her.

The food was brought forward with style; a swan on a platter with various vegetables surrounding its base on the tray, platters of beef, poultry, and fish, loaves of bread, and more than enough ale and wine for all to drink.

Rhoslyn fanned her fingers and stared at her ruby ring. She watched the glimmering reflection of the flickering flames of the candles dance in the precious stone.

Jayden noticed his wife admiring the trinket. "So, you're pleased with the ring?"

"Yes, very much so."

"Mother wanted you to have it."

"It's a very kind and thoughtful of her to think of me so. I'll be certain to let her know how much I appreciate her gift."

After a meal filled with merriment, plenty of food, and drink, the musicians took their place and awaited their cue.

Jayden stood and offered his hand to his wife. "My dear, may I have this dance?"

She placed the palm of her hand within his. "Yes, and all of the others that follow for the rest of my life."